TAKE CARE OF YOU

TAKING CARE BOOK 1

GIANNI HOLMES

A GOOD DADDY TAKES CARE OF HIS BOY.

Editing by Ann Attwood Editing and Proofreading Services
Proofreading by Barbara Ingram
&
Lori Parks
Take Care of You © 2019 Gianni Holmes

GIANNI HOLMES

LOVE KNOWS NO BOUNDARIES

❀ Created with Vellum

Warning

This book contains sexual content that is intended for a
mature adult audience

Hi Reader,

I'm excited to share my new release, *Take Care of You*. I started this story because of a lack of a younger daddy in the daddy kink world that we so love. I find Declan to be the perfect younger daddy and Owen to be the exact mature fit for Declan's boy. Together these men have done me proud, and I hope you feel the same.

This book started off being a standalone novel. I had no intention of making it a series, but as happens with authors at times, our characters often have a mind of their own. As a result, *Take Care of You* is the first book in the Take Care trilogy which will cover the full story of Owen and Declan's relationship.

Book 2 should be available at the end of April.

The books that will be in this series include:

Take Care of You: Book 1

Take Care of Me: Book 2

Take Care of Us: Book 3

I sincerely hope you enjoy reading about Owen and Declan. You can sign up for my newsletter at http://eepurl.com/dFTPDD to keep updated on their progress.
Love
Gianni

Thanks to Anna for the support and encouragement she doled out in generous portions while I was writing this book. This book would not have come to fruition without you.
Special thanks to Claudia for helping me with information about your beautiful country and ensuring I got the translations all right.

Age is an issue of mind over matter. If you don't mind, it doesn't matter.

Mark Twain

PROLOGUE
OWEN

The second I entered the house, I knew something was wrong. I couldn't say what yet, but the conversation I'd had with my wife last night rang in my ear. I hadn't thought of it all day, because I believed talking about it had solved the issue, but now I had major doubts.

"Jenna?" I called softly, not wanting to wake the kids, because it was late. I didn't bother to shrug out of the jacket of my chauffeur's uniform but hurried along the hall. When I heard the television on in the living room, I sighed in relief.

"You wouldn't believe the crazy day I've had, love," I remarked, sighing. "I swear rich people are the worst, and they prove me right every single time. Too bad…" I trailed off, frowning at the dark head resting at the back of the sofa. Jenna was blonde and had always been a blonde since we met in middle school. Her hair was also kept short in a bob, not the long tangled curls that I was looking at.

The person on the couch turned, and I recognized our regular babysitter Anna who lived down the block from us. The sixteen-year-old girl rose to her feet and muted the television.

"Mr. Long, I didn't hear you come in," she said, giving me an apologetic smile. Anna was a good kid who did a stellar job in watching our three rambunctious children, and I was always happy to have her around, but I didn't remember an arrangement for her to be here tonight.

"Where's Mrs. Long?" I asked her, shifting my weight to the balls of my feet.

"She didn't say," the girl answered with a shrug of her slim shoulders. "She just told me that you'd get in lateish."

"Oh, okay." Hoping she didn't see the tremor in my hands, I fished in my pocket for my wallet.

"It's fine. She already paid me. Do you mind if I wait here? I'll call my brother Claude to pick me up."

"Sure, that's fine, Anna. Take your time. I hope they weren't troublesome tonight."

"The usual, but I kept them occupied."

I smiled, a tight little jerk of my lips in opposite directions. "You're a real natural."

"Lots of experience with my brothers and sisters."

I nodded, then excused myself to check on the kids. Once at the stairs, I took them two at a time, my heart hammering in my chest.

"Owen, I'm not happy. I think we made a big mistake."

Those words came back to me as I replayed my conversation with Jenna last night. She had expressed her unhappiness of our life together, and I had talked her into believing that it was just a phase. Just the blues. I had made love to her, and if it felt like something was missing, we'd both not mentioned it afterward.

The truth was that I understood Jenna's misgivings, but now wasn't the time to voice them when we had three little ones depending on us.

Although I planned to check on the kids, I stopped at our bedroom first. My eyes swept the four corners, noting everything was neatly in place. The bed had been made with fresh covers today, and the rug at the foot of the bed had been vacuumed. I marched over to the closet, yanking the door open.

"No, no, no." I didn't want to believe it, but the empty spaces in the closet where her clothes had mingled with mine proved it. She was gone. Her shelves of shoes I usually teased her about were gone too.

I left the closet door hanging and ran over to the dresser. I yanked her drawers open and found they were all empty. I ran my fingers through my hair, feeling sick. She had left me. She had left our kids.

I think we took the easier road ten years ago, and it's single-handedly the worst decision we've made.

"Jesus, Jenna, don't do this to us."

I needed her. There was no way I could do this on my own. Jenna had been a constant in my life since we met in middle school and became friends. When we found out each other's peculiarities and were able to accept each other, something had changed between us. It was our acceptance of each other which had forged a bond and understanding between us. Everything that happened in the following years had seemed natural. Dating, going to the prom together, coming out together as bisexuals, getting engaged, marrying and starting a family.

Having come from a small town, we had found in each other what we hadn't been able to discover in our families. That was what she had meant about us making the worst decision of becoming lovers instead of friends. We had been convenient for each other.

I blinked at the tears that formed in my eyes, pinching the bridge of my nose hard. I worked my ass off to give us a better life. I did my duty by her and the kids. I did it out of love. How could she abandon us? We had given each other leeway in our marriage to see other people. She got her regular fix when she craved a woman. All I had asked of her was to be discreet because of the kids. They weren't exactly at the age to learn about our open marriage.

Our marriage hadn't always been open, but I had sensed her restlessness, so I had done what friends did best. I thought about what would make her happy. Why hadn't she been able to do the same for us?

My eyes dropped to the dresser, and I froze when I saw the white envelope. I hadn't noticed it before in all my frantic worry. Snagging the envelope, I opened it and took out the single sheet inside.

I will always love you and our kids. Please find it in your hearts to forgive me. I understand that it will take some time.

Love, Jenna.

This was it? Our life summed up in three sentences? Nineteen years of friendship. Eleven years of marriage. Eight years of parenting together and this was it?

"Daddy, there's a monster beneath my bed."

At the little voice behind me, I turned to face my three-year-old daughter, Summer, who had her thumb in her mouth and her blankie in her other hand, trailing on the floor. Her ringlets of blonde curls stuck about her head like a golden halo, and her eyes were droopy.

Our baby girl. How would I raise her on my own? Every little girl needed their mommy.

I dropped the paper back to the dresser and crouched on the floor with my arms outstretched. Summer trotted over to me, her gait unsteady from sleep. Once she was in my arms, she trustingly placed her head on my shoulder and smiled. My throat constricted with emotions, and my heart squeezed. I loved my kids so much. I would have done anything for them.

Why wasn't this enough, Jenna?

"Will you scare the monsters, Daddy?" she asked on the cutest little yawn.

"Always, my little monkey. Daddy will always scare your monsters away."

And I would do it alone too if that was what it took.

1

DECLAN

"Remind me why your father has to have a bachelor party again?"

I wondered the same thing but tried my best to answer my best friend Ridge's question the way Charles would have expected. "Every man needs one last night of debauchery before committing himself to sleep with the same woman every night."

My response was dry, complete with an eye-roll, and Ridge erupted into laughter. The glass of whiskey he held sloshed perilously close to the edge, and I frowned, hoping it didn't spill.

"This is what? Wife number four?" he asked. "Charles wouldn't know how to sleep with the same woman every night even if she crawled into his bed."

I should have been offended, but I couldn't be when Ridge spoke the truth. Charles was an irresponsible and selfish man who I had spent much of my life taking care of instead of the other way around. I ensured his little fuck-ups remained exactly that… little. And, if they ever got to epic proportions, I took care of it discreetly. No biggie.

"Wife number five," I replied, sipping from my glass of Scotch, as I took a seat on the elegant couch in the sitting room on the second floor. This was my favorite room in all the house since it overlooked the rose garden.

"Isn't there a cap on how many people you can marry?" Ridge asked, coming to sit by me. His leg pressed to mine, he leaned forward and kissed me. I kissed him back half-heartedly, glad for the contact. Although we were friends, we'd kissed and fucked around a little, but it had been a couple years since we'd done the latter. He had no expectations, and neither did I. We both knew what we wanted in a partner was different from what we could ever be to each other. Still, it was nice to have somebody I could call over if I felt out of sorts. Somebody who knew me inside out.

"Thanks. Needed that," I told him as he pulled back. "And to answer your question, if there's no cap, there needs to be one for people like Charles. I understand him wanting to change women, but he doesn't have to marry every one of them."

He squeezed my thigh sympathetically. "You're wound up about this, aren't you?"

"More like trying to control the situation. It's not easy having a father who acts like he belongs to a frat house. Instead of getting better with age, it's getting worse."

"Maybe you coddle him too much? He knows you'll always be there to bail him out, so he doesn't need to use good judgment?"

He was absolutely right. "Yeah, but I can't help it."

"I know. Wish we could find someone for you."

I smiled at him gratefully. "I've given up hope. Seems not many are interested in my particular kink."

"I wish I was older for you."

I scoffed at that and drained my drink. "No, you don't. We both know you like being the annoying bratty boy that raises his Daddy's blood pressure."

He grinned at me and winked. "You're right about that. It's just so much more fun."

"You're almost as bad as he is," I said, rolling my eyes. "I need someone a bit more mature to handle."

"I'll keep an ear out for you." He pressed his hand dangerously close to my groin. "Want me to suck you off? It might improve your mood."

I pushed his hand away gently. "Can't. I'm really not in the mood, and in a sec, I'll have to make some calls to ensure we pull off everything for the night. I'd forbidden Vegas for his bachelor party, but now he wants me to make Vegas come to him. Perhaps I should have just hired a jet and sent him on his way. Without me."

He chuckled. "He would have enjoyed that, but I'll take a raincheck. I feel like we never get a chance to fool around anymore. You know I love acting your part."

I could feel my cheeks heating at Ridge's words. Two years ago, when I engaged in my first Daddy/boy relationship, I had come out to Ridge about my unusual kink. He had tried not to show his surprise. Daddy/boy kink was popular in our community, but not the reverse way I liked it. I liked my boys to be older. My last partner had been thirty-five, twelve years my senior, but I had wielded the power play in our relationship. I'd loved it. I thrived on it. Too bad after a while he had lost interest in being the submissive to a younger man.

That was my dilemma. Finding a man old enough to pique my interest and submissive enough to not mind my Daddy fetish. At one point, I had been ashamed of it, but I'd already worked it all out in therapy. Charles's habits might have driven me to my mindset of managing older boyfriends, but there the similarities ended. Charles was a pain in the ass. I preferred older men who acted mature and deserved my affection and pampering.

"Been busy with the wedding planning," I answered. Given my mindset to micromanage everything, I'd been on the heels of the wedding planner since Charles was adamant about his fifth wedding happening. Everything had to be perfect. Even if I did predict this marriage wouldn't last very long. They never did.

"It's okay. I got that. Plus, I've a new Daddy now anyway. He doesn't seem to like sharing."

I raised an eyebrow at that. In the past, Ridge had picked Daddies who didn't mind him having other Daddies on the side or random hookups. He was that kind of free-spirited guy who believed in sex positivity and no sex-shaming regardless of preferences. That was the reason we had become such good friends. He might not understand the reason I preferred older men to be submissive to me, but he didn't criticize me for it.

"We'll have to all go out sometime," I told him. Despite his penchant for drama and to stir a hornet's nest, Ridge was a sweet guy, and I didn't want to see him hurt, especially not by a Daddy he put his trust in.

"Meh. I'll think about it. Don't think he'll be your cup of tea."

"Hmm." He didn't seem like he wanted to share more, so I dropped the subject. "Just know you can talk to me about anything."

"Yup, already know that." He cleared his throat. "Need any help taking care of Charles's party?"

"Did you think you'd be excluded?" I asked, amused. "We'll split the list of things we have to do. He asked for a very specific cake, so I'll have to check the pastry shop got that right. Then there's confirming the strippers will be there, and that they are to his specifications, double-checking the venue, transportation, the long guest list. Yup, we have a full day ahead of us."

Most of the things on the list had already been done, but I was quite anal about double, okay, triple-checking everything. It was a little obsession of mine to have everything go according to my plan. As the heir to Charles's finance company, I had grown up managing things. It was in my blood and had trickled down to my personal relationships.

Ridge made the duty list less monotonous, and we did most things over the phone. Almost everything was going fine so far without a hitch. I gave the strippers' profiles a quick overview and decided they were to Charles's forty-nine-year-old specifications. There was a mix-up by the caterers that I corrected and was assured would be fixed by the time of the party.

"Declan, we've got a problem."

I ended my call with the catering company and turned my attention to Ridge who was sitting on a chair with the front legs tilted in the air. I frowned, biting back my command for him to stop. He wasn't my boy. I didn't have any right to tell him what to do. Still, he must have seen how much it bothered me, because he immediately righted the chair.

"What is it?" I asked.

"The limousine company you hired has the date mixed up," he replied. "They thought the party was next week."

"They can't have the date mixed-up," I growled at him. "I called them twice to confirm it."

He shrugged. "Want to talk to them and use that toppy voice to get what you want?"

I snagged the phone from him and wagged a finger in his face. "You be glad I'm not your Daddy."

He chuckled and fluttered his eyes at me. "I should be so lucky."

"Hello?" I barked into the phone. "This is Declan Moore. What's this nonsense I hear about you mixing up the date for my father's bachelor party?"

"Uh, Mr. Moore." I could hear the nervousness in the employee's voice as he addressed me by name. Our finance company did regular business with the limousine service, so they knew the revenue they got from us consistently.

"Well, what seems to be the problem?" I prompted.

"We don't have the number of vehicles you require, sir," the employee answered. "We've been booked out for a function put on by the mayor."

"Are you saying you can't deliver what you promised?"

"We can on the nineteenth."

"Except we need you to deliver tonight."

"I'm really sorry about that, sir."

"What's your name?" I asked, pacing the length of the room. We needed at least a dozen limousines for the event. Charles insisted on having his guests picked up and escorted to and from the venue. I knew the companies that offered this service would be stretched thin on short notice, so I had called in advance to ensure I secured the vehicles. I had even paid the full price already instead of just the required deposit.

"It's Joseph, sir."

"Joseph, do you know how special tonight is?"

"Umm." He gave a noncommittal answer.

"It's very special, Joseph." It really wasn't. Just the third bachelor party I was conducting on behalf of Charles, but he wanted it perfect, and as the dutiful son, I complied with what he wanted. "It's the night before my father gets married. Now we need a fleet of twelve limousines, and you're going to need to produce them fast."

I heard the shaky breath Joseph took over the phone, and I almost felt sorry for the guy. Almost.

"Uh, umm, perhaps you can try Cush, sir? They have a wonderful fleet."

"Are you recommending your biggest competitor to me?"

"In this case, I think it's appropriate, sir. I do apologize for us having the dates mixed up, and you can rest assured that we'll find the employee responsible."

"Don't bother on my account. The damage is already done. I'll take my business to Cush."

"What if we offer you a fifty percent discount on your next order?"

"Not interested. I don't need a discount. I'm in need of a dozen limousines which you can't deliver. Have a good day, Joseph, and give my regards to management."

I hung up and placed my hands on my hips. "Can you believe these people?"

"*I* can't believe how hot you sounded," Ridge moaned, pointing to the crotch of his pants which was snugger than usual.

"Behave, I still need to get another fleet."

I had Siri search for Cush's contact number and dial them. The phone rang two times before it was picked up.

"Cush Luxury Transport Service. This is Lionel speaking. How may I help you?"

"Lionel, let's get straight to the point. I need a fleet of a dozen limousines tonight. Can you deliver?"

"Uh, let me check on that for you… may I have your name, please?"

"It's Declan. Declan Moore."

"Just a minute, Mr. Moore."

I could hear the clicking of computer keys. I caught a glimpse of Ridge watching me and lightly stroking himself through the crotch of his pants. I scowled at him, and he dropped his hand while rolling his eyes. I knew he was craving me to fuck him, but I was trying to pull away from that side of our relationship and work on a more permanent situation.

"Mr. Moore." Lionel came back on the line. "You're

in luck. We can provide you with a dozen limousines for the night. Given such short notice, however, there will be an additional fee for express service."

"That's fine. As long as you can deliver."

Crisis averted, I got down to business. I just needed tonight and tomorrow to go well, then I would get a much-needed break from Charles. He wasn't just getting married this time but planned to enjoy a year-long cruise with his new wife. That meant I had full control of the company. I needed this more than anything, to not have him underfoot, distracting me from the business. Plus, with him gone, perhaps I could focus on my own personal needs for a change.

2

OWEN

"Popcorn's almost ready!" I called out to Summer. "Did you find a movie?"

When I didn't get any feedback from my nineteen-year-old daughter, I went to investigate. The popping sound coming from the microwave at my back, I padded barefooted to the living room where Summer was supposed to be setting up for our big movie night. Our last movie night of her living with me.

I tried not to choke up at the thought of my baby girl moving out. I had promised not to cry. One would have thought that already seeing two kids out the door would have prepared me for this, but Summer was my little girl. Of all three kids, she had stuck to me most, always having a hand in whatever I was doing. My identical twin sons, Oscar and Auggie, had moved out together to their own apartment five years ago which should have prepared me for the inevitability of Summer moving out as well. It hadn't. Our home

would no longer be the same, and that was discon-
certing.

Tomorrow she would move out all the way to
Columbus where she would share an apartment with her
girlfriend Penelope. I had known before senior year what
their plans were, and when they got accepted into their
first choice, Ohio State University, it had become set in
stone. Even though she and Penny had been joined at the
hip since both girls were twelve, I worried about Summer
making such a life decision at her age. She had barely
had time to explore. Penny had been her constant
throughout her teen years, and although I had always
sensed there was more to their friendship, she hadn't
opened up about it until two years ago.

The memories that conversation with her had
brought back.

"Summer?" She wasn't in the living room, but the
television was on, and the movie title Jersey Girl was
frozen to the screen.

"Shit." We had come across this movie once before,
but we hadn't even made it through the first half an hour
before she broke down. We hadn't attempted to watch it
again, because of the bitter memories I knew she still had
about her mother abandoning us.

I had tried to make Jenna's abandonment easy on the
kids, but it had hit her harder than the boys. That whole
girls needing their moms thing was not a myth. Once she
had come out to me, she had explained that she had
struggled with being a lesbian because she didn't want
anything that had to do with her mother. Not even her
sexual orientation, and Summer had apparently strug-

gled with hers for so long before she finally accepted herself for who she was.

The whirring of the microwave had stopped, signaling the readiness of the popcorn. I ignored it and took the stairs pretty much the way I had done that night Jenna had left us, two at a time. Worried about the mood she was in, I knocked on the door to Summer's bedroom.

"Summer?"

"Come in."

I pushed the door open and found her sitting on the bed, surrounded by her mountain of pillows. I had lost count of the number of throw pillows she owned. Birthdays, Christmases, whatever occasion, she was happiest when she got a decorative pillow, especially when they were personalized.

"Hey, you okay?" I asked, moving toward her bed to sit beside her. She shuffled over to lay her head in my lap.

"We should watch it," she replied, hugging a pillow to her chest.

"But we don't have to, especially if it's only going to make us sad. I don't want to be sad with you on your last night here."

"Yeah, that makes sense," she said on a sniff. "I'll probably watch it at our new place with Penny. She's great with my waterworks."

I smiled down at her and brushed the curls at her temple. "You know I love you, right?"

"I love you too, Dad," she replied on a sigh. "I know you're not the happiest about me moving in with Penny, but it'll be okay."

"I'm just worried about you. I can't help it. I don't want you to be hurt, and you already love her so much."

"She loves me too."

I nodded, but didn't say anything. I didn't want to shatter her dreams by pointing out that Jenna and I had loved each other too. Before she just woke up one day and stopped loving me. In the fifteen years since she had left us, she had never once contacted us, never wished the kids a happy birthday, or Merry Christmas. Nothing. I had no idea if she was dead or alive, and that was one of the hardest things I had to deal with.

"You're thinking about Mom, aren't you?"

"Maybe."

"Penny is nothing like her," she continued, her tone a little forceful. "Our situation is very different. She wouldn't abandon me as Mom did us, and plus, we don't have any kids in the equation, which would make it easier even if she did."

"Thank god for small favors," I said jokingly. "There's no risk of you making a baby with Penny."

She chuckled. "You know, it should be super weird talking to you about things like this, but it's not."

"Yeah, well, when I've been doing tampon duty since you were twelve, we kinda got over it."

"Seriously though, Penny and I will have kids someday, I'm sure. Just not now. When we've finished university, have jobs and can afford kids."

"Sounds like a good solid plan."

She patted my cheek and sat up. "You want grandkids, right?"

I groaned. "I just got you guys out of the house. At least give me a few stress-free years first."

She laughed. "Well, Oscar's got a girlfriend, so you should be lecturing him."

Like me, Oscar was bisexual, although he'd only introduced me to one boyfriend in high school. His other partners had been girlfriends so far. At least as far as I knew. I still couldn't say about Auggie who was tight-lipped and had never been in a relationship. He was the most reserved of all my kids, and sometimes I had the feeling Jenna's abandonment had affected him more than he let on. He was the most mature of the three and the reason I hadn't fretted unnecessarily about their move. He would keep Oscar, who had a bit of a wild streak, in line.

"Auggie will keep him in check," I answered, getting to my feet. "Come on, let's find a different movie. Preferably something funny."

She groaned as she followed me from the bedroom. "Which reminds me, this is probably the last time I'll get the opportunity to watch a rom/com. Penny hates rom/com."

"Well, if she really loves you, sweetie, she'll watch a few rom/com movies just for you."

Relieved that I had diverted the crisis upstairs, I sent her to find a new movie while I ran the popcorn for another few seconds. I microwaved another packet before dumping both into a large bowl—our movie bowl. I grabbed two cans of pop from the fridge and joined her. My ass had barely landed on the couch when the phone rang.

"I'll get it," she said, and jumped to her feet, shuffling by me to get the phone on the side table. I brought up the metadata for the movie she had selected and half-listened to her end of the conversation.

"Hello? You'd like to speak to my dad? Umm, hold a sec, please."

I frowned at her as I got to my feet. "Who is it?"

"Trevor from the car company." Her face fell, and mine nearly followed. Trevor never called for pleasantries, and if he was calling this late, then it had to be an emergency. I had asked for today and tomorrow off so I could spend the time with Summer.

"Hey, Trevor, what's up?" I answered, once I took the phone from her.

"Owen, I'm sorry, man, but we have to call you in."

I groaned. "Come on, Trevor, I told you how it is this weekend."

"And we tried to avoid it, but we can't," my supervisor remarked. "We've got a huge request for a bachelor party tonight. Twelve drivers. Initially, we left you out and added Tony, but Martin's wife went into labor, and he has his little girls."

"What about Ray?" I suggested. Anything to get out of duty tonight. "Ray's sick. Chicken pox."

"And I'm the only one available?"

"Yeah," he answered. "You know I wouldn't have called you if it wasn't urgent. This is a huge request, by Declan Moore."

"Doesn't make sense when you drop names, Trevor. They always fly over my head."

"Well, this guy stands to inherit a billion-dollar

company, so we can't not deliver. You're one of the best drivers we've got."

"So, what's the occasion?"

"Bachelor party. You'll need to be at the location by ten. It's a late night affair."

"Shit. I promised to drive my daughter to Columbus tomorrow, Trevor."

"I'm sorry, but there's a wedding tomorrow too. A bunch of important people will be there, and they're transporting them in style."

I glanced at Summer and her crestfallen face. We'd been really looking forward to that drive to Columbus together. I wanted to see her apartment, check out the neighborhood where she would be living, and if possible give her fatherly advice.

"It's okay," she mouthed to me. "I'll be fine. I'll call Penny, and we can drive together."

"Hang on a minute," I said into the phone, then pressed the mute button so I could speak to Summer. "I wanted to take you, honey."

"But your job's important," she replied. "I'll be gone, and it's probably the only thing that will keep you company for a while. Just come down to visit me next weekend."

"Are you sure?"

She nodded. "Yes, I'm sure. In fact, we can invite the boys too, and make a family reunion of it."

I liked the idea of that. Although I spoke to Oscar and Auggie by phone often, I hadn't seen them since Christmas. "Okay. I'm really sorry."

"It's fine, Dad."

I nodded and unmuted the phone. "Trevor, you still there?"

"Yes, so I'm going to send you the information. Check your email."

"Alright. But if I do this, I get next weekend off, even if it's the end of the world. I'm going to have to make it up to my daughter, big time."

"Yes, that's fine. We just can't screw up this request. The Moores are big, like, fucking huge."

"I got it, Trevor. Send me the info. I'll have to iron my uniform."

"Thanks, man. Knew I can count on you."

I grumbled into the phone and ended the call.

3

DECLAN

"**F**or God's sake, Charles!" I said, waving at his naked torso. "Button your shirt, will you? The limo is here, and you aren't ready yet."

My father, Charles Moore, turned to assess himself in the full-length mirror in his bedroom. His face took on a pleased look as he returned his attention to me. "Why can't I leave it open? I take care of my physique. Surely I get to show it off even a little."

"Then make it be a little," I told him. "You can leave the top two buttons undone. Strippers like a little mystery. Not that I think you should be having strippers at your bachelor party anyway. It's kind of tacky for…" I trailed off when Charles gave me a warning look. I didn't bother finishing my thought that he was too old to be acting like this.

At least he listened and started doing up the buttons to his shirt. At the same time my phone rang, and I dug it out of my pocket. I was trying to stay calm and handle the night with as much finesse as possible so everything didn't end in a disaster. We hadn't even arrived at the club we had rented for the night and my father was already being a handful.

I groaned when I saw my future step-mother's face pop up on my phone screen. I would have ignored it if I thought it would have stopped her calling, but Poppy could be rather insistent. She would keep calling until I eventually gave up and answered the phone.

I knew she was worried about tonight, possibly thinking that my father would call off the wedding for some stripper he met. I couldn't say that I blamed her. Charles was quite fickle with his affections.

"It's your future wife," I announced, before answering the call. "Yes, Poppy?"

"Declan, your father won't answer his phone," Poppy remarked, her tone panicky. "Is everything alright?"

I ignored Charles who was desperately waving his hands in a no signal that he didn't want to talk to her.

"Everything is quite fine, Poppy," I answered. "Aren't you getting ready for your own bachelorette party?"

"How am I supposed to enjoy it when I'm worried your father will get into all sorts of trouble?" she moaned. "You have to promise to keep an eye on him, Declan. Don't let him take home any skanks. That wedding is happening tomorrow."

"Of course, it will. I've put a lot of effort into this." And married they would be, even if it meant a divorce a week later.

She gave a dismal laugh. "Sometimes I wonder why

you couldn't be straight. It would have been so much easier falling for you than your father."

I rolled my eyes, and my father frowned, probably wondering what his soon-to-be wife was saying to me. Judging by her words, it was impossible that their marriage would survive, but the worst thing to do was try to talk Charles out of something. It was much better to give him enough rope to hang himself with.

Too bad he never learned from each episode.

"Have a great party, Poppy," I wished her. "Our ride's here. Got to go."

Before she could respond, I hung up. Charles's face relaxed into a smile.

"Thanks for handling that, Declan," he said. "You always know exactly what to do."

"Right, and for that reason, I'm telling you that it's time to go. Unless you no longer wish to have your bachelor party."

"Like hell I don't."

That got him moving, and with a sigh, I followed him out of the guest bedroom where he was staying until tomorrow when he got hitched.

"Did you get all those bills I asked you to fetch?"

"Yes, Charles. I have your hooker money right here in my wallet."

He laughed, delighting in my words instead of taking insult. "Ah, my bad. I should have told you to hire a male stripper just for you. Too bad you didn't think of that. Then you could have let your hair down a little, had a lap dance by a hunky dude you could take home later. Might put you in a better mood for my wedding tomorrow."

I didn't take offense at his words. Too many years of his ribbing had made me immune. I had long since given up on the idea of having an actual father-figure. I had settled for the one I had, who wouldn't even allow me to call him dad.

"Makes me feel old. Just call me Charles," he had told me when I was fourteen. I hadn't called him Dad since, which hadn't been hard considering he hadn't been much of a father before that anyway.

"David, don't wait up for us," I told our butler who saw us out.

"Okay, sirs. Enjoy your night."

"I will, David, my man!" Charles said, loud enough to wake the dead.

Shaking my head, I followed him down the steps and toward the white limousine parked in the driveway. But, it wasn't the limousine that snagged my attention. I had tested out more than my fair share of luxury vehicles in my life. What I hadn't tested out was the gorgeous driver who stood leaning against the limousine. At our approach, he straightened and tugged at the jacket of his uniform.

Thanks to the well-lit yard, I was able to take in all of him as we approached. Although we were about the same height, give or take an inch or two, he was bigger than me. Not in a completely muscular way, but not fat either. He was large, a big-boned man. Judging by the lines on his face, he was probably the same age as Charles.

All the blood flooded to my crotch unexpectedly. I wasn't expecting him at all. Our eyes met, and his widened in a flicker of surprise. I saw the flaring of his nostrils, the slight ruddiness of his complexion that his neatly trimmed beard could not completely hide.

I didn't need a male stripper after all.

"Declan Moore?" he asked, his voice deep and gruff around the edges as he eyed my father.

"Don't look at me," Charles replied, coming to a halt and pointing his thumb at me. "That's this guy over here."

His attention turned to me. "I'm Declan Moore," I confirmed, stepping forward. "This is my father, Charles Moore."

He extended a hand toward me. "Hi, I'm Owen Long, and I'm your designated driver for the night. I trust you'll have a grand time."

I heard his words, but they didn't process. Not when his huge hand swallowed mine in a handshake. Damn, if just our hands touching made me feel so electrified, I didn't want to think about other parts of our bodies touching. I lifted my gaze from our hands and landed on his thin lips. The bottom one was just a little curvier than the top. As though he could fathom my thoughts, his teeth sank into his lower lip oh so briefly before he caught up on himself and released me.

"Well, are we going to stand here all night, or get moving?" Charles asked, breaking the connection.

Owen dropped my hand quickly, and I curled it into a fist, wishing his touch was a tangible thing I could take with me. It had felt nice. Electrifying. It reminded me of what I always knew. He was exactly the kind of guy I was interested in. Older, bigger, good looking, and enough interest in his eyes to make me hopeful that what I wanted wasn't impossible.

"This way, please." Owen cleared his throat and walked over to open the door for us. Charles eagerly slid inside, already chattering about the strippers he would bring back in the limousine with him. I didn't even respond, knowing it wasn't going to happen on my watch.

Before getting into the car, I turned toward Owen. I paused when I found how close we were. If I made one step, we would be touching in interesting places. Tension strained between us. The good kind of tension that usually ended in something explosive beneath sheets, sweaty bodies and throat raw from face-fucking and moans.

"Before I forget," I said, my voice low and huskier than usual. "There are two of Charles's friends that we'll have to pick up on the way to the club."

"The addresses?"

He reached for a small notepad and pen from the insides of his jacket and jotted down the addresses I gave him.

"That's it?" he asked.

Yes, I'd like to see you on your knees. Naked. I shook off the crass thought. "Yes. For now."

I heard the hitch in his breath at the "for now." I slid into the backseat of the limousine with Charles, and Owen shut the door. I repeated his name in my head, liking it. A solid, dependable name. I wondered what he was like as a person. I had sensed the attraction between us, but of course I couldn't be certain if what I felt was one-sided. My gut said it wasn't, but even if he turned out to be gay, he didn't have to be into my kind of kink. In fact, I decided he was definitely not the kind of guy who would be into my kink. He looked like a guy who took charge of situations, very much like me. Instead of this being a turn-off though, it was the biggest turn-on. To have such a big, older, powerful man submissive to me was hot.

I spent the first leg of the journey blocking out Charles, his excitement, and willing my hard-on away. I declined the glass of complimentary champagne in the cooler of the limousine.

We picked up Charles's long-time friends from college. They were every bit as excited about the bachelor party as he was. They were glad to be away from their trophy wives for a night, to skirt the edges of their wedding vows. I tuned them out and kept my focus at the back of the driver's head. I hadn't put up the partition between the driver and passengers in the back of the limo, because I wanted to look at him. I couldn't see much except how his dark hair at the nape of his neck curled.

He drove carefully, handling the huge car with ease and familiarity. I wanted to ask him how long he had been in the business. I wanted to ask him to be my boy. I'd buy him his own damn fleet of limos if that was what he wanted. But he was different. I could sense it. This was no man who could easily be turned by the green of my money.

At a stop light, he glanced in the rearview mirror at the same time I did, and our eyes clashed. He frowned, possibly trying to figure me out. I smiled ruefully at him and nodded. His eyes widened again, and though the conversation was silent, I understood it fairly well. He was debating with himself whether or not it was interest he had sensed from me. When I nodded at him, I had confirmed indeed it was . But what would he do with the knowledge? The little shake of his head as he turned his attention back to the road said he refused to believe it.

We had rented out an entire club, the parking space as well as that of the lot next door to it, so all the limousines would be in the same location. Owen drove up to the club and let himself out to come around to open the door. I allowed the other three men to go ahead of me before I exited behind them. They trotted eagerly toward the club, but I hung back, satisfied no one else was around.

"You should come in," I said, making it a statement instead of asking him. "All the drivers are welcome to join us. The more the merrier."

He shook his head. "I'd rather not. It's not really my crowd."

"You don't go to strip clubs?"

He scratched the back of his neck and frowned at me. "Not what I meant. We're from different circles. I try not to fraternize with clients. It keeps the boundaries intact."

I had a feeling he went through the whole explanation for my benefit. "So, what are you going to do? Stay out here all night? Knowing Charles, he will not want to return home until the wee hours of the morning."

He shrugged. "That's fine. I'll be here. I'm used to waiting."

I frowned at him. "That's ridiculous. What do you plan to do? Sit out here in the car all night?" I pointed toward the front of the club where a couple of men dressed in the same uniform as him were entering. "See, everyone else is joining us."

"There's a coffee shop just a block from here," he replied, sticking to his guns. He removed a small device from the inside of his jacket. "Audio book I'm listening to is four hours long. It should be perfect."

Damn stubborn man. The pleasure it will give me to punish him when he refuses to listen. I wondered what his kind of punishment should be. Would he be open to getting his ass spanked? As a Daddy, I liked punishment the least, but I didn't hesitate to mete it out when it was needed.

"Perhaps you should give me your business card or your number?" I suggested. "Just in case there's an emergency, and we're ready to leave before we anticipated."

His eyebrows rose, but he removed a wallet from his pocket and plucked a card out. "Cush requires us to bring them around." He circled something and handed it to me. "That's my personal number you can reach me on. The others will go straight to the office."

One glance at the number he circled and I already had it committed to memory. I tucked the card into the top pocket of my shirt.

"If you change your mind, feel free to come in and mingle." Even as I said it, I knew he wouldn't take up my offer. I was all the more interested in him for it.

4

OWEN

"Shit," I muttered and paused the audiobook I was trying to listen to. This was turning out to be a big waste of my time. I had thought for sure I could spend some time at the coffee shop, or in the limo listening to a good book. The conditions were right. The coffee shop was peaceful with a few people trickling in and out. I was tucked away in a far corner, so I wasn't distracted by all the movements, my Kindle was fully charged, and I was in the middle of a hot sex scene. So why the hell did I keep re-reading the same paragraph?

Declan Moore.

I couldn't get him out of my head. It wasn't like he was the first man I had been attracted to since Jenna left. While I hadn't taken any guys home with me, there had been quick blow jobs in public places and in cars to take care of my needs. I hadn't had full on penetrative sex with a man though, since my one foray in high school.

Since Jenna and I had married young, it hadn't

seemed important in the grander scheme of my kids' lives. To be honest, I had been obsessed with raising my kids, wanting to fill the hurt of their mother leaving. I hadn't wanted to bring anyone new into their lives to further upset the dynamic.

But, there was something different about Declan Moore. I hadn't expected the interest in him, because he was younger for one thing. Way too young. He didn't look older than the twins. It had been embarrassing to find I had physical desire for a guy who looked half my age. At first, I had been a bit worried he would have seen my interest because it had taken me by such surprise that I hadn't masked it well. Then his own interest had shown, which had puzzled me.

Declan Moore and I were as different as night and day. That dynamic was impossible. Yet he had insisted I join them at the club, and the damnedest thing had happened. The sexual desire had sparked at the commanding way he spoke. While having been a bottom the first time I explored, I'd never been into being bossed around or anything, but he'd almost made me want to do what he said.

The ringing of my phone startled me. I half-expected it to be Declan since he now had my number, but sighed with relief that it was only Auggie.

"Hey, Auggie. What's up?" I answered.

"Hey, Pop. Just calling to see if everything's good for tomorrow."

I grimaced. "Change of plans. Penny and Summer will travel together. I got a gig I couldn't get out of."

"Oh man. I was looking forward to seeing you."

That sent off alarm bells in my head. Auggie was the self-sufficient one. He never really needed me like the other two. "Why? What's wrong?"

"I-I just... I wanted to talk to you about something."

"Well, you can tell me now," I told him.

"Nah, it'll wait till I see you."

As much as I wanted to, I didn't push him. Auggie needed to come to me in his own time, although I suspected what he wanted to talk to me about. As far as I knew, he'd never been in a relationship, but I felt in my bones that he was gay. I'd heard from my side of the family that I was to be blamed for my kids all coming out as anything but straight.

"You're bisexual, and you married a woman who left you for another woman. Those kids didn't even stand a chance. They have the queer genes from both sides of the family."

After enduring one too many comments at my mother's last birthday, I had cut all ties with most of my family members. I loved my kids for who they were, and they were good kids. They deserved to be identified for more than just their sexuality. Oscar was a talented artist, Auggie was philosophical, and Summer was... well, she was a kind soul. I wouldn't have wished for different kids.

"There's a big chance I may be visiting Summer next weekend," I told Auggie. "I'm hoping to see you and Oscar there so we can have dinner together as a family."

"That sounds perfect. I can talk to you then."

"Great." I was really looking forward to dinner with my kids. My life would be empty now they were all out of the house. If I didn't find new hobbies and perhaps make new friends, I would go out of my mind from the loneliness.

Declan will be an interesting hobby. I pushed the thought from my mind. I couldn't wait for this gig to be over so I could get rid of Declan for good. Now that Summer would be gone tomorrow, maybe I could go barhopping and find a willing dude to take home for the night. That idea sounded interesting.

"Summer tells me Oscar has a girlfriend," I said, steering my mind back to my son. "Is it like serious?"

"Actually, he *and* another guy are dating her."

"Huh? What?"

"I shouldn't say anything. He'll explain when you see him."

I groaned, thinking about the shenanigans Oscar was probably getting into. "Just remind him to be safe, will you?"

"Don't worry. I ensure his supply of condoms never runs dry."

"Thanks. I know I ask a lot of you in being there for him."

"Well, you've done enough for us." There was a pause, and I could imagine him frowning, his brow knotted as he thought deeply about whatever he wanted to say, but trying to find a nice way about it. "Do you think you'll date now that we're out of the picture?"

"Hey, what do you mean out of the picture? You might have all decided I'm no longer fun as a roommate, but I'm still Dad. You'll never be out of the picture."

"But, you have the house to yourself now. Don't tell

me you've not met anybody interesting, or thought about it some."

"Well, maybe a little," I answered honestly. I never lied to my kids even if the truth was difficult. I helped them to deal with it. "But I'm not looking to jump into a relationship with anyone right now." *And especially not with a kid young enough to be my son.*

"Just so you know, I won't have a problem if you want to date again. Woman or man that is."

My heart swelled with affection, and I wished he was close by so I could hug him. "Thanks for letting me know that, Auggie. I appreciate it."

"Yeah, well, I gotta go now. I'll call you sometime next week to find out about your trip here. And don't worry. We'll keep an eye on sis."

"I know you will. Love you, son."

"Love you too, Dad."

Auggie hung up, and my night so full of frustration changed. My turbulent thoughts settled after the conversation I'd had with my son. I was able to return to my audiobook and get my mind off Declan.

At one, I decided to walk back to the club and continue reading in the car, especially since the battery of my Kindle was dying. I kept the earphones in my ear, hands tucked into my pocket as I walked the ten minutes back to the club. The night was busy as was to be expected on a weekend out in this part of Cincy.

Back at the club, I located the limousine I was in charge of and slipped into the driver's seat. I reclined the headrest a little, locked up, plugged in the Kindle to charge and continued listening to my book. When it ended, I wrote a quick review and opened the next book in the series.

Reading romance novels, especially LGBT ones, was my little secret that no one knew about. I had gotten into the habit after Jenna left and I needed something to occupy my time, something I could have done from home while I took care of the kids. Since they had been so young, I couldn't have left them to go partying. I took to reading which passed the time as well as gave me a little hope about romance and love. When I started working as a driver, I'd turned to audiobooks which seemed more logical for time on the road.

The party broke up around three to my relief. I wanted to get everyone home and drop off the limousine at the depot. That, in itself would be another tedious process as the vehicles were thoroughly checked before we were cleared and signed off for the day job. Although the vehicles had insurance, any significant damage that didn't have a rational explanation, generated a fine taken out of our checks.

I got out of the limousine to attend to my passengers, barely containing my disgust at the drunken guests that we would have to escort home. I had driven enough wealthy people around to know what to expect. Some got verbally abusive when intoxicated. At least seeing Declan this way would kill any attraction I harbored. I disliked entitled rich people who thought they could treat people like crap because they had money. In my experience, the majority of them were the same.

They spilled out of the club with skimpily clad women hanging on their arms, laughing at the top of their voices. It didn't escape my attention that the strippers they had hired were far from drunk. That was amusing as I already knew their habit. By the end of the night, they would have gotten as much as they could from the drunken old sods.

"Owen, man. Need a favor."

I turned to one of our drivers, Morgan, and groaned when I smelled the stench of alcohol on him. I quickly checked out the other drivers, as many as I could see to find out if any of them were drunk. They seemed to be functioning efficiently to my relief.

"What the fuck man!" I growled at Morgan. "You're drunk. You know better than to drink when you're expected to drive."

"I'm so-oorry." His words were distorted as he burped loudly. "I was-I don't know what happened. Can you carry my people?"

"How many were in your vehicle?" I asked, already trying to sort out the mess.

"Six," he answered while holding up seven fingers.

"Look, I'll ask the Moores if they can ride with us. Then I'll call Trevor to arrange a pick up for you and transport the limo back to the depot. Man, you're going to be in a fuck load of trouble."

"Is everything alright?"

I spun away from Morgan to the very sober tone of Declan Moore. I startled to find him not only sober, but as impeccably dressed as when he had entered the club. He didn't seem to have a hair out of place, and I couldn't smell any liquor on him.

"I'm sorry, but one of our drivers can't make the

journey back," I replied, trying not to make my stare accusatory. If *he* hadn't invited all the drivers in with them, this wouldn't have happened. "I'll take his passengers in our ride, if that's okay with you."

He nodded. "Of course. Where are they? I'll get them in the limo."

Morgan mumbled that they were in his ride before he proceeded to hurl. I grimaced at the condition he was in. He was as good as fired. Declan moved off to take charge of the situation, while I called Trevor who was none too pleased. He yelled in the phone until I reminded him I was simply the messenger. Eventually, he hung up, promising to come himself to collect Morgan and the limo.

I was surprised to find Declan shepherding the drunken partygoers to their respective rides. I was too much in awe to help. He moved with the grace of a man who knew what he was about. Not one time did he seem at his wits' end. Not even when a skimpily clad woman deliberately tripped into his arms. He simply righted her and turned her in the direction of our ride.

As a result of Declan ensuring everyone was taken care of, we were the last ones to load into our ride. His father and the other two guys were only too grateful for the three women who were now included in our ride home. I tried not to listen to their lewd talk as everyone got in.

"I think that's everyone," Declan remarked, then he frowned at Morgan who was sitting on the ground, moaning and clutching his head. "What about your friend? We can't just leave him here."

"More of acquaintances than friends," I replied. "My boss is on his way to get him and the limo."

"I probably shouldn't have invited them to the party, huh?"

"Nope, you shouldn't have."

"But they could have turned down the offer. You did."

"Every man has his own weakness."

He raised his eyebrow. "And yours is?"

I was saved from answering when a cab drove up, and Trevor appeared. He was apologetic to Declan who assured him it was fine. He even managed to praise Morgan for not attempting to drive, but speaking up.

"Ready now?" I asked Declan, as Trevor moved on to speak with Morgan. I didn't want to catch wind of that conversation.

"Yes, I'll sit up front with you."

I paused at that. No way in hell could I have him sit up front with me. He was distracting enough already.

"You'll need the addresses for the others who have joined us," he said, his eyes twinkling as though he figured out I was going to disagree. "I can make this ride easier for both of us if you let me."

I frowned because his words struck me as a double entendre. One I chose to ignore. "Okay then. Let's get this show on the road."

To my complete surprise, Declan stopped at the driver's side of the limousine and opened the door. At first, I thought he meant to drive the vehicle which I, of course, couldn't allow. Instead, he held the door wide open for me like I had done for him earlier. Like it was his duty to do. Not mine.

His eyes turned hard, challenging me to say something about it. Even if I wanted to, I couldn't. My throat was too tight, and I wanted more than anything to get him home. Far away from me. So I mumbled, "thank you," and prayed he didn't see how flustered I was.

"You're welcome," he said, closing the door firmly after me.

My hand shook as I tried to start the car while he walked around to get in. By the time he was settled and his seatbelt firmly in place, I had needed to make three attempts before I was able to start the car.

He recited the first address for me, and I set off, calculating that I would be the last person at the depot tonight. I would have to wait in line to get cleared to go home. Not to mention the fact that I would have to be up early tomorrow as well, to transport the groom's party to the venue where the wedding would take place.

"How was your book?" he asked on the way. "Did you get to finish?"

"Yes, and started a new one."

A loud feminine squeal followed by the rumble of male voices and chants of, "take it off," came from the back. I dared a glance in the rearview mirror, because they hadn't bothered to raise the partition. A young woman in her twenties, flashing her boobs, was being egged on to remove her top.

"You sure you don't want to write down the addresses and join the fun in the back?" I asked, hoping he would say yes.

He scoffed. "Perhaps if it was a dude wearing a jock-strap, then yeah, I might have enjoyed saying 'take it off.'"

My palms started to sweat on the steering wheel as his meaning struck me. He had just confirmed he was gay.

"And you? Which would you have joined?"

"Both," I answered without thinking, then wished I could have taken it back. This was no conversation for me to have with a client. All he needed to know about was my ability to drive and follow directions. The guy didn't need to know I swung both ways.

"Ah, have a preference of the two?" he asked.

I swallowed hard before answering. "Look, I'm not quite comfortable with our conversation right now. I think it's chalking that line I told you about earlier."

"You're not comfortable talking about your bisexuality?"

"I'm uncomfortable talking to *you* about it," I answered. "How old are you, anyway? Twenty-three?"

"Twenty-five."

"Well, my sons are twenty-three and my daughter nineteen," I replied. "You can understand from that why this is all a little uncomfortable."

"Hmm, it doesn't have to be, but I'll let it go for now."

I sighed with relief, sure he had to be toying with me. I was twenty-one years older than Declan. He had to know there was nothing that could come of this, and if it was a casual hookup he was looking for, I wasn't inter-ested in someone so young.

It didn't matter that I liked his commanding voice. He was only two years older than my sons. I doubted when Auggie had given me the greenlight to date again he had meant someone who could be his own boyfriend.

Tomorrow couldn't come fast enough for me to forget Declan Moore.

5

DECLAN

"Earth to Declan!" Ridge snapped his fingers in front of my face, and I scowled at him.

"You do that again, I'm gonna put you across my knees," I snapped at him. I was full of tension, wound up by the fact that I was about to see Owen again so soon after last night. I didn't have much patience for Ridge and his usual antics when I was contemplating the best approach to wining over Owen.

Ridge grinned at me and reached for the buckle that held up his dress pants. "Where do you want to do it? Here?"

I shook my head at him, slightly bemused despite how tense I was. "Apparently your new Daddy's not being heavy-handed enough with you if you're still being such a flirt," I told him. "Stop antagonizing me and help me with my tie."

He approached me with a dramatic sigh and held the two pieces of my tie while I tended to my cufflinks.

"You seem even more testy than usual," he observed aloud. "Did something happen at the party last night? I wanted to go, but I was being rude, so Daddy grounded me to stay in."

I remained silent as I contemplated whether or not I should tell him. Ridge was my oldest and most trustworthy friend. If I couldn't tell him about the interesting man I had met, I couldn't talk to anyone about it.

"Last night I met a man. I want to make him my boy."

His hands stilled on the tie, and he raised his head. "You're not joking, are you?"

"No. He's perfect for the part, Ridge."

"Perfect how?"

"Perfect image. Perfect attitude. He's older. Lots older, and although he did argue some things, I don't think he will be opposed to taking orders once he gets into the habit. I can't wait to break him in."

He abandoned the tie altogether and placed a hand on my chin, adjusting my head so I looked at him. "This sounds serious."

"There's still a lot of work to be done," I answered, trying to downplay the excitement that was buzzing through my veins. I hadn't felt so invigorated by the possibilities of a relationship in a long time. "He might be a bit difficult to manage at first. I don't think he's the kind of guy who knows when to let someone take care of him for a change."

"You got all that in one night?"

"In just a couple hours really."

"So, what else do you know about him?"

I frowned and caught the abandoned tie to do it myself. "He's got three kids."

Ridge gave a mock shudder. "Yikes. Good luck with that."

"They are grown. The youngest is nineteen."

"Yeah, but it still makes things sticky. What if his kids disapprove? Is the mother in the picture?"

"Those are the questions I need to find out today, my friend."

My tie fixed, I stared into the mirror and patted my dark brown hair. I used to get mistaken for a submissive twink when I came out as gay. I still carried a slender frame, an athletic body, but working out in the gym had given my form definition and muscles. I still couldn't grow facial hair, and my face would probably always look a little on the boyish side, but what I lacked in appearance, I made up for with my commanding presence—or so I had been told.

A knock sounded on my bedroom door, startling me out of my thoughts.

"Come in!"

The door pushed open and David, my fulltime butler, poked his head in. "Your ride is here, sir."

My heart skipped a beat in anticipation. I glanced at the clock on the wall, pleased to discover Owen was ten minutes early. "Has he been waiting long?"

"No, sir. He just drove up."

"Excellent. I'll be down in a little while."

Since my bedroom overlooked the courtyard, I moved to the balcony and stared out at the same white limousine from last night. Owen was lounging against the vehicle, dressed formally in the dark suit of his uniform. A warm feeling settled in my gut as I watched him unnoticed. His lips were moving as though he was talking to himself, and I would have killed to know what he was saying.

"What's so interesting?" Ridge asked, coming up behind me. He rested his hand on my waist and took in the sight of Owen.

"Who's that?" he started to ask before he glanced back at me. "That's him, isn't it?"

"Yes, that's Owen. Man of my fantasies."

"You start saying shit like that and I'll be inclined to believe you fell in love at first sight."

I scowled at him. "Who said anything about love? Love's overrated."

"Not when it's the right person." Ridge returned his attention to the driver. "I still don't get why you like older guys so much. I mean, I can see the appeal. He's hot as fuck, but he looks like someone who belongs on top. Not the other way around."

Because we had engaged in this conversation so many times before, I didn't bother to respond. I didn't expect Ridge to get it. There was something powerful about claiming an older man's body, taking charge of that relationship and having our roles reversed. An image of Owen kneeling in bed, naked, face flushed with passion and need flashed through my mind.

Fuck me, Daddy.

The mental picture was so hot I immediately became hard. It didn't matter if Ridge got it. The fact was that it fucking turned me on. Adjusting my cock, I backed up from the balcony. "Do me a favor," I threw at Ridge as I headed for the door. "Check on Charles and ensure he's ready. Have everyone down in fifteen."

"You owe me for dealing with your father!" he yelled after me.

I ignored Ridge and tried not to show my excitement as I descended the stairs. Owen didn't immediately see me when I walked out of the house. He was checking out the yard, his head turned to the side, and the sunlight glistened on the silver strands at his temples. I loved seeing those silver strands, yearned to kiss the hair at his temples. I wanted to kiss him all over until he begged me to make him come.

"I like a man who's punctual," I said as I walked toward him.

He didn't immediately turn to face me. His jaw tensed, and he inhaled deeply before he slowly turned. His eyes swept over me and the formal attire of my wedding suit, but I couldn't tell what he thought, because his eyes were deliberately shuttered.

"Mr. Moore, good afternoon," he greeted me all formally.

So that's the way he's going to play today.

"I trust you got enough sleep?" I asked, noting the circles under his eyes. They weren't prominent, but I was observant when it came to him—to most things really.

"Enough to function for the day," he answered.

Before I could say anything else, his phone rang. He reached into his pocket and took out the outdated device that didn't even have a camera. He glanced at the screen then back at me. "Sorry, this is kind of important."

"It's fine."

"Hey, sweetie," he answered the call, and my insides froze. I hadn't even given much thought to him being in a relationship already. I had taken one look at him and decided that he was mine.

"Alright, don't forget to grab your inhaler," he continued, and paused before adding, "Call me when you get there. Auggie says he'll pop over later to ensure you're settled." Pause. "Yeah, well, get used to it. They are your big brothers, and I can sleep well at night knowing they are close by. Otherwise I'd have to pack up and move to Columbus too." Pause. "Okay, just kidding. Maybe. I'm on the job right now, so I have to go." Another pause. "Love you too, Summer."

By the end of his conversation, I realized he had been talking to one of his kids.

"Family crisis?" I asked, giving him the opening to talk about his family so I could learn more about him.

"Not really. My last kid's leaving the nest. I was supposed to go with her today."

While I couldn't be entirely unselfish because I was glad to see him today, I could feel a bit of empathy for him not being there for his daughter. I had no idea what that was like. My grandfather had been the strong influence in my life before he died. Charles rarely ever gave a shit.

"And because of me you can't," I stated, giving him what I hoped was an apologetic smile. "I'll make it up to you."

He gave a half-laugh, half-choke. "I'm just doing my job, Mr. Moore. A job. Nothing more."

I dismissed his meaning. "So, with your kids all gone, it's just you and your wife?"

"I'm a single parent."

I was impressed. "Of three kids? Must have been a handful."

"Doesn't matter if they were at times," he answered, his tone full of affection. "Twenty-three years of parenting have paid off. They are wonderful young adults now, and if there were sleepless nights, busting my ass off working to ensure they had what they needed, it was all worth it."

At the end of the impassioned speech, it was as though he caught up on himself. He blushed, and his eyes took on a vulnerable look. I wanted to ask him who took care of him while he was taking care of the kids? I had the impression he had been going at it all alone.

The front door of the house opened, breaking the mood I had been creating between us. I frowned as Ridge, Charles, and his two friends made their way toward us.

"We'll continue talking about this later," I said softly so no one heard. I felt him stiffen beside me, but he didn't protest. He transformed into work mode, opening the limousine door for us. I didn't bother to ask to sit up front with him this time. I would rather give him the space to think. He was aware of the attraction between us, but he was feeling guilty about the age gap. Somehow, I would have to let him get comfortable with the idea of us, and what I wanted to do to him. *My God, the things I want to do to this man.*

"Let's go marry your father off," Ridge announced,

giving me a wink. I frowned, wondering what he was up to, but then he reached up and smacked a kiss to the corner of my mouth before ducking into the limousine. I glanced up at Owen who stood holding the door. His body had gone even more rigid, and he refused to look at me, but I saw the ticking in his clenched jaw.

Ridge was right. I damn well owed him.

Owen closed the door just a little too hard before walking around to the driver's seat. I watched him, listened to the rumble of his voice as he asked if everyone was comfortable before backing out of the driveway.

"The answer is yes," Ridge whispered to me in a low voice. We sat in the far corner, leaving Charles and his friends to their conversation.

"To what question?" I asked Ridge.

"If he wants you too," he replied. "I sensed jealousy when I kissed you."

"You might have warned me before you did it," I said, but smiled at him. "Thank you. I think you're right."

6

OWEN

I startled as the front passenger door of the limousine opened and Declan slipped inside, closing the door behind him. I flushed because even though I had my earphones in to listen to one of my audiobooks, I had been immersed with thoughts of this bewitching young man. I didn't want him. I had drilled that into my head last night, but when I had seen him this morning looking ravishing in his wedding attire, all the longing mocked the mental exercise I had gone through last night.

Thankfully, I had three kids and knew what to do about self-control. I was used to making sound decisions, so I had made one when I subtly told Declan earlier that I was only here to do my job. *If that's true, why did you get jealous when the other guy kissed him?*

My gut tightened as I remembered the kiss. There was very little to it to be honest, just the slightest brush of lips against lips. Still, my reaction scared the shit out of me. It had been so long since I had been jealous of anyone. To find myself envious over someone kissing this young man was unnerving.

Throughout the drive to the five-star hotel where the wedding took place, he and his friend had sat with their heads close to each other, talking in low tones. From the way I caught them glancing at me in the rearview mirror, they had been discussing me. That had left me even more bothered, and all I wanted was for the day to end.

"Hey, you okay?" Declan asked, shifting to make himself comfortable while facing me.

I swallowed hard. "Shouldn't you be at the reception? What are you doing here?" As the vehicle carrying the bridal party, I had parked on the hotel's parking deck after unloading everyone. He was meant to call me once the event was over so I could pick up the bride and groom. I would drive them to a private helipad so they could embark on their honeymoon.

Then that would be the end of me seeing Declan. And no, that was definitely not a pang of regret in my gut.

"Answer my question first," he said. "Are you okay?"

His question unnerved me. I was the one who usually asked people if they were fine, not the other way around. People took one look at me, saw that I was a big guy, and immediately assumed I was able to take care of myself. I was unsettled by the way Declan asked the question, as though expecting an honest answer.

"I'm fine," I answered, my face growing hot. "This is my job, you know. I'm used to sitting and waiting."

"Must be boring," he replied, shifting slightly to face me better. "Thought I'd keep you company."

I groaned. "Not necessary."

"I assure you, it is. Here, I brought you something."

I blinked at him as he extended a closed box in my direction. I looked at it suspiciously, and he laughed.

"You don't have to look at it like that. It's just cake."

"You brought me cake?" I shook my head at him in wonder. "Why?"

He shrugged. "I thought you'd like it. Will you take it from me? I swear I haven't added love potion to it or anything."

Jesus, he's killing me. Because I couldn't be bothered with the back and forth between us, I took the cake box from him, hoping he would leave afterward. "Thank you. That was thoughtful."

"I'm a thoughtful guy," he remarked. "Go ahead, taste it. Let me know what you think. I picked it out. I picked out every damn thing for this wedding. One would think it was my own."

"Maybe it's good practice for when you and your... err... boyfriend tie the knot."

His eyebrows rose. "Boyfriend? Hmm. I'm not in a relationship. Trying, but not quite there yet."

I looked away from him because the interest in his eyes gutted me. Was he crazy? Didn't he know that I was way too old for him? My mouth twisted bitterly. Who was I kidding? Rich little boy probably thought he could toy with the limo driver, get him into bed for a night then discard him.

I tried the cake and ignored him. I was prepared to

just chomp on it, but the delicate cake crumbled into my mouth revealing a buttery inner cream that exploded with flavor on my tongue. A moan slipped out before I could stop it. I had a sweet tooth, and this cake hit all the right spots going down. I stuffed another piece of the cake into my mouth to cover it up, fearing it was already too late anyway.

"Good?" he asked with a big grin that revealed he hadn't miss the moan.

I swallowed. "Yes, amazing."

I finished off the last piece, giving myself some time to think about how to tell him nicely, but firmly, that I didn't need his attention.

"I thought about bringing you a drink too, but figured you wouldn't drink even one glass," he said, with a slight shrug.

"That's fine. I always keep my bottle of water here."

Before I could get to my bottle, he shifted further toward me, his hand coming up to my face. "You have a bit of crumb here." I froze as his fingers brushed the side of my mouth. His lips curved into a small smile, but he didn't just stop at brushing. I imagined he had brushed away the crumb already because now his thumb teased the corner of my mouth. He slipped that errant thumb over my bottom lip, and my mouth went dry. I raised my eyes to his and saw the stark hunger there. It was predatory. Hot. Fuck. I needed to stop this.

"You've a nice mouth," he said softly, and every word was a tick of the timebomb of want ready to explode. Tick. Tick. Tick. Timed to the beating of my pulse. "I'm going to kiss you, and you're going to let me. You know why?"

The sound that came out of my throat should have been a growl, but sounded more like a moan to my ear.

"Because, you've been thinking about this as much as I have."

His hand slipped from my face to the back of my head, urging me forward. The hold he had over me left me breathless even before his lips crashed into mine. He kissed me boldly like a man who knew what he wanted and wasn't afraid to go after it. Even as my brain demanded that I pull away, his mouth coaxed me to open up for him.

The cake box tumbled from my hand when his tongue plunged into my mouth. I grabbed at his shoulders, feeling the long moan rip from my throat and not able to do anything about it. My body had found a master it had not known it needed.

My nipples tingled and blood surged into my groin. His fingers tightened in my hair, the painful tug exciting me. It had been so long since I'd felt so heated. So long since I wanted to settle on my knees and pull down my boxers. His kiss reminded me that it had been too long since I had been fucked. There was no mistake about his kiss. All this time I had thought he would want me to fuck him, which I wasn't completely averse to, but his kiss said that he wanted to possess me, to own me, to fuck *me*.

The extent of his desire heated my blood while at the same time it frightened me.

His hand released my hair, and he sank his teeth into my bottom lip as he palmed my cock through the material of my trousers. So good. So fucking delicious. I could hump his fist and spill my release right there. I wanted... needed... My hips nudged upwards, pressing into his touch, craving more.

"Please." The plea fell from my lips as my harsh breathing filled the space where we were. He continued kneading my cock through my trousers, hand digging into my flesh, squeezing and releasing.

He licked the line of my jaw up to my ear. "I don't want our first time to be in a car," he murmured, a shiver running through my spine as his breath filled my ear. "Nope. I want you in bed, beneath me, staring into my eyes while I fuck you senseless into the mattress. I want you to call me Daddy, and you'll be my boy. You'll be a good boy, won't you, Owen?"

I was with everything he said until the Daddy part. I jerked away from him, confused. "Wha-at?"

He smiled like he hadn't dropped a bombshell in my lap. "You heard right," he answered.

I shook my head. "Can't have. I thought I heard you say you want me to call you Daddy?" I wanted him to deny it, because then, maybe I could give both of us what we wanted. Just one night. What would one night be? Good sex. Amazing sex. I felt it between us. The undeniable chemistry. After that kiss, there was no sense in pretending I wasn't attracted to him. My cock was still tenting my fucking pants. He'd had that same hard cock in his hands, caressing it, just a minute ago.

"Yeah, is it so hard to think of doing it? Age is a matter of semantics."

He was serious. By god he was serious and expected

me to call him... Daddy? I'd never called anyone Daddy in my entire life, and I wasn't about to start calling a man almost the same age as my sons Daddy just for him to get his rocks off.

I wiped the back of my hand across my lips as though that could make it go away. It didn't. I could still taste the unique flavor of Declan Moore who had disturbed my quiet life. "You're two years older than my sons," I replied, trying to go for calm and reason with him. It couldn't be so hard for him to see why nothing he said made sense.

"I already know that," he answered, just as calmly. "I won't insist in you calling me Daddy if it makes you feel uncomfortable. You can call me Sir instead."

I gaped at him. "You want me to call you *Sir?*"

"Why not? You already call me Mr. Moore."

I fell back into my seat and scrubbed my hand over my face. He was confusing the hell out of me. It didn't help that my brain was still muddled by that kiss. Fuck, he was a good kisser. His lips and tongue would feel good all over my body. I had forgotten what that felt like.

I cleared my throat and tried to regain control. "Look, that kiss should never have happened." I expected him to interrupt me, and when he didn't, I turned to face him. He was looking at me, a small smile on his lips that unnerved me. It was like, although he heard my words, he knew what my body wanted.

"But it did," he replied. "And it won't go away. You know what else it did, Owen? It confirmed what we both know. That we want each other."

"Yeah, well, we don't always get what we want. I'm just here as your driver."

"But you want me to be so much more." He placed a hand on my thigh, stroking, and my muscles bunched beneath his touch. "I don't want to make you uncomfortable, Owen. Believe me, that's not my intention, and I'm going to back off because I know it's a lot for you, but don't make any mistake about it. I'll see you again after today. I'll give you some time to think about it and what I want to offer you. You can stay home and listen to all the audiobooks in the world and let me take care of you."

I turned red at his words, and this time it wasn't from embarrassment. It was from anger. I should have known it would boil down to this. He had all this money and thought he could buy my ass with it?

"I'm not interested in your money, *sir*," I added the last word for good measure. "I'm not for sale, and if you weren't a client, I'd tell you just where you could stuff your money." Right up his rich entitled ass.

Instead of being pissed off, he grinned at me, and damn if it didn't make me more upset and aroused. "It'll give me great pleasure to tame you. I'll see you around."

He left the car, and I slammed my fist into the steering wheel. "Fuck!" This could not be happening. Had I been out of the game for so long that I was allowing myself to be bested by someone like Declan? I'd always been versatile. Even in my relationship with Jenna, I'd allowed her to peg me. I had enjoyed it, being the bottom and feeling so sensual while getting pounded.

For fifteen years I had not gotten my ass fucked though, which was a long time for someone who enjoyed that activity. That had to be the reason I was falling for Declan's honey-dripped words. Despite him being young, the man had a sort of control and commanding presence that usually turned me on. That made me want to do whatever he asked to feel more of those scorching kisses. To feel his hands on me. Lips on me. Body on me. In me.

But no. Hell no. I refused to call a man just two years older than my sons, Daddy. Not gonna happen.

7

DECLAN

"Fuck. Why are we here again?" I asked the man shimmying beside me as we entered the club.

"Because you need cheering up," Ridge replied, placing a hand around my waist. "You've been brooding more than usual of late."

I scowled at my friend, plucking his arm from around my waist, but he gave an I'm-not-gonna-apologize-for-saying-it shrug. I didn't argue with him, because he had a point. I had been out of sorts this week. Thanks to Owen Long. I'd tortured myself all week between calling him or not. I had his number. I had even toyed with the idea of calling Cush and requesting him, but I decided against it. If he didn't want to play my game, I had no reason to chase him. No reason to seek him out. It would be better for me to find someone else who appreciated my kink. Someone who didn't mind calling me Daddy and enjoying it too.

I rubbed a hand at the back of my neck and followed

Ridge's shimmying hips. *He* was clearly in the mood for partying. I wasn't. I had partied some during college but since joining my father's company, work had become more important. I took my responsibilities seriously, although I enjoyed having fun too. The club could be an agreeable place with the right entertainment.

I'd had only one condition when Ridge had asked me to go out. I didn't want to hit up our regular spots. I'd wanted somewhere low-key where no one would recognize me. All the expensive clubs knew me by name and face. This club, Reprobate, was in the middle of the ones I used to visit. Not sleazy enough to admit everyone, but not having the usual uptown crowd either.

"I've found us a booth!" Ridge cried, waving me over. He was wearing skinny red leather pants and a white cotton shirt with most of the buttons undone. He looked like a little slut, and he loved it. I shook my head as I watched him slide into the booth. I followed him, sitting on the opposite side. The club was already in full swing despite it being quite early at some minutes after ten. The music was loud, but not so much where we were sitting. The dance floor and deejay were at the other end of the club.

"When's Vincent meeting you?" I asked about his new Daddy. We had already met last week for dinner so I could check out the guy. He seemed okay enough though I predicted Ridge would burn a hole right through him in no time and move on.

He glanced down at the Rolex on his wrist. "In about fifteen minutes," he answered. "Enough time for me to get up your ass about finding a guy already."

"I found a guy."

"Yeah, but he's not interested."

I didn't believe that at all. Not after the way he had kissed me back in the limo. His body had recognized the call of passion we were all slaves to even if his brain had denied it. I had no idea why people were so hung up about age. Charles, for instance was forty-nine years old, and he didn't act his age. He behaved like an eighteen-year-old with raging hormones. While at twenty-five, I had taken on more responsibility than most people my age. I almost ran our company single-handedly.

"I wouldn't say he's not interested," I replied. "Just needs a little persuasion to forget about our age difference."

"It *is* a huge age difference."

I scowled at him. "That man who's fucking your ass tonight is almost sixty. Wanna keep digging at my age fetish?"

Ridge raised his hands in surrender. "Sheesh. Don't snap my head off. It's just the natural order of things in our community that the older guy takes care of the younger guy."

"Says who?" I challenged him.

He rose to his feet. "Says every single Daddy who's looking for a twink to coddle. You could be a twink if you want, but nope. You'd rather be a Daddy even though you're just fucking twenty-five." He rolled his eyes at me. "Do you know how many daddies are already out there who would love a chance at you?"

"Except I'm not looking to be fucked by anyone," I reminded him. "I like it quite fine the other way around, and I'm not going to change my preference to suit anyone. That's like asking you to fuck the same guy for the rest of your life."

He had a funny expression on his face. "Hey, I may find someone who gets me to commit." His face broke into a grin. "Who am I kidding? I can't see that happening either. You're probably right. You *are* good at fucking." I grinned at the man who appeared over his shoulder, but didn't say anything as he continued. "Would let all that goodness go to waste if you suddenly become a bottom. At least not indefinitely. A little bit of versatility wouldn't kill you though, you know."

"Are you offering?" I couldn't resist asking.

The man behind him tapped his shoulder. "I'd think twice before I answered that question if I were you."

Ridge startled, his face going red as he spun around to face his Daddy. He tried to adopt a sweet expression, pushing out his bottom lip and letting his lithe body go bendy. I had to admit that sex with Ridge had been flexible. He was bendy as fuck and could balance in all kinds of positions while having sex.

"Daddy!" Ridge cried, resting his hands to the man's pudgy stomach. "You're early."

Hearing Ridge call his man Daddy carved out a longing inside me. Why was it wrong to want to be called Daddy by an older man? No one frowned on it if it was the opposite.

"I sensed you were up to no good," Vincent replied, "Remind me to punish you when we get home." Vincent then turned to me and nodded. "Moore, fancy seeing you in this club."

"Change of scenery does a man some good," I replied.

He shook his head at me. "No one would think you two are the same age. A pity some of your responsible nature didn't rub off on this one."

"Well, we all have our own roles to play," I remarked. "You two going to dance?"

Vincent glanced down at Ridge who nodded up at him. "Yeah, let me bump and grind against you, Daddy."

"Lead the way."

I watched Vincent and Ridge walk off toward the dance floor. There was a certain man I wouldn't mind bumping and grinding against, but first how to get him to want me enough to agree to call me Daddy and be my boy?

A twink came over to my booth, scantily clad in jock strap and body glitter that would be a bitch to get off.

"Lap dance?" he asked, his pink lips stretched in a lascivious smile.

It was on the tip of my tongue to tell him no, but then I remembered Ridge imploring me to let go of my fetish, try something new. Maybe it would catch on if I let go of the hope of finding a more mature guy.

"Get on with it then," I told the boy.

"That'll be thirty dollars," he said. "An extra twenty if you want to touch me while I'm all over you."

I gave him a fifty just in case Ridge was right, I was wrong, and I wanted to touch him. The boy didn't seem a day over twenty. In reality, he should have been perfect for me. We weren't far apart in age, and he was an eager little thing as he gyrated on me. Slender, long limbs void of hair wrapped around me, teasing me. He had a skinny ass that fit his frame well.

To be fair, he was rubbing on me, so my dick responded at first, but the longer he kept at it, the more my interest waned. It became too evident that he was not right. He was too slender. His face too smooth, his body too hairless. His brown eyes were all wrong. They weren't the piercing blue I craved.

I couldn't tell exactly why I peered at the bar. I just felt compelled to look. It was probably my subconscious letting me know I hadn't had a drink yet since dropping by. Whatever it was, I found those piercing blue eyes I was just thinking about watching me. I sucked in a deep breath, excitement coursing through my veins at the sight of Owen scowling at me.

The stripper's hand brushed over my cock. He pressed closer to me, and I grabbed his ass cheeks, squeezing hard. I had paid to touch after all, which I hadn't planned to do, but knowing Owen was watching was incentive enough. He looked on us like he had done when Ridge kissed me. Why would he look so upset if he wasn't interested? The heat in his gaze just now wasn't of a man who wanted to keep his distance. It was of a man who wanted to be fucked. To be owned.

Blood flowed to my crotch at the thought. This seemed to excite the stripper. He started slipping down my body, under the table, hand reaching for my zipper.

"I'll blow you for a hundred," he said, licking his lips. "And you have to wear a condom."

"I'll pay you two hundred if you stay under the table just like that," I told him, glancing up to verify that Owen was still looking at me. He was, although he tried to look away fast when I noticed. "Just for five minutes."

His eyes narrowed. "You sure you don't want me to suck you? I don't mind."

"I'm sure. Just stay under the table."

I leaned my head back against the booth like I was basking in the pleasure of having my dick sucked. One hand remained on the stripper's head beneath the table. Half-masting my eyes, I kept my gaze on Owen, watching every play of emotion that crossed his features.

8

OWEN

Tearing my eyes away from Declan who was having his dick sucked by the same twink I had turned down for a lap dance, I grabbed my drink and knocked it back. I grunted as the liquor went down hard. *I don't give a fuck*, I tried to tell myself. Good for him that he could get a blow job out in the open like that. I had at least used a bathroom stall, or behind the building in a dark alley, the couple of times I'd had my junk sucked off at the club.

My chest constricted into an uncomfortable tightness as I tried not to glance back at them. Fucking bastard. I had known he was toying with me, and I should be glad I had turned him down, but I had already made a fool of myself by kissing him back at his father's wedding. Now he was probably having fun at my expense, showing me that he didn't need me after all. He could fuck whoever he wanted.

Earlier after I got off work, I had convinced myself

that going out would be a good idea. I had been sick and tired of being in the house alone, haunted by the memory of Declan's lips on mine, his hot breath brushing my ear, his hand on my thigh. I had convinced myself that I needed to go to a club, get semi-wasted, bring a guy back home with me for the first time in over twenty-three years and fuck all night until the demon-clawed memories of Declan left me alone.

It could not be healthy to obsess so much about one man.

I had the urge to leave the club, but if I left now, he would know it was because of him. No, I'd keep my ass seated at the bar like I didn't have a care in the world. Like I didn't have any insecurities about what he really had wanted from me.

I hadn't dated much before Jenna and I became a couple, so I didn't know what to expect. As a teen, the short relationships I had formed had mainly been concerned with groping and experimenting. The one other semi-serious relationship had been with a guy that had involved sex way too soon before we broke up.

At forty-six, I couldn't have flighty expectations. I didn't want life in the fast lane. I needed a steady man. Or woman. Although the way my interest was shaping up these days, I was pretty sure I would end up with a man. All *he* could offer was one night of bliss. Fuck. Bliss. I grunted at the thought of what his lips would feel like over my naked body.

If only I could get Declan out of my mind so I could set my eyes on someone who would be more suitable for me. Someone who could join me at dinner with my kids.

Bringing Declan to dinner with mine would be nothing short of awkward. How would my children even look at me?

And yet, a deep part of me, the part that had enjoyed his kisses, wanted me to be the one under the table sucking his cock. Not that my bulk could have fit under the table anyway.

"Need another drink?"

I stiffened at the hot breath that fanned the side of my face as the forbidden subject of my fantasy whispered next to my ear.

"I'll take care of it," I answered. "You seem busy, so don't mind me over here."

He ignored me, leaned on the counter and signaled the bartender. He smelled damn good, so good that it distracted me from saying no when he asked the bartender to bring me another glass of whatever I was having. While he waited for the bartender to return, he pointed at my glass. "Finished with that?"

"Yes." My reply was curt.

He snatched up the glass and scooped out an ice cube, sucking it into his mouth. I watched the way his throat worked, his Adam's apple prominent as he chewed up the ice and swallowed.

"It's quite hot in here," he stated, leveling me with his eyes. "Fancy seeing you here. You don't strike me as the club type."

I grunted a noncommittal response and decided instead of playing petty, I'd have the drink after all. I would show him that nothing he had just done bothered me. *Kissing me one day and kissing someone else the next.* I gave him a tight smile when the bartender placed the drink before us. "Thank you for the drink."

"You're welcome. Have whatever you want. I'll put your tab on mine."

"Let me guess. I have to pay you back on my knees, right?"

He drank thirstily from his glass, unbothered by my comment. "Do you want to get down on your knees?"

"That wasn't the question."

"It is now."

I bit back a nasty retort and brought the glass to my lips instead. Silence ensued between us, and although I wasn't looking at him, I could feel him watching me. I wished he would stop as heat was beginning to flood my face.

"Were you jealous?"

I sputtered my drink over the counter. I was, but hell if I was going to admit it to him. The bartender muttered under his breath as he wiped down the mess. I apologized and decided right there and then that Declan was hazardous to my common sense. I needed to get out of there and home to my lonely bed. My cock was already well acquainted with my right hand, so I doubted it would put up much of a fuss tonight.

"Why would I be jealous?" I asked.

"Hmm, because I would be if that had been you getting blown by a stripper in a bar."

I sucked in a deep breath once more, my brain scattering at the outlandish things he said.

"Yeah, well, I tend to mind my business, and this is none of mine."

"If it's any consolation, he didn't suck me off."

I narrowed my gaze at him. "You'd stoop that low and lie to me because you want me in your bed? I saw you."

"You saw him under the table and me slipping him a couple hundred bucks to stay there."

"What? Why'd you do that?"

"Err, I wanted to see what your reaction would be."

There, I confirmed he was teasing me. That was all he wanted me for. To make fun. He must have known how attracted I was to him, and now he was using it to debase me.

I slid off the bar stool, grabbed my jacket I had placed on the back and shrugged it on. "Get this in your head, Declan. I'm not some puppet you can wind up when you want, okay. I'm a grown-ass man old enough to be *your* dad."

Instead of cowering under my glare, he licked his lips. "You're going to be a handful managing, aren't you? Thank god, I like a challenge."

Frustrated that he still refused to get it into his head that I wasn't interested, I stalked away from him. I didn't look back, but I felt disappointed when he didn't try to call to me. If he really wanted me as badly as he claimed, he would have come after me, wouldn't he? I snorted in disbelief because I didn't want him to come after me. I swore I didn't.

Once outside the club, I sucked in a deep breath, cursing because I hadn't taken my car. I had plans to drink more than what was acceptable for driving tonight, so I'd left the car at home, opting for a cab. I had planned to either hitch a ride with whatever man I dragged to my bed, or call another cab to pick me up.

I dug into my pocket for my phone and came up empty. I didn't have either my wallet or my phone. I patted the pockets of my jacket and my jeans again. Fuck. Did I leave them at home? No, I had paid the cab driver from my wallet. I had checked the time on my phone right then too. I'd had both on me. I hadn't taken them out in the bar, so I couldn't have left them at the counter, and if I had, they would be gone by now.

"Something wrong?"

I closed my eyes tightly at the bane of my existence. He was persistent. I had to give him that.

"My wallet and phone are gone," I replied, still feeling my pockets as if they would magically reappear.

"Maybe you left them at home?" Declan asked, approaching me.

I glanced up at him and became temporarily distracted by how good looking he was. Nicely sculpted cheekbones and a spectacular body. *And he wants to fuck me?*

"Well, did you?" he prompted.

"I'm quite positive I had them on me."

"Want to go back into the club and check if you left them at the bar?"

I shook my head. "Even if I did, someone would have snatched them already."

"What are you going to do now?" he asked, hands deep into his pockets.

If he was anyone else, I would have asked him to give me a lift home, but I couldn't. I would be playing right into his hands of all this nonsense about taking care of me. I was a six foot tall strapping man who was bigger than him. Why did I need him to take care of me?

"Ask me."

I blinked at him. "Ask you what?"

"To take you home. There's your solution right there."

I opened my mouth, but no sound came out. I couldn't. I shut my mouth, my frown deepening. If I accepted a ride from him, it wasn't like he was big enough to hold me against my will. But I didn't trust myself around him. Not one bit. I had a penchant which seemed to go weak at the sound of his voice, and the way he spoke with such calm, like he believed everything would eventually go his way.

And, well, if he took me home that was one step closer to getting me into bed. I had meant to bring home somebody tonight, but not him. Never him.

His sigh was long and heavy. "We'll have to work on your ability to ask for things you need," he said, and placed a firm hand at my lower back. "Come on. My car's this way. I'll drop you home."

I dug my heels in. "It's fine. I'll find a way to get home."

He paused before me. "Owen, don't be stubborn. Let me help you."

"I don't need your help. You only have one thing in mind."

He threw his hands up in the air, the first time I was seeing him even a little ruffled since we had met. "I swear to god, Owen…"

The way he growled at me was supposed to upset me, not screw with my brain. Heat pooled into my belly and flooded my cock. He was so fucking hot when he glared at me. I had the sudden urge to argue with him as much as possible just to push his buttons. To be a brat. His brat.

Holy hell, he'd infected my brain. I had no other explanation for the thoughts running through my head. I'd never been anybody's brat. Never. I had grown up a solid and dependable guy. And this was a perfect sign that I shouldn't get into Declan's car with him.

"You swear what?" I heard myself test him.

"I swear if you continue with this nonsense, I'll put you across my knees the first chance I get." Staring into my eyes, he bit his bottom lip and added, "I'll spank your ass red."

Sweet holy hell, I was losing all the oxygen from my brain. Every bit of it was draining into my cock. No wonder my stupid brain had me visualizing myself over Declan's knees, my bare ass to the ceiling as his beautiful slender hands crashed down onto my backside.

"You're being ridiculous again," was the only thing I could manage to strangle out.

"Maybe. We can talk about the ridiculousness of it all when we're driving to your house. Let's face it, Owen. You need to get home. You don't have any cash on you. Don't fight it, or I'm going to start thinking you don't trust yourself around me."

And how could I continue turning down his offer if that was the impression I was going to leave him with?

9

DECLAN

L ust pounded in my blood to have Owen next to
me in my car. It was a heady feeling, more than
just want. It was also power, pride, and pleasure
at having him so close to me, letting me take care of him,
even if it was just to bring him home. His hands were
really tied, and he wouldn't have accepted my offer if
he'd had a better option, but he had none. I was glad he
had none as it forced us together, and even if the journey
wasn't more than half an hour, it was still more time
with him.

"Do you go to that club often?" I asked him, because
the silence in the car was thick, and it made the desire
that much more evident. Nervous energy was bouncing
off him.

"Nope," he answered, and said nothing else. He had
buckled his seatbelt which I didn't have to remind him to
do unlike Charles. I never realized before just how a
small responsible act could make my heart melt.

I glanced at Owen's profile. He was so tense, sitting ramrod straight and staring ahead. If he didn't need to blink, he probably wouldn't have.

"You can relax, you know," I told him.

"I am relaxed," he answered.

"No, you're not," I contradicted him. "I won't bite." Then I added in a softer tone. "At least, not tonight."

His sharp intake of breath filled the car, and I grinned. As much as he fought the attraction between us, he wanted me. If he hadn't been interested in me, I would have left him alone from the moment we had met. I was determined to break down whatever constraints he had about us because of societal brainwashing about age-appropriateness for dating.

"It's been a while since I was driven by someone," he remarked, ignoring my statement.

"Because you're always the one driving people around," I commented, understanding. "Is that why you're so tense? You don't like giving up the driver's seat, do you?" The question was a loaded one, and I waited for him to respond.

"It's not a matter of liking it or not," he finally answered after seconds ticked by. "I stay in the driver's seat because it's my job, my responsibility. I don't have to like it, but I do it because it's there to be done, and people are relying on me."

"I'd have thought because you drive for a living you would relish the opportunity to be in the passenger seat when it pops up."

"But the opportunity rarely does. It's not just about a job. It was me driving my kids to soccer practice, rehearsals, recitals and such. With three kids, I pretty much had my butt planted in the driver's seat all the time even when I was off schedule."

"What are they like?"

"Excuse me?" He seemed taken aback like he didn't expect me to have interest in his kids. They were his. Everything about him interested me, and his kids were obviously close to him.

"What are your kids like? You said your last just left home?"

"Oh, yeah, Summer. They are good kids."

He didn't say anything else which was disappointing. I let it go and allowed the rest of the drive to continue in silence. We arrived at his house way too soon— an average-sized home for a small family. I parked, having no intention of letting him get away just yet.

"Thanks for the lift, man," he said as I released the lock. "This saved me walking home."

I frowned at him. "You don't have a friend who could have come to get you?"

He shrugged and opened the door. "Not really. Having kids doesn't really allow you much time to socialize."

"But your kids are adults now."

"There are a few guys from work," he answered with a shrug. "I should go in. Good night, Mr. Moore."

I rolled my eyes at him. "Call me Declan at least."

He quirked an eyebrow at me. "Not Sir, or *Daddy?*"

I laughed at his mocking tone. "I don't want to force you into it. We'll get there in good time."

"You're not giving up, are you?"

"I just got your address," I told him with a grin. "Does this seem like I'm giving up?"

"Fuck."

He rubbed a hand over his face like it had just dawned on him that I now knew where he lived. I didn't bother to inform him that I could easily get that information. I could also find out all I needed to know about his kids, but I preferred him to tell me in his own timing.

"May I use your bathroom before I get out of your hair?" I requested.

He scowled at me. "You don't really need to use the bathroom, do you?"

No, I didn't. "Yes, I do."

He groaned. "Alright, come on, but as soon as you're done, you can leave."

"Not very hospitable, are you?" I asked as I got out of the car and shut the door. I followed him up the steps of the porch and watched him walk over to one railing. He pressed his hand beneath and plucked a key that had been taped there.

"My guests until recently were rambunctious teenagers," he answered. "I usually keep a spare key here if the kids lost theirs."

"Practical."

"I'm a practical man," he answered, inserting the key into the hole. "And that's why you need to give up this crazy notion of yours that I'll somehow wind up in your bed, calling you Daddy."

He stepped inside the house, and I followed, making no effort to put distance between us as he closed the door.

"You know," I said, observing the attractive green shade of the walls in the hall. "If you keep mentioning this Daddy thing, I'm going to think you're really interested."

He scoffed. "I don't have a bathroom downstairs, so we'll have to go up." At the foot of the stairs, he gave me a glance over his shoulder. "And I don't have a Daddy fixation. Never had a Dad in my life."

"The two aren't the same, Owen."

"Well, I can't separate them, so you'll have to get your Daddy kink on somewhere else."

"But you'll get it on without the Daddy kink?" I teased, as I watched how the material of his jeans clung to his round ass. *Lucky jeans.* I could watch the outline of his ass cheeks as he climbed the stairs all night.

"You don't give up, do you?" he asked, when we were at the top of the stairs.

"Never," I replied. "I always get what I want. I don't mind the work I have to put into it."

He grunted, then pointed out a closed door. "Congrats on your work ethic. Bathroom's here. You can let yourself out when you're finished."

Before I could say anything else, he disappeared into a bedroom that I only got a quick glimpse of. With a sigh, I went to use the bathroom because now I really needed to take a leak.

Like what I had seen of his house so far, the bathroom was neat and sparkling clean. Knowing the little I did about Owen, I wasn't surprised that a single male, who efficiently raised three kids all by himself, had color-coordinated his bathroom. There wasn't a speck of dust on the mirror and the hamper was empty.

Impressed, I finished my business, washed my hands and left the bathroom, closing the door quietly behind me. I descended the stairs but didn't leave as he had suggested I do once I'd finished. After a quick glance in the small but tidy kitchen, I detoured to the living room.

I glanced around, taking in the space I imagined must have been a little cramped for a grown man and three teen kids. The television was dated and the sofas a little worn, but everything was neatly arranged. My eyes landed on the mantel which featured several framed photographs. I approached and took in the pictures of Owen and his kids.

There were individual photographs of a younger version of his kids and another with all three of his children grown. His daughter, Summer, wore a gradua-tion gown and had an arm around Owen's waist. Two young men who had to be his sons crowded them together in the photo. They were all smiling in the picture, genuine happiness displayed on their faces. Owen stared into the camera with pride and affection in his eyes.

I reached for the photo and brought it closer, studying that happy face of his. What would it take for him to look at me like that? Right off the bat I had sensed he was special. Seeing the love he had for his kids captured on camera moved me more than I would have thought.

"You're still here."

At Owen's voice, I turned to regard him. He had

changed into sweatpants, a gray T-shirt, and went bare-footed. Even his hair was mussed for a more relaxed look.

"Yes, still here," I responded, then gestured toward the photograph I still held. "Your boys bear a striking resemblance to you."

He walked over to me and plucked the photograph from my hand, resettling it on the mantle. "Why are you snooping around my home?"

"Not snooping. Trying to learn more about you."

"For God's sake, why?"

"You know why. Have you forgotten our kiss? I haven't."

He rubbed two fingers at his temples. "It was just a kiss. You must have kissed a dozen guys in the past. It's no big deal."

"Isn't it, Owen?"

I placed a hand in the center of his shirt. "Declan." My name fell from his lips in the beginnings of a protest that didn't come to fruition. I tugged and he didn't resist as we met chest to chest, toe to toe. I ran my hand up the solid wall, feeling the ridges of his muscles. His heart pounded in his chest, and I smiled because he wasn't stopping me. I circled his neck with my hand, teased his bobbing Adam's apple with my thumb before gripping him by the back of his neck.

"This is so wrong," he murmured as our lips drew closer.

"Why?" I asked. "Aren't we both consenting adults?" I rubbed my lips against his back and forth, and when he inched closer, begging for me without words, I avoided his lips.

"It just feels so wrong," he answered. "So, so wrong."

"Then let me remind you how right it can all be when you're not overthinking things."

He didn't protest, so I took that as my answer. I slackened my hold on his neck and kissed him, giving him the opportunity to slip away if that was what he wanted. He responded by moaning into my mouth, a guttural sound of acceptance. And I felt fucking ten feet tall even though we were the same height. The yearning inside me for him doubled, no, tripled. I kissed him harder, showing him with my lips and tongue just how much I needed *him*.

Owen's kiss was hesitant at first, but the more I probed with my tongue, the more he relaxed. With a groan, he completely gave in and moved even closer to me. I gripped the short strands of his hair, wrapping my other hand around his back to grip his ass. He gasped, not expecting that move, but I wasn't in the mood to play coy with him. I needed him to know exactly what I wanted—to devour all of him. Not just his body, but his mind, and soul.

I released his neck and brought my other hand down his back. He jerked against me as I caressed both his ass cheeks, my breathing shallow at how round he was.

"Fuck, Declan," he gasped, tearing his lips away from mine.

"Feels good, doesn't it?" I asked, and before he could lie, I pressed him forward so our groins rubbed against each other. His cock was solid against mine. It was useless for him to deny the desire thrumming through his veins.

"Yes," he finally agreed. "It's been so long."

And because of his admission, I needed to make this

good for him. When I left tonight, I wanted him thinking about me. I didn't plan on being another one-night stand, a distant memory.

I liked Owen. I liked his dedication to his job and kids. I liked his strong set of morals, even the way he clung to the stupid belief that he was too old for me. Older guys who had opted for me to be their Daddy had been driven to it by my wealth. I hadn't minded, because I had that in droves, but Owen was different. He didn't seem to care.

"You've been taking care of everyone else," I murmured, backing him up to the nearest sofa. "Who has been taking care of you, Owen?"

He licked his bottom lip, his eyes trained on mine, and I knew he wanted me to kiss him again. "I have."

"Well guess what? I'm going to take care of you tonight."

10

OWEN

I caught a glimpse of my exposed dick sticking up toward my stomach and was at a loss at how I'd wound up in this position. My sweatpants and boxers were both around my ankles, and I vaguely remembered Declan giving me a push on my chest which had me sprawling onto the sofa. I could have resisted the move, but allowed my body to go with the motions because it all felt so good. I wasn't kidding that I hadn't been with anyone like this in a long time. Not since Jenna walked out on me.

Sure I had the occasional hookups, but I hadn't kissed any of them and made out like I'd just done with Declan. The way he stood over me, staring at me spoke volumes. I swallowed at the raw desire in his eyes. I still had no idea what he wanted with me.

He wants to fuck you that's what. Well, I knew *that*, but why? He was a damn fine-looking man with all the money that could get the attention of guys more like him. I was a washed-up has-been dad, trying to make sense of my life now that I didn't have my kids around me anymore. It certainly couldn't be with this young man who wanted me to call him Daddy. Even my kids had stopped calling me that years ago.

And why are you still thinking about it? You're considering it, aren't you?

"You're thinking again," Declan said, approaching me. "Don't. Just feel."

"I can't help thinking," I murmured, wishing I could turn off my brain as he wanted. "I'm naked, and you're fully-clothed."

He smiled at me in that heart-stopping way of his. He was so self-assured. I had to give him props for that, and it made me like him a little. Not a lot. Just enough to give in to him going down on me.

"Tonight's about you," he remarked, and knelt between my legs, his hands on my thighs. "I'm going to make you come so hard you may even give in and ask Daddy for more."

"If you keep up that Daddy talk, you're going to make my boner disappear," I warned him.

He chuckled and placed a kiss on my right inner thigh. I cringed, wishing I wasn't so hairy all over. "It won't. Your cock likes the thought of being owned by a Daddy. Can't you imagine it, Owen? You belonging to me, controlling your pleasure, punishing you when you're being stubborn, but spoiling you rotten?"

"I don't want anyone to spoil me rotten," I said as his lips continued pressing kisses up my thick thighs.

He glanced up at me. "So, you're not opposed to the rest? I'll take that as progress."

"I—" My clarifications went out the window as his hand wrapped around my cock. I sucked in the deep breath I would have needed for speaking and tried not to act like an inexperienced virgin at the tightness of his palm around my arousal. I couldn't tear my eyes away from his hand as he moved it, slowly at first.

"Like that?" he asked, when I made a strangled sound.

I moaned a response, because how could I vocalize that his touch made all two hundred pounds of me turn to liquid? I was melting into the sofa, trying to contain my moans by grinding my teeth together.

"Don't hide what you feel from me, Owen," he remarked, gripping my cock by the base. "I want you to say my name, over and over while I'm sucking you."

He didn't give me a chance to respond as his head bent, and he slipped the head of my cock into his mouth. I desperately tried to contain my groans and grunts, but when his lips slid down my shaft, I was left undone. I fucking trembled beneath him, my eyes falling to closed slits as he sucked me reverently up and down.

He released me, and my eyes shot open in protest. I wasn't ready for him to be done yet. Not by a long shot.

"That's right. Don't close your eyes," he instructed, tugging at my sweatpants and underwear until they were completely off. "I want you looking at me, seeing the things I make you feel with my mouth on you."

I clutched the edges of the sofa as he claimed me once more. A heavy languor overtook me, and I would have closed my eyes again, but I didn't want him to stop. His lips felt amazing. He sucked me down wet, deepthroating me.

"Dec-lan," I cried out his name at the powerful sensations, but he didn't stop. His head bobbed up and down my cock, his lips twisting down my shaft, tongue trailing on the underside, teasing the prominent throbbing vein. He dipped his head to kiss my balls while his hand worked my shaft up and down hard. He sucked the heavy sac into his mouth, letting them go one by one with a pop.

"I-I'm gonna come," I grunted, because I could feel it building up inside me. It had been too long since I had experienced such pleasures with another person, male or female.

At my warning, he released the pressure of his hand. "You don't come without my permission," he said.

I groaned. "How am I supposed to do that? I've not had this in such a long time."

"If I'm going to pleasure you, we need to do this on my terms," he told me. "You keep it within you until I tell you to come, Owen."

His mouth settled over the head of my cock again, and although I knew it was coming, nothing could have prepared me for the wetness of his lips sliding down my shaft.

"Holy hell!" I cried out, because it was that intense. He knew the exact pressure to use up and down my length. He toyed with the head, taking my hisses and groans for encouragement. I was no longer fighting the lethargic spell he had me under as I couldn't tear my eyes away from him sucking me down his throat.

In a move that I would have never anticipated, Declan grabbed me by the hips and pulled me further down the edge of the sofa with my legs in the air. Before I could decide what to do with my legs, he caught them and placed them on his shoulders. A sliver of embarrassment went through me at the way I was sprawled opened up for his pleasure. He could see everything, and my god all that hair! If I had known I would be in this position, I would have taken the time to shave. *Liar, you went out tonight for a hookup. You just didn't care about shaving until now.*

I had no idea what was happening to me. Okay, I had some idea. Declan was turning me inside out and exposing every lie I had told since we met about me not being interested in him. Hell yes, I was interested, but was concerned he was too young. Plus, I still didn't fully understand this Daddy fetish thing he had going on.

Despite his youth, he was clearly experienced in the art of sucking dick, and there *was* an art to it. He was precise, knowing when to let me slide down his throat, when to lightly graze me with his teeth and when his tongue would add even more sensation. He watched my every reaction, figured out what I liked and continued doing it until soon I was struggling not to blow my load in his mouth. Seriously struggling.

"Declan," I gasped his name. "I'm not sure how much longer I can wait. Please."

To my frustration, he released me, but allowed my dick to rest vertical to his lips. It was maddening that I could feel his lips on me, but not in the way I wanted it.

"I suppose I could make you come now," he said as though in contemplation. "How bad do you want me to make you come, Owen?"

I hated the way he wanted me to admit these things aloud. I would have much preferred a lack of conversation as he sucked me off, then made his way home, so I could sooner bury my head in my pillow and curse myself for my weakness.

"Answer me," he said, a bit sharply, startling me when I took too long to respond.

To my surprise, his hard tone only kicked my heart into gear. I stared fully into his face. Damn, he looked sexy when he had his straight face on.

"I need to come now," I finally admitted. "Please, don't stop."

My face turned red at my begging. I had never begged a man for sex before, and I certainly shouldn't be begging Declan either, but he had me right where he wanted me. Just a little bit frustrated at being brought to the brink, then left hanging. I was desperate for him to continue.

"Declan, do something or let me up," I growled at him.

A sharp slap rang out in the living room as Declan reached beneath my body to spank my ass. It stung, but was more startling than anything. I remembered the promise he had made earlier at the club. *Had he just spanked me? Like really spanked me?*

"What the fuck?" I cried. "What was that for?"

"You don't give the orders here. I do. Now if you be good, I'll make you come the way you want. Will you behave yourself for Daddy?"

Him and this Daddy fixation. Jesus. Would he ever let up? Then I decided to use his alternative to throw him off. "Yes, *Sir*, Mr. Moore."

I never anticipated the effect hearing that would have on him. His eyes locked with mine, heavy with desire. His nostrils flared, and his hands tightened around my legs a fraction of a second, but I didn't miss it.

"Say it, again," he prompted me.

I didn't plan to repeat it. I was just yanking his chain, but then I heard myself say it again. "Yes, Sir, Mr. Moore."

He groaned. "You don't know it yet, Owen, but you need this as much as I do. You'll see. Now come for me."

Before I could voice that the only thing I wanted right now was his mouth back around my dick, he spat in his hand and brought it to my crack. I tightened up at the feel of his fingers probing, but then his mouth settled over my cock, and all the emotions became a tornado of lust, and something close to affection that I was beginning to have for this man and his unwillingness to give up.

Declan's middle finger slipped into my tight ass while he continued sucking me harder, deeper. He fingered me, pushing in then out, over and over, deeper and deeper, crooking his finger to brush the little rough lump inside my body which meant he had found my prostate.

"Uh!" I grunted, hips jerking. "I'm coming."

Declan's response was to suck my cock even harder. A keening cry left my lips, and my back arched, head pressed back into the sofa as I spilled and spilled. I raised my head in the throes of passion, watching him suck harder, his hand gently squeezing my sensitive balls as he sucked every drop out of me.

I'd had guys take me in their mouth before, but as soon as I pulled out, they were off to the bathroom to flush it down the drain. Declan swallowed before releasing me, then trailed little kisses over my length and finally to the head. I didn't even know when he'd withdrawn his finger.

"Fuck!" I cried, my legs shaking in the aftermath of my powerful release. It was more than embarrassing, but he didn't make fun of me, the older one who should have been more experienced. He lowered my legs and moved in for a kiss. I closed the distance between us and kissed him back, expecting a hard, sexual kiss, but it wasn't. The slow tender press of his lips against mine freaked me out more than him going down on me and fingering me.

"Your phone's ringing," Declan said against my lips. Yes, it was, and I hadn't even heard because my senses had been drugged by his kisses. Damn, I was screwed.

"I need to get it," I told him, shifting beneath him, but he wouldn't release me.

"It's late. Let it ring to voicemail."

I was tempted. His mouth was definitely so close to mine that I just wanted to latch on again, but then the machine beeped an incoming message.

"Hey, Dad!" Summer's voice came over the answering machine, and I froze. "I'm surprised you're not there. Anyway, just want you to know that I can't wait to see you over the weekend. I know you'll be staying with the twins because Penny's and my apartment is too

small, but at least we'll all get to meet up for dinner. I
hope you're still coming. I miss you. And turn on your
cellphone. I tried calling you a dozen times!"

Complete silence followed the voice message. Reality
hit me hard that I wasn't exactly in a father-like position
at the moment. What if the kids found out I had brought
someone over? What if they found out that person was
just a few years older than them?

"I can sense you're freaking out," Declan declared.

"No, not freaking out. Just wondering what the hell
did I just get myself into?"

He smiled at me. "As long as you don't try to extricate
yourself from whatever the hell this is."

"Get off me, will you?"

With a sigh, he moved back and allowed me to
upright myself. I refused to look at him as I grasped my
clothes, stood and quickly dressed before turning back to
him. He rose to his feet, his eyes on me, and a lump
formed in my throat. He was so damn young. And sexy.
Why did he have to set his eyes on me?

"I take it you won't be free this weekend then," he
stated, sounding disappointed.

"Yeah, that's right," I answered, relieved I had made
plans. I didn't trust myself to say no to him especially if
he promised more blow jobs like the one he had just
delivered. Now I was curious about his other skills. "I'm
visiting my kids in Columbus."

His frown turned into a grin. "Really? Columbus,
huh?"

"Yeah, that's where they moved."

He closed the distance between us, and I seriously

wanted to bolt, but I maintained my stance. He reached for a corner of my shirt that was tucked haphazardly in my waistband and pulled it out.

"How about I pick you up tomorrow and drop you off?"

I stepped away from him. "Uh... Of course not."

"Unless you have a backup driver's license somewhere around here, I'd say you don't have much of a choice," he stated.

I stilled. Shit, he was right. With my wallet gone, so was my driver's license. There was no way I could drive all the way to Columbus without it. As a professional driver, I couldn't blatantly disobey the road code. There was no way I could get a new one either since it was the weekend.

"Crap. The kids will be so disappointed I'll have to cancel," I murmured, more to myself than to him.

"Then don't cancel. I can drop you off. I have business in Columbus anyway, and I was going to ask you to join me for the weekend."

"I can't."

He quirked an eyebrow at me. "You can't see your kids? Or you won't?"

He grinned at me, and I scowled at him. "You know what I mean."

He chuckled softly. "You look sexy when you're mad."

"See! That's why I can't go with you. It'll be non-stop flirting, getting me to do things I don't necessarily want to do."

He rolled his eyes. "Fine. I'll try not to flirt with you.

I'll drop you off at your kids like the saintly virgin you've suddenly become. Be ready by seven, and don't make me wait."

Well, if there was no flirting involved, I figured I could live through an hour and a half drive with him. The kids would be disappointed if I didn't show up. Plus, Summer had been calling often and each time she did, she mentioned it. Then there was Auggie who wanted to have a serious talk.

"Okay, seven's fine."

He nodded. "Good. Now walk me to my car."

He didn't wait for me to respond, but turned away, taking it for granted I would do his bidding. Who did he think he was that after one lousy orgasm he expected me to do his bidding? Okay, lousy orgasm was stretching it a little. A lot. But still, he didn't have to be a dick about it.

I willed my feet to remain where they were, but they charted a path right behind him although I was bare-footed. I sighed, admitting defeat as I caught up to him at the door. In silence, we continued to his car. He unlocked the door, then turned to me, a half-smile on his lips that wreaked havoc on my heart.

"I enjoyed tonight," he said, then leaned forward to kiss me. To give him credit, he gave me enough time to move away if I wanted to, but I remained standing where I was. While I didn't close the gap between us, I heard his frustrated sigh when his lips finally closed over mine. I hadn't moved away either.

I wished I could just live in the moment, enjoy this for what it was, knowing eventually the passion would burn itself out. But, I wasn't made that way. I was the guy who had married his best friend and never bothered to become seriously engaged again since our separation.

Declan's tongue slipped into my mouth, and then I was no longer thinking about past relationships. I wasn't thinking anything at all beyond all the butterflies swirling in my stomach. When he released my lips, I was panting against him, my hands clutching the front of his shirt, crumpling the material. It took a while for me to work my fingers loose to release him.

"See you at seven, Owen." As if he couldn't resist, he kissed me hard again before getting into his vehicle. I stood there in the driveway and watched after his car, feeling more confused than the night my ex-wife had walked out on me and my kids.

11

DECLAN

W hen I rang Owen's doorbell the next morning, I expected him to be dressed and ready to go. He hadn't believed me last night that I had business in Columbus today, but it so happened that it was the truth. Not that I wouldn't have conveniently come up with an excuse to take him even if I hadn't had business in the city. The plan was for us to head out early so I could make any detour we needed to in order to drop him off at his children's place.

Last night I'd slept better than I had in a long time. I had trouble sleeping at times because I was usually concerned about Charles and his handling of the family business. I had even been prescribed sleeping pills by my doctor, but I loathed taking them, so nine out of ten times I suffered through the insomnia until I collapsed from exhaustion. My doctor was concerned I worked too much, and that the odd feelings I had in my stomach were a result of stress, but there was so much to do that I couldn't slow down.

I had been anticipating this morning since Owen didn't protest my offer of assistance last night. I had fallen asleep quickly, but had been up by the ass-crack of dawn, getting everything prepared for today. Although this was a spur of the moment decision, it didn't have to feel like one.

My regular driver, Silas, who had been with my family since I was a boy, waited in the car given I had opted not to drive. I intended to get as much as possible out of the long drive to Columbus.

I frowned at the length of time it was taking Owen to answer the door. He hadn't exactly confirmed that he would go with me. I hadn't given him the opportunity to say no. I had taken last night to mean progress, but what if I had scared him off by being too forward?

Maybe I could have given him more time to get used to the idea of me, but last night had presented itself as a perfect opportunity for me to show him the possibilities that existed once we were together. I thought I had done that quite well, given his moans and eager kisses.

Just when I began to think he had already left for Columbus without me, I heard soft footfalls followed by a bolt sliding and the doorknob turning. Owen stood before me, deliciously mussed from his bed hair to his bare feet. He was still wearing the clothes I had left him in last night. He blinked at me owlishly. "Shit!" he muttered, eyes flying open as he recognized me. "What time is it?"

"You're not dressed," I said on a frown, wondering if

he had deliberately made himself late to see what I would do if he weren't ready.

He scrubbed a hand over his morning's stubble. "My phone usually alarms, but I don't have it, so was relying on my internal clock to go off."

"Seems you don't have an internal clock."

His eyes landed on the bouquet of roses I had brought for him. Sappy, I knew, but I would bet he'd never been given flowers before.

"I-It was a long night," he answered, still staring at the flowers. "What the hell is that?"

"I believe we mere humans call them roses," I answered, extending the small bouquet toward him.

He made no attempt to accept the flowers. "You brought me flowers?"

"Yes. Why are you so surprised? I thought I made my intentions clear last night."

His face turned red, and he coughed into his fist at my mention of last night. "I guess."

"There's no guessing about it, Owen," I remarked and pushed the flowers at him. "Now you're going to be a good boy and take them, place them in a vase with water, and hopefully they will still be in good condition when you get back from your trip."

"I guess... I mean I should say thanks." He brought the bouquet up to his nose and sniffed for a few seconds before he realized what he was doing. He jerked the flowers away. I didn't think he could get any redder than before, but I was wrong. I grinned as he looked everywhere but at me. Seeing him so flustered was oddly a turn on for me. "Uh, I'm not ready, so I guess you'll have to go without me."

"And how would you get to Columbus?" I asked him. "Come on. I'll make you some coffee while you take a quick shower."

He didn't protest when I entered his house and closed the door behind me. I trailed after him as he made his way to the kitchen, his sweatpants riding temptingly low on his hips. My eyes glued to his ass, appreciating its hard fullness, and I felt the first stirrings of desire as I thought about spanking it for him not being ready like he should have been.

Once inside the kitchen, I watched him open a cupboard and take out a tall glass which he brought over to the sink. "I don't have a proper vase. Flowers didn't seem like the most necessary thing with three kids in the house."

"And now they're grown, you get to do all the things you've never been able to do, like investing in a flower vase."

He frowned as he turned, trying to figure out where to place the flowers. He finally decided and placed them next to the window where a stream of sunlight peeked through. I had almost changed my mind about bringing him the flowers, but now seeing the thoughtfulness he took in finding the perfect place to rest them, I was pleased I had gone with my gut. It made me feel like my instincts about him in general were right.

Before he could turn, I was behind him, crowding him. His body went rigid, but I didn't give him time to figure out what was happening. I rested a hand on his right hip to keep him in position.

"I told you I don't like being made to wait," I said, leaning forward to whisper in his ear. He leaned forward which placed his lower body in just the right curve for me.

"Technically, it's your fault," he remarked. "I couldn't sleep after…" He trailed off, and as much as my heart softened to know he had been so affected by me making loving to him last night, I had to punish him. He still had no idea how serious this was, and I would have to build him up to accepting our relationship for what it was if this was going to work.

I slid my hand from his hip to grope his ass. He clenched but didn't tell me to stop. BINGO. I had him right where I wanted him.

"Not good enough an excuse," I told him as I circled the waistband of his sweatpants, inching my thumb into the elastic. "Do you know what happens when you disregard orders?"

"Orders?" he grunted, pushing his ass back into my hand before he caught up with himself and stilled.

I tugged at the waistband of his sweatpants, dragging his underwear down over his taut butt, exposing him. "I'm going to have to postpone my meeting until later today because you aren't ready."

As if caving in, he leaned forward some more on the counter so his ass jutted out. I grinned with satisfaction as I rubbed his butt. He had no idea what was coming to him.

"You actually have a meeting?" he asked on a groan. "I thought you made that up to…"

"To get a piece of your ass?" I finished for him.

"Fuck, not again," he said, and started straightening, but I planted a hand in the center of his back and pushed him forward.

"Stay. You don't move until I say."

"We're late," he protested half-heartedly. "I should take a shower and get dressed."

"We're already late. And you'll take a shower after."

"After?"

I drew my hand back and slapped his ass hard.

"What the hell!" he howled, jerking upright. His hand came down to cover his ass where I had slapped him, and he glared at me over his shoulder. "What do you think you're doing?"

"Hmm. I must be losing my touch if you have to ask. Now bend over."

"Declan—"

I pushed into his back for him to lean forward again. "Humor me," I told him, brushing his hand away from his ass. I rubbed the area where I had slapped him, soothing the sting he had to be feeling. "Prove to me that after spanking you a dozen times, you won't be turned on."

"I won't," he argued.

"Then let's test the theory."

"This is humiliating." His growl turned into a groan at my hand connecting hard with his ass again. Whether intentional or not, his head fell forward along with his torso which made his ass that much more accessible.

"It's beautiful," I told him. "Seeing my handprint all over your lovely ass." I slapped him again, my own hand stinging, but the pain was welcomed at the sight of his cheeks spotted red.

I resisted grinding against his ass with my arousal as I delivered yet another slap harder than the last. He made a sound between a whimper and a "fuck." The redder his ass was, the harder I became. His body stiffened in anticipation of each slap, and my excited breaths blew out hard and fast to match his.

With only a couple more slaps to go, I stopped fighting the urge and grabbed him by the hips, grinding my groin to his ass. My cock throbbed heavy with need, and I allowed him to feel how much I desired him. I had the idea he didn't truly believe this was real, as if he expected one day to wake up and I would be gone.

"Feel how much I want you, Owen," I growled at him, undulating my hips against the hardness of his butt.

He mumbled unintelligibly, but his body communicated well enough for me. His hips moved, his ass twitched backward, seeking out the thickness of my length.

"Please," he begged. "I'm so hard, Declan."

I knew what he wanted, but he didn't deserve to come. Not when he'd kept me waiting. I pulled away from him, delivered the last two slaps to his ass before reaching for the waistband of his sweatpants and tugging them back into place.

"You've fifteen minutes to take a shower and get dressed."

At my words, Owen straightened and turned to me, eyes narrowed. "What?"

"Fifteen minutes, Owen," I told him, moving away to get the coffee that I had promised him started. He wasn't the only one with a swollen dick, but the next time I had him naked, we would *really* fuck, and now wasn't the time.

"B-but... you...I-I..." he stammered, hands folded into fists as he glared at me. "You don't rile a man up, then leave him hanging."

I smirked at him. "Thought you weren't going to get hard."

He opened his mouth to argue, and I quirked an eyebrow at him, daring him to deny what was so evidently tenting the front of his sweatpants. He thought better of it and stalked stiffly from the kitchen.

"And don't think about jerking off in the shower either!" I called after his retreating back. "I'll know if you do."

12

OWEN

Half an hour into our drive to Columbus, I kept my head averted from Declan because I was ashamed that I had allowed him to spank me. That wasn't even the worst part. Nope, that would have been the mortification of my arousal, of the precum that had stained my boxers when I had finally escaped to the bathroom. Who was I kidding? I hadn't escaped. *He* had rejected me, left me hanging with a cock pumped full of blood that I hadn't even been able to touch when I was alone in the shower.

I had tried to ignore his warning that he would know if I had jerked off, but in the end, I hadn't been able to give in to my urges. I had taken a cold shower, steeled and conditioned my mind for this hour and a half journey, only for him to unsettle me once more by making me a cup of the most delicious coffee that had ever been brewed in my coffee maker.

In the shower, I'd thought I had worked off the

embarrassment enough to appear before him and function as if nothing untoward had happened. Thank God, he had been busy making phone calls, pacing in the kitchen while I drank my coffee. I shouldn't have minded how distracted he had been, yet I couldn't help feeling annoyed that he wasn't affected in the least by what he had done to me. I would never be able to use my kitchen again without the memory of Declan spanking my bare ass.

I tried not to squirm, but failed miserably. The sting had receded to a light throb, but it was a constant reminder that at forty-six years old, I had gotten my ass spanked by a guy young enough to be my son. I stole a glance at Declan only to find him still tapping away at his phone. He had apparently been serious about business in Columbus. He hadn't been off his phone since we left my house, and it unnerved me more than it should have.

With a frown, I brushed an imaginary speck of dirt from the knee of my jeans. I didn't know what to do with my hands. Usually they were wrapped around a steering wheel as I drove clients around, but here I was being ushered around because of Declan who wanted a relationship with me. But, what kind of relationship could we have? One where my ass took a pounding whenever he thought I broke one of his rules?

I shifted as my cock twitched at the thought of him giving me a hiding. Declan was so virile. His commanding presence exuded such confidence. It was rare that a young man had so much confidence without the usual cockiness behind it. Yet, he didn't have a cocky air at all. Just a man who was used to being in control and solving problems.

He seemed older than his twenty-five years. I imagined guys at Declan's age were busy getting their weekend on, but here he was snapping into the phone in that all-powerful way of his that made a shiver run down my spine.

I imagined the person at the other end of the line was scurrying to do his bidding. Hadn't I fallen into that trap last night, then this morning as well? I couldn't even blame it on the lack of sleep, just waking up and then being surprised with flowers.

Of all things, why had he brought me roses? Better yet, why did it affect me so greatly that he had given me something so simple, but which I had never received before? I wasn't the flowers kind of guy, though I secretly liked the gesture.

Declan's long groan was unexpected, and I glanced over at him where he sat beside me. He punched at his phone furiously before pocketing it. "I'll turn off this goddamn thing, or I'll end up spending the entire drive trying to fix one thing or another."

He closed his eyes and leaned back against the seat. I couldn't tear my gaze away from him and the lines that furrowed his brows. There were further tiny lines at the corners of his eyes and bracketing the corners of his mouth. He seemed stressed.

"Uh, everything okay?" I asked, out of genuine concern.

He cracked an eye open and gave me a lazy smile. "And he speaks."

I frowned at him, wishing I hadn't said anything. "Even if I had wanted to, you've been on the phone since you handed me the cup of coffee."

That made him pause, and he blinked as if he hadn't realized. "Sorry. I didn't mean to ignore you. I just had some work to do."

"I'm not complaining," I rushed to explain.

"Still, I'll make it up to you," he stated, then stretched his arm at the back of the seat until his fingers were sifting through the hair at my nape. "I sometimes get so caught up with business that I don't always pay attention."

I stiffened at his fingers in my hair. It was either that or purr into his touch, and I wouldn't do the latter. Dear lord, I needed to keep my guard up around this man who was hellbent on knocking down my defenses.

"About the ride back from Columbus," I stated. "One of the kids can drive me home so you don't have to go out of your way and wait on me or anything."

"It's no problem at all. We leave at seven Monday morning. Understood?"

"I'll try to get my internal clock to work this time," I said drily at his tone.

He leaned close to me. "If you don't, I'll be inclined to think you're just hankering for another spanking. Maybe I'll use my belt the next time."

I sucked in a deep breath. I had walked right into that one. "There won't be a next time," I ground out. "You caught me by surprise."

"But you liked it." Although I was no longer looking at him, I sensed the laughter in his voice.

"We agreed you weren't going to flirt with me on this trip," I reminded him, taking the coward's way out of answering that question.

"This is hardly flirting," he scoffed. "Besides, have I kissed you yet, even though I've wanted to all morning? No, I haven't, so I've definitely been sticking to my end of the bargain." He paused, allowing that to sink in, and that it did. Then he added, "Although should you want to change the terms and conditions of this trip, I'd be more than happy to oblige."

"Nope. The terms and conditions remain the same."

He chuckled, reached across the seat and squeezed my thigh briefly before letting me go. "Then it's pretty useless for me to persuade you to stay in my hotel suite in Columbus, isn't it?"

I rubbed a hand over my thigh where his had just been. "And how would that fit in with our current terms?"

"I have self-control, you know," he answered. "I might want to fuck you until you admit the feelings here are very much mutual, but I'll refrain unless you ask me to."

"Jesus!"

"Plus, I find myself with urges for something a bit different," he continued. "It's been a long time since I've ever dreamed of going sans condom, but I already know I want to fuck you raw. To own every bit of your ass and brand you as mine. That will require both of us to be tested before sex, so rest assured, Owen, it's going to happen, but not this weekend, so it's safe to stay in my suite."

I threw a panicky look at the back of the driver's head and felt my face burning at the thought that the man could probably hear every single word that we were saying.

"New topic," I said, and he laughed, the sound gravelly like he hadn't done that in a while.

"Sure. What do you want to talk about?"

So much. I wanted to find out about this Daddy fixation of his, but that would be a conversation better left for when we were alone. I'd learned not to open a can of worms if I was afraid of dipping my hand into the whole squiggly mess.

"What kind of business are you into?"

He groaned. "Finance and insurance, but can we talk about anything else other than business? That for me is kind of like you not wanting to talk about how much we both want me to umm—" he cleared his throat when he saw the glare I aimed his way, "—do things to you," he ended.

"You grew up in Cincy?"

"Pretty much, although I went to boarding school and college out of state."

"Hmm. Where did you go?" I asked, relaxing a bit under the new direction of our conversation.

"I studied Banking and Finance at Harvard," he answered. "Seems light years ago now."

"Couldn't have been *that* long ago," I couldn't resist pointing out. Despite his maturity, he was only twenty-five. *He's only twenty-five years old. You cannot want him.*

"When you start college at seventeen, it seems that way."

To say I was impressed was an understatement. Declan continued to surprise me. Not only was he wealthy, but he hadn't just been given a place in his father's business because of nepotism. He was smart. Just what I needed. Smart, sexy, and domineering. What the hell was he doing trying to get the attention of a man with very little to offer besides his body?

"Declan."

His hand fell from my hair to rest on my shoulders. "Hmm?"

"Tell me you're doing all this to satisfy some curiosity. I won't be mad. I get it."

"Why would I lie?"

He shifted the conversation then to other mundane topics, and gradually I relaxed as we moved away from discussing anything that remotely sounded like a relationship. When he wasn't talking about fucking me raw, he was a guy I could talk to in an easygoing manner.

By the time we arrived in Columbus, I knew all sorts of unimportant facts about him. The time had flown by so quickly, and I was stunned for a second as we approached Abbots Cove Blvd where my sons shared a townhouse. I glanced out the window at the brick structures that became our view, and felt a sort of panic that this was it. Our time was up.

I couldn't remember the last time I had gotten to know somebody new. The drive had almost felt like a date.

"We're here," I announced, the nervous energy that had disappeared during our conversation reappearing. Did I shake his hand, thank him for the ride and grab my overnight bag? That seemed a bit too formal after last night and this morning for a guy who had stuck his finger up my ass.

"You sure you don't want to take me up on my hotel offer?" he asked, glancing skeptically at the houses set up in this housing scheme development. "The hotel is in the heart of downtown which is less than a fifteen minute drive. These apartments don't seem to be very spacious. You could be back and forth with little time lost with your kids. I'll even leave Silas at your disposal for getting around."

I directed Silas to the townhouse and while he parked, turned to address Declan. "I'm not sleeping with you."

"And that's fine for this trip. I booked a double suite. I'd even hand over the key so you can ensure the door stays locked between us all night."

"I'd have the original, but what about the spare key?" I grunted. "Would you hand that over too?"

His shoulders shook as he laughed which ended on an attractive snort. "Will you consider staying with me if I promise to hand over those too? I snagged a lake view. The hotel's all-inclusive, so you'll have access to the luxury spa, a private heated pool, a tennis court. You name it. You can truly enjoy the weekend."

"I intend to enjoy the weekend," I replied. "As lovely as all that sounds, I'll stay with the boys. This weekend is all about them."

His sigh was one of disappointment. "And I wouldn't be able to meet them, right?"

"What?" He continued to shock me each time. "You want to meet my kids?"

He shrugged. "I'll have to meet them sometime. You can't keep them in the dark forever. I'm not saying it has to be now, but eventually."

"Maybe." I didn't bother to elaborate that I didn't see me ever telling my children about him. How would I even begin to explain my attraction to someone so much younger?

"Anyway, my offer is available all weekend, so call me if you change your mind about the sleeping arrangements."

"No phone, remember?"

He turned to the briefcase beside him. "I almost forgot." He popped the lid, took something out and handed it to me. I stared down at the rectangular box with the logo of that well-known apple, then at him.

"What are you doing?" I asked, my throat tight.

"I'm giving you a means to contact me if you need to get a hold of me over the weekend," he replied nonchalantly. "Plus, no need to rely on your non-existent internal alarm clock on Monday when I drop by to pick you up."

I made no move to take the box from him. I was appalled at the very notion that he had bought me something so expensive. It was the latest model too, and I only knew that because Summer had been going crazy about not being able to afford one. *Didn't these things cost over a grand?*

"I can't accept that."

He groaned. "It's just a phone, Owen, and you so

happen to need one. Sometimes plans change, and I may need to call you. You don't want me driving all the way here just to tell you about a change of plan, right? Of course then I'll probably meet your kids."

"I know what you're doing," I growled at him.

"And what exactly is that?"

"Using common sense to win this argument," I scowled at him.

He didn't fight his outburst of laughter this time. "I always win, Owen. I always get what I want in the end."

I had the feeling he wasn't just speaking about the phone, which he proved when he shuffled closer and cupped the back of my head. I swallowed hard, eyes zeroed in on his lips, and there was no sense in pretending his kisses from last night hadn't lingered in my mind all day. Aside from the spanking he had given me, he had been true to his word and not pushed for anything more.

"I *always* get what I want," he repeated.

"I should go." But even as I said the words, I kept watching his lips. *Kiss me.*

"I want to kiss you first," he replied. "But, I promised you I wouldn't come on to you. Unless you want me to. You know what you have to do."

Beg him to kiss me after he left me high and dry back home? No sir.

"Kiss me, Dec." *Uh-wait, were those words coming from my mouth? Didn't I just—*

Declan didn't give me the chance to change my mind. My consent was all he needed before his lips were on me. His fingers at the back of my head curled into my hair, pressing me closer to him. Everything ceased to exist except for the press of lips against lips, breathy pants, soft moans and growls of frustrated desire. Tongues tangled into a tentative dance that became bolder and pushed the limits of my self-control. I wanted to climb into his lap, settle my ass over the erection I knew rivaled my own and feel him sink inside me.

I gripped his arms to steady myself because I was falling. Hard. I had to tear my lips away from his to suck in a deep breath because I had forgotten to breathe. I kept my eyes closed, but it didn't help, because although I couldn't see him, I could feel him, scent him, hear his needy pants. We were shrouded in a blanket of desire so thick it felt almost suffocating. I needed space to breathe… to think.

"If I didn't know how important being with your kids this weekend is to you, I'd have made you change your mind," he whispered. "I'm also hoping you'll use some of your time to get used to the idea of us."

He cupped my cheek and ran his hand down my neck, the starved look on his face making it clear how much he wanted me. I felt something in my hands and glanced down to find that while we had been kissing he had transferred the phone to me. The sneaky, pushy bastard. He should be grateful I was still reeling from our kiss, so I wasn't thinking properly, or I would have given it back to him.

"Thanks for the lift," I croaked out, opening the car door.

"Don't mention it."

I exited the car and grabbed my duffel, feeling like I

had just been dropped off at home after a very hot prom date that I didn't want to end. I watched the car drive off, taking Declan away with it. I wished I had been able to accept his hotel invitation, but there was no way I could without feeling guilty. The boys' house was small, but we would be together as a family, and that was all that mattered.

So what if I had passed up the opportunity to stay at an all-inclusive hotel—something I hadn't done in years? The last time I had almost gone to a hotel was as an employee of the year. I had received an award for a weekend at a hotel out of town, but with no one to mind the kids, I hadn't gone. Instead, I had given away the tickets and stayed home.

I glanced at the box in my hand, still ambivalent about taking the gift from him, but he was already gone. Plus, I wanted to keep in touch with him over the weekend just as he had requested. There, I had admitted it. I had taken the phone so I could maintain contact with Declan.

13

OWEN

"Dad!"

When I opened the door later that evening to let in Summer, I barely got a glimpse of her before she flew into my arms, a head of blonde hair greeting my face. Her arms tightened around me, and I bit back the teasing words when I saw how emotional she was. I stroked her hair and wondered if it had been a good idea for her to move out so soon. We had both thought she was ready for the move, but she had been gone only for such a short time, and her response to seeing me wasn't exactly encouraging.

"Hey, Summy girl, what's up?" I asked, squeezing her to let her know I missed her too. After the boys had left together, it had just been us for a while, and we had grown closer because of it.

"Fine now that you're here," she answered, releasing me to push her hair back from her face. "I couldn't wait to see for myself that you were here. I kept expecting something else to prevent you from coming."

Something had come up, but thanks to Declan I had still made it to Columbus to see my kids. If not for anything else, I was extremely grateful for that and would let him know the next time we saw each other, which should be Monday morning at seven. Just to be safe, I had already set my alarm for six which should give me enough time to be ready by 6:45. I wasn't about to allow another spanking which should have never happened in the first place.

"Hey, Sis," Oscar called, passing me to give Summer a brief hug. He checked her out. "Did you get here straight from work?"

"Nah, I stopped at my apartment for a quick shower first," she replied. "Where's Auggie?"

"Trying to preserve dinner," he answered. "I think the lasagna is a lost cause, but you know Auggie. He won't be satisfied until after he's at least tried to salvage our meal. Luckily, there's an Italian restaurant just a mile and a half from here where we can eat without a reservation."

I had been looking forward to eating at home with my kids. I didn't want to share them with the outside world tonight. It would have been just like old time's sake at home, but Auggie and Oscar had refused my help in the kitchen. Given the acrid odor in the air, I had no hopes of us eating in tonight, which probably wasn't a bad idea. Maybe, being out I wouldn't be inclined to think about Declan so much.

Apart from sending me one text that he had arrived

at his hotel okay and hoped I enjoyed my stay with my kids, I hadn't heard from him. I had ignored the message at first as I spent the day with Oscar, catching up on what was going on in his life. Then, Auggie had arrived home from work, and the conversation started from scratch. As much as I had enjoyed being updated on my kids' lives, I had drifted from the conversation at times, wondering what Declan was doing.

The most thought about question seemed to be whether or not he would be enjoying someone else's company because I had turned down his offer to sleep in his suite at the hotel.

"Soooo, dad, there's something I was hoping to talk to you about," Summer announced, grabbing my arm and hauling me off to the small living room. Once inside, she released my hand and turned to me. "Hey, I didn't see your car just now. How did you get to Columbus?"

Despite having explained this to both boys before at separate times, I still felt a bit guilty about my answer which wasn't even a lie.

"A business colleague of mine was heading this way," I answered. "And since I lost my wallet with my driver's license, there was no way I could drive myself here, so he offered, and as I didn't want to cancel again, I accepted."

She dropped herself onto the couch, and I followed suit to sit beside her. "Does this mean one of us will have to drop you home?" she asked. "I'm free on Monday, so I can volunteer myself."

I smiled at her. "Thanks, but not necessary. My business colleague will be traveling back to Cincy, and he's offered me to tag along as well."

"That's awfully nice of him."

"It's really no big deal," I responded, trying not to show how much I felt like I was lying. It was a big deal to be getting involved with my first guy since my divorce. *And I was getting involved no matter how I try to convince myself otherwise.*

This wasn't another quick blow job in some seedy bathroom, or in a dark alley. This, whatever this was, because I wasn't able to define it yet, included rescuing me when I was stranded, flowers, the best goddamn coffee I'd had in a long time, a drive to see my kids, and a new phone. And the sex. Fuck, the sex.

"Are you sure you're okay?" I flipped the questions her way to avoid discussing Declan. I wasn't certain the kids could ever know about him. "You seem a little jumpy," I remarked.

"Actually, it's nice out here," she replied with a tight smile.

"Everything okay between you and Penny?"

The way her eyes dropped to the floor answered my question. I usually tried not to pry. I gave each of my children breathing room to make their own mistakes and learn from them, but seeing her hunched shoulders alarmed me.

"It's a lot different than I thought it would be," she finally answered on a sigh. "It's a lot harder for one. We argue a lot these days and sometimes it's over petty things."

"Do you want to come home?"

She straightened and shook her head. "No, I don't. I love her, you know. I just think maybe I suck at this relationship thing and living together with someone. It's a lot different from us just dating. I really don't want to screw up and hurt her."

I frowned at her. "The arguments are a natural part of you two finding out how to share your space. As long as you're both open with each other and respectful, you'll get over those little squabbles in time."

"You think so?"

I reached across to hold her hand and squeezed it. "You love Penny, and she adores you. That's the first hurdle out of the way. I just have to ask though, why do you think you're going to hurt Penny?"

She shrugged. "I don't know. I don't have the best example of a relationship to emulate. Mom supposedly loved us, but she hurt us anyway. Apparently, love isn't a guarantee you won't hurt the people you love."

Her bitter tone surprised me. I always knew her mother's disappearing act bothered her, but not to the extent where it was causing problems in her own relationship. I caught her chin when she tried to look away and turned her face gently in my direction. "You're not your mother, Summer. There's no reason to fear your relationship morphing into mine."

"I-I've just been thinking a lot of late about all the things that could go wrong and how hurt I'd feel if we didn't work out. It's been causing me to do shitty things to Penny and pushing her away. That's where most of our arguments come from. The sex isn't the same either."

Talking about sex with my daughter had never been a comfortable subject, but I did it because she needed advice, and I wasn't about to let her down. Nevertheless, these were the times I wished Jenna was still around. Maybe I hadn't done such a good job and that was the reason she was feeling insecure. What the hell did I know about two girls having sex? And one of them being my daughter didn't make it any better.

"Eew, so gross, Sis," Oscar remarked, walking into the living room and hearing the latter part of the conversation. "I think I should go help out Auggie."

"Oscar, we could use a little help here," I said, beseeching him to sit it out with me, but he wasn't having it. He backed out of the living room.

"Trust me, Dad. You do not want my opinion about my little sister's sex life. If it was left up to me, it would be nonexistent, and she would be locked up in a convent."

"Seriously, Oscar? That's what you can contribute to this conversation?" I asked him in exasperation.

He shrugged. "Told you I was useless at this. Holler if you need anything else."

I shook my head at his retreating back and turned my attention back to Summer. "Have you at least tried to talk to Penny about how you feel?"

"I don't want to worry her. She always thinks I have my shit together."

"Language."

She sighed heavily. "Sorry, Dad. I'm just a little stressed out at the moment."

"Talk to your girlfriend about it, Summer," I encouraged her. "You'll be surprised how many problems we can solve just by talking them over." That was what I had hoped for with their mother, but Jenna hadn't seen fit to stick around and discuss the void that had existed in our relationship. It still hurt that after years of friendship, she hadn't been able to come to me for us to reach an amicable solution.

"Okay, maybe I'll do just that," she stated with a sigh. "This is one thing I miss about not living at home anymore. I miss the great advice you always give, and I know some of the conversations tend to be uncomfortable, but you always listen and try to help anyway."

"Well, that's what I'm here for, kiddo."

After our talk, Summer felt better and was back to her usual jovial self. She followed me to the kitchen to check out what we were going to do about dinner, and everyone, even a reluctant Auggie, decided we would eat out.

We took two cars, Summer and Auggie driving the five minutes to McKinney Avenue. Apparently the pizza place was Auggie and Oscar's favorite place to eat, and I could understand why. The setting was laid back and extremely casual. The tables and chairs were pretty basic, and the menus looked cheap, but Oscar swore the pizzas were five-star quality.

Dinner was just as delicious as they had promised and the banter reminded me of home. I used to wonder where they all put the food they consumed in great proportions, and apparently that had not changed. Amongst the four of us, we all shared two large pizzas, mozzarella sticks, and cheese and bacon fries.

Oscar stuffed his face as usual, cramming slice after slice of pizza into his mouth like his belly was a bottomless pit. Summer was only slightly better, and her brothers now left her alone since she had socked Auggie good when she was fourteen for making a sexist remark about her eating so much for a girl.

Auggie was his usual quiet self, but even more so than usual. I couldn't help noticing his frowns. He picked at the pineapple toppings on his pizza, popping them into his mouth, but not much of anything else. We hadn't been able to speak privately since I got to the house, and I kept replaying his conversation in my mind that night he had called me when I first met Declan.

As though the universe had sent him a message that I was thinking about him, my phone chimed. I wiped my hands on the towel and removed the phone from the inside pocket of my light blazer. My heart skipped a beat at the message that appeared on the screen.

Your bed is waiting. All you need is to call me.

Three pictures popped up as well which I opened eagerly, the beauty of the luxurious suite he had taken a picture of, robbing me of my breath. The last picture was of him standing on the balcony of the hotel room, a glass of what looked like whisky in his hand, and looking at the view so only his profile was shot. He looked powerful, beautiful. He looked like he was waiting on me to show up.

But who had taken the photo of him? I wondered if my instincts were right, and he already had someone to share his weekend with. If that was the case, why had he sent me those pictures? For me to be jealous? I deleted the photos and didn't respond to his message.

Frowning at Declan intruding on dinner, I raised my head to find three pairs of eyes regarding me. Their eyes shifted in stages from me to the phone, and I understood.

"Oh my god, Dad, you bought the latest iPhone?" Summer squawked, her eyes wide.

"That's what it looks like to me," Oscar replied. "Must be good to no longer have to take care of three kids."

Even though his tone was joking, I quickly got rid of the phone. "Don't be ridiculous, Oscar. It's just a phone."

Summer made a choking sound. "You told me you'd never spend more than a couple hundred bucks on a phone dad."

I didn't know how to respond to that. It wasn't like I could tell them that they couldn't ask me questions anymore because I was their Dad and I said so. That line hadn't worked on them since years ago.

"Will you guys let up a minute?" Auggie asked, drawing attention to himself, something he rarely did. "Dad's more than entitled to buy himself an expensive phone."

"Of course he is," Summer agreed. "It's just so weird."

"Well, there's something I need to talk to everyone about, so if you could just listen for a minute," Auggie stated, as if she hadn't spoken.

Oscar turned to Auggie, a strange look on his face. He was being serious, something unheard of for him. When he'd broken his leg playing soccer, he had made a game of it, but here he was looking uncertain at what Auggie wanted to say.

"I really don't think this is the best time," Oscar told his twin.

"It's eating me up inside," Auggie replied. "They

deserve to know what we have been doing and with whom."

I frowned from Oscar to Auggie. "What did you guys do? I hope it's not anything criminal."

"It's not, but you may think so."

I had no idea what they were talking about. "Are you a part of this too?" I asked Summer.

"No, I'm just as confused as you."

"Okay then, we don't keep family secrets," I announced. "Spit it out."

When Oscar shook his head, Auggie turned to us. "I-um, while living here we discovered something we think you may be interested in." His Adam's apple bobbed in his throat as he fought to find the words to express himself.

"You'll take forever to do this," Oscar remarked, then shifted his gaze to me. "What he's trying to say is that we've been... well, we've been seeing mom behind your back."

I lost count of how many times I blinked as I tried to put into perspective what Oscar had just said. The words sounded like he was trying to say he had been in touch with their mother, but that was impossible. They would have never hidden something like that from me. Not after all that we had been through together.

"What?" It was the only word I could manage until I figured out what was going on.

"I swear we didn't look him-her up or anything," Auggie rushed to explain. "It was completely coincidental. A few months ago, I ran into uh-her at a gas station. I couldn't believe it was umm-her, but she recognized me, and we got around to talking."

I was at a loss for words. I had completely struck Jenna out of our lives after she had disappeared for years without making even an attempt to stay in touch. If she had needed some time apart, *that* I could have accommodated, but what she had done to us was despicable. I couldn't help feeling betrayed by my sons that they had been speaking to her with me none the wiser.

"How long?" I croaked the words out. "How long have you been in touch with her?"

Oscar looked away uncomfortably, and Auggie dropped his gaze to the table. He whispered something I didn't hear.

"I can't hear you, son," I said, surprised at my steely tone, but unable to temper it. "Speak up!"

"Ten months," he answered loudly. "Please, don't be mad. I-we-she wanted to get to know us."

I stared at my boys like I didn't even know them. Sure they had kept things from me a lot when they were growing up, but nothing this monumental. As much as they had their secrets back then, they would always let me know the big ones. Yet, here they had grown up into adults who had found their mother and had not mentioned it to me, especially knowing how I would feel about it.

"You've been talking to your mother for almost a year and didn't say anything to me?"

The guilty look in their eyes should have made me feel better, but it didn't. It really didn't. Suddenly, I wanted to be out of that restaurant, to catch some air and clear my mind to let their news sink in. Their mother who had abandoned us over fifteen years ago was back in their lives, and they hadn't seen fit to tell me.

"Dad, we wanted to tell you," Auggie stated. "We just knew you'd feel strongly about it, and we wanted to get to know her without the added pressure of making you feel bad about it."

Beside me, Summer finally stirred, having been shocked into speaking. I had the feeling she hadn't believed the twins at first. They had pulled enough pranks on her that she would be wary of them, but this was a serious matter they couldn't be joking about.

"You've been talking to Mom and you've said nothing to me?" she asked, her voice raised. "How could you do that and be so selfish? You weren't thinking about anyone else but yourselves!"

"It's not like that, Summer," Oscar replied, coming to the defense of his other half. "We knew if we told you that you would tell Dad."

"You could have avoided all that by coming to me and telling me about this earlier," I stated, disappointed almost to the point of anger. I felt betrayed. Why did they even want to entertain a mother who had walked out on them? I was the one who had been with them all these years.

"We weren't sure how you would react," Auggie remarked, looking miserable. "We didn't want your opinion on the matter to influence our decision, Dad. We had to decide on our own whether we wanted to form a relationship with her or not."

"Why would you even want a relationship with *her*?"

Summer snapped. "In case it escaped your memory, she left us, dumped us on Dad. It's a little too late to want to play Mom now, isn't it? We don't need her."

"She wants to meet you, Summer," Oscar stated.

"Hell no!" Summer cried, jumping to her feet. "She abandoned us! She has no right to walk back into our lives, expecting us to accommodate her. I fucking hate her, and you can tell her that."

"Summer!" I called after her, rising to my feet.

"I'll go after her," Oscar stated, and was already off to tend to his sister. I sank back into my chair and stared at Auggie.

"Why?" I asked him. "Why did you even want to talk to her after what she did?"

Auggie blinked furiously, and I knew he was trying to suppress tears when he pinched the bridge of his nose. "Because she's my mother, and nothing will change that. Regardless of what she did, that remains. I wanted to know why she left us."

"Well, let's hear it," I said, pissed that once more Jenna was fucking with my kids' emotions because it suited her to reappear now. Had she been in Columbus all the time, less than a two-hour drive away, and she hadn't seen fit to drop by to see how the kids were doing?

Auggie shook his head. "It's not my place to talk to you about it. She says she will talk to you when she's ready."

I gave a snort of laughter, staring at my son as though he was a stranger. A part of me was trying to understand why, but I couldn't. I couldn't fathom how Jenna could be forgiven for her actions. She had ripped our family apart that night I found she had skipped town on us.

"So, now she has you keeping secrets from me?" I asked him. "This is rich, Auggie. Real rich. After fifteen years of raising you on my own, this is the thanks I get?"

A brief flash of pain crossed his face. "Dad, that isn't fair."

He wanted to talk about fairness? Where was fairness when I had to raise three kids on my own? Non-existent. I had raised them out of love, doing my goddamn best by them.

I rose to my feet as anger surged inside me. I couldn't be around them right now. I needed some time and space to think.

"I need to go check on your sister," I remarked, and turned away from him. I saw the tear that finally managed to streak down his cheek. My heart tore into several pieces, wanting to go to him and comfort him, wanting to find out why? Why did he still hunger for the attention of a mother who had abandoned them? Had I not been enough? Had I done a shitty job as a single-parent that he ran to his mother the first chance he got?

14

DECLAN

Eyes shifting around the room with boredom, I barely acknowledged the man beside me who was sulking. The party was in full swing, laughter ringing out with the occasional clinking of glasses. My hosts were gracious and had extended the invitation to their cocktail party once we had concluded business this afternoon. I hadn't been in the mood for a party then, and I still wasn't. However, I figured it would be a good enough distraction so I wasn't consumed with thoughts about a certain older man who had probably forgotten me by now.

He had ignored all my text messages to him. I wasn't fond of texting in the first place and would have called him, except I didn't want to put him in an awkward position if he was around his children. Text messages were less intrusive and he could get around to answering them later, but he hadn't gotten back to me, and it pissed me off in seismic proportions.

"This party is a bit boring," Ridge whined beside me, snagging another glass of wine he didn't need. He was already half-drunk, and a sober Ridge was already barely manageable.

"You invited yourself along," I reminded him. "I don't even know why you're here."

He sidled up to me like a kitten seeking attention. "Because, I need some comfort."

Ah yes, his Daddy had cut ties with him, and although he hadn't shared why with me, it was always the same reason. Ridge was a spoiled brat. Not just any spoiled brat. *The* spoiled brat who didn't know when to give it a rest. It could be cute at first, but his Daddies usually realized sooner or later that it wasn't just an act. Ridge was a handful. He would need a staunch disciplinarian Daddy to manage him.

"What you need is a proper spanking among other things," I said quietly so the couple next to us, talking animatedly, didn't overhear our conversation.

Ridge placed a hand on my waist and frowned, his drink in the other. "Let's go back to the hotel and get me across your knees," he replied, his eyes hopeful. "You know just how hard I love it."

I stared at Ridge for the first time in a long while. Really stared at him. *Fuck.* That hero-worship look he always had in his eyes was almost rife with desperation. When I had spoken to him earlier, he had volunteered to drive to Columbus to spend the weekend with me because he was bored and had no other friends in the city. The latter was true, so I hadn't given it much thought. It was also no hardship offering him the vacant room anyway since Owen had decided to stay with his kids.

"Ridge, you've been drinking too much," I told him. "Maybe I should take you back to the hotel suite to cool off."

"And spank me?" he asked hopefully.

"No spanking," I replied, with a frown. "You know I'm not much into the disciplinary side of being a Daddy. I do it when it's necessary, but I much prefer rewarding to punishing."

"Then I'll be a good boy and you can reward me with a good fuck."

I groaned. "Ridge, we can't fuck around like we used to. You know that." Besides, it had been almost two years ago since I last touched him like that, and we had both been drunk. One of the rare occasions I had let loose.

"Why not?" he sulked.

"You know why. I'm not going to fuck up this thing I've going with Owen. I'm pretty sure he's not the sharing kind. Frankly, neither am I."

"But you shared me," he whined.

"But you weren't mine." The longer the conversation continued, the more alarmed I became. "Please tell me we're on the same page about this, Ridge. I don't want to make things weird between us. You need to stop pushing your Daddies away."

He glanced away, snagging another drink from a passing tray. "Yeah, we're good. I'll just find someone else to hook up with tonight. No big deal."

"Ridge," I trailed off when my phone vibrated. I reached for it to shut it off so I could continue my conversation with him, but it was Owen. I glanced from Ridge to the phone screen. Why did it feel like I was making a choice between my best friend and a new love interest? *Love. Is that what Owen is? A love interest rather than just an interest?* Only time would tell.

"I need to take this call," I told Ridge. "We're not finished with this convo."

"Whatever."

"I just need five," I told him, winding my way through the throng of bodies to the double doors leading out to the patio. I swiped the screen to answer the call before it rang off to voicemail. No way was I going to miss his call when I had been anticipating it all day. Hell, I'd not thought he would call. I had expected a text message at the most.

"What took you so long?" I growled into the phone as I abandoned the party, leaving the laughter behind me. Some of the chatter carried outside to the patio, and I moved further along the cobbled stones.

Other than his deep breathing, silence answered my question. I was about to tease him about the heavy-breathing call, but something in the way he sounded alarmed me.

"Owen?" I asked. "Are you there?"

He cleared his throat, so he was definitely there, but again, nothing. Every bone in my body became taut with unease.

"Owen, talk to me," I urged him.

"Declan." I had never heard my name called with so much pain before. "Are you busy?" he asked.

"No, I'm not," I answered. "Why? What's up? Did something happen?"

"I need a favor," he remarked. "I know I had said no before, but do you still have that extra room available?"

I didn't, but there was no way I was going to tell Owen that, especially when I could tell something was wrong. Owen wouldn't be asking to stay with me instead of his kids if everything was fine. He was nothing if not a devoted father, and when he had told me that this trip was for his children, I had believed him.

I would rather book Ridge another room and Owen not be the wiser.

"There's always room wherever I am," I told him, indirectly answering his question. "Where are you? Do you want me to come get you?"

"I'm in the hotel lobby," he admitted. "I walked out from the restaurant."

"Why did you do that? I would have come by to pick you up, Owen, or sent Silas."

"I know."

I sucked in a deep breath, overjoyed by those two simple words and wondered if he knew how much he had revealed to me. All he needed to do was call and I would be there for him. That was one lesson I had been trying to teach him since the first time I laid eyes on him. It was the first step to him acknowledging that he was mine. Mine.

"Don't move," I told him, backtracking toward the sliding doors of the house. "I'll be there in ten."

"What? You mean you're not in?"

"Not quite," I answered, "But I'm not far out, so I'll be there in ten."

"Declan, if I've caught you in the middle of something, you don't have to rush over. I can find somewhere else to spend the night."

I wanted to ask him why he needed somewhere else to spend the night considering he had accommodation available at his kids' house, but I preferred hearing it in person. If he wasn't staying with his children though, something had to have gone horribly wrong.

"I'm on my way, Owen," I told him. "Just hang tight until I get there."

"Alright."

Even though he had agreed to stay put, I didn't like the hesitancy in his voice. I hurried back inside the house, scanning the room for Ridge to inform him we were leaving. I needed to figure out what to do with him for the night.

The minute I entered the room, I spotted Ridge in one corner with a guy who looked like he wanted to eat him alive. Ridge was unsteady on his feet, laughing a little too loudly, the drunken sound carrying over to me from across the room. The brat had another drink in hand when he should have quit many glasses earlier.

I groaned as I tried to make a quick decision. The longer Owen was on his own, the more likely he was to change his mind and find somewhere else to spend the night. He sounded so distressed on the phone that I couldn't let that happen. At the same time, I couldn't leave Ridge on his own to deal with guys like the man leaning over him. As drunk as he was, his decision-making skills were too impaired.

With determined steps, I moved toward Ridge, shuffling by others blocking my path. When I finally arrived, he was smooching with the guy I had seen him with. The guy was practically holding up Ridge's drunken ass.

Normally I didn't like to intervene, but hell if I was going to be late in getting to the hotel because Ridge decided he wanted to get laid tonight. If that was his intention, he should have been sober to make that decision. I couldn't do anything about this shit when he was alone, but he was on my time, which made me feel responsible for him. Sometimes assuming all this responsibility without being asked could be a fucking pain, but I did it anyway because that was just me. Responsibility guy. *The one people turn to when things go wrong.*

I, at least, waited until they came up for air. Ridge blinked when he saw me, like he was having difficulty remembering who I was. That was how drunk he was.

"I'll take my friend here home," I announced, grabbing hold of Ridge's arm.

"I think he wants to go home with me," his companion barked, tightening his hold on Ridge. "We're kinda not done here for the night."

Another night I might have been amused, but the man I was starting to care for way too much in such a short time was waiting for me back at the hotel, and I couldn't let him down. I put on my best glare and gave Ridge's companion my full attention.

"My friend is drunk," I enunciated clearly for him.

"There's no way in hell he's going anywhere else tonight, but back to our hotel room. Now if you'll excuse us."

I didn't wait for a response, and I was relieved he hadn't challenged me. Ridge had yet to say anything, and he didn't protest when I removed him from the other man's arms and led him from the house. I didn't encounter Steven Vascianne, my host, but neither was I going to hunt for him.

"I wassh tryna get laid," Ridge slurred, leaning heavily against me. His steps were all over the place, and I was grateful he had a lithe form, or we would have done more than stumble a few times.

"Then do it sober, you ass," I growled at him. "I'm not going to have this on my conscience by leaving you here with a stranger to take advantage of you. Seriously, this is fucked up, Ridge. You need to be more responsible."

"Fuck res-pon-sib-ilty." He hiccupped, then giggled. "S'all you talk 'bout. Respon-spilty. You should have fun sometimes."

I bit back a sharp retort that if he and others were more responsible, then I wouldn't have to always be the one in charge. I didn't grow up wanting responsibility. It had been dropped into my lap from a tender age, and there was no going back now. It was deeply ingrained in me.

Now I had to do the responsible thing in getting him to bed to sleep off the alcohol, while trying not to leave a bad impression on Owen.

15

OWEN

"Declan?"

Climbing to my feet, I stared at Declan who had entered the hotel lobby, but what I was really looking at was the man plastered all over him. It was the same guy from his father's wedding— the one who had kissed him. They were both dressed up as if they had gone out together, and that made me pause. I couldn't readily identify the emotions swirling inside of me, but I registered shock and uncertainty at what I was doing here.

"Owen," he said, turning his head in my direction. He looked pissed off. Maybe I had interrupted something after all.

"You should have told me you had company," I said, eyeing the exit and trying to come up with a graceful strategy to get the hell out of there with my dignity intact. Served me right to think a guy like him really meant us to be serious. Or maybe it was my fault for rebuffing his invitations.

"I didn't know I would have company," he answered, frowning at the man in his arms. "Grab his other arm, will you? Bastard's drunk and a dead weight."

I didn't move from where I was. *He wants me to help bring his friend—lover— whoever this guy is up to his suite?*

"It's not what you think," he stated, using his head to gesture at his charge. "I'll explain when we get up to my suite. Just for God's sake grab his other fucking arm or I'm going to drop him, although, it would serve his ass right."

Despite what I thought or *didn't* think, he was perilously close to dropping his *friend,* so I moved toward the pair and steadied the guy between us. A stench of alcohol wafted up my nostrils from the knocked-out guy. For a guy who looked so lithe he was heavier than expected, and I could see how his weight would have been a bother for Declan.

"We're on the nineteenth floor," he told me as we headed for the elevator.

We didn't speak further as we rode the elevator to his floor, and all the time I wondered what the hell I was getting myself into. I tried to remember if Declan had ever clarified what his ties to this guy was, but I couldn't recall. All I could remember was the kiss shared between the two, and that was no friendly kiss either. My male friends, the few that existed, didn't go around kissing me on the lips.

I should have bailed out, found another means of

working through all the craziness of tonight, but I couldn't find the words to tell him that I was backing out of this— whatever the hell this was. Carrying a drunk man between us to his hotel suite wasn't what I had signed up for. I didn't even know what I had signed up for. One thing I was certain of was that I could no longer pretend I had accepted Declan's offer of a ride to Columbus just for the kids.

"Can you take most of his weight while I get the key?" Declan asked once we had stopped at his door.

"Yeah, sure." Like I didn't find it awkward as hell to have a strange man in my arms.

"Thanks," he answered. "I know you didn't expect this, but I couldn't leave him at that party drunk for some dude to take advantage of him like this."

I grunted a response that was unintelligible because I didn't understand enough to give a reply. He finally got the door open, and we lugged his friend inside. I almost got distracted from how nice everything was, but he tugged me through the living room and in the direction of a bedroom where we dumped his friend unceremoni- ously on top of the covers. He pulled off the guy's shoes, dropped them on the floor and turned him on his side with a scowl. I watched the domestic scene, feeling uncomfortable and a little sick to the stomach that Declan seemed too familiar doing this.

"Uh... I should go," I said, backing up as fast as my legs could carry me.

"Owen, wait!"

I didn't quite make it to the door as Declan's hand clamped down on my shoulder from behind. His hold was tight, and I cast a longing look at the door before turning back to him.

"Why should I wait?" I asked him, my face flushed and confused. "You've got somebody in your bed."

"He's just a friend," he answered, running his hand from my shoulder and down my arm.

"Are you trying to fuck with me?" I demanded, reaching my limit for the night. "Because that's the same guy who kissed you the day of your father's wedding. Now he's in your bed. That doesn't seem like a coincidence to me."

Owen frowned at me. "Look, I'm going to explain this once, and you're going to listen to me, then we'll end this discussion."

"You don't get to—"

"Owen!"

He didn't shout. He didn't need to. The sharp way he said my name shut me up, made me want to sit on my hands and promise to be a good boy. My cheeks blazed at the realization of where my thoughts were leading. *My god, what is he doing to me?*

"That's better," he remarked and rubbed a finger at his temple. "Ridge is a friend. We've known each other practically all our lives. He recently broke up with his partner, so he came out here because he was not feeling his best. If I had known you would take me up on my offer, I would have had him book a separate room, but you led me to believe there was no way you would consider my offer."

But he's lying in your bed, I wanted to argue, because how was I supposed to feel about that? His friend Ridge was a gorgeous guy who made me feel like a fucking extinct dinosaur. Why would Declan want the outdated T-rex when he could have for himself a beautiful chameleon?

"Okay, you've explained," I remarked, because he was waiting for some kind of response from me. "I still think I should go."

"The townhouse is about a half hour walk from here, Owen. What are you going to do? Walk?"

"I'll call a cab."

He came up to me and hooked his fingers into the neckline of my shirt, tugging just a little. "No. What you're going to do is sit with me at the wet bar. We can share a drink while you tell me what's going on."

I pushed my hands into my pockets, reminded of why I was there in the first place. I glanced to the bed dubiously then back at him. "Seems like you already have your hands full."

"Owen, I can see that something happened tonight. Don't be stubborn. Come on. We both need this drink, I think."

He walked away from me to the wet bar. I glanced at the door. Now was the time for me to make my escape. I scowled at the thought that I was thinking of it as an escape. It wasn't like he had me against my will. I had walked all the way here without his knowledge, and I could leave any time. So, why didn't I?

I trailed after him through to the sitting area where a fancy wet bar was set up against one wall. There were four white and steel stools in total set up around the counter opposite each other. I claimed one of the stools and watched Declan as he mixed our drinks without even asking me what I'd like. I didn't volunteer since I didn't have an eclectic taste when it came to liquor anyway. I usually had a Chickow, but just looking at the regal stance of Declan, I could tell he wasn't a beer kind of guy.

He turned toward me, drinks poured into two glasses and pushed one across the counter toward me. Before he sat down, he removed the expensive jacket he wore and threw it across the other stool on his side. He wasn't wearing a tie, but he worked a few of the buttons on his shirt loose, getting comfortable before he claimed the stool across from mine. I couldn't decide if I preferred having the counter between us since it meant he was facing me directly. There was nowhere else to look except at him, so I stared down into the clear liquid in the glass. He had dropped a few ice cubes in the drink, and I was grateful for that. It didn't take a lot to make me tipsy since I wasn't used to drinking as a habit. I'd needed to be sober to take care of three kids.

"What happened?" he asked after taking a sip from his drink. "When I dropped you off this morning you were excited about seeing your kids. Now you're here, and not that I'm not glad you are, but this wasn't in your plans, so something had to have happened."

"Yeah, I didn't mean to intrude," I mumbled, taking a small sip of the drink. It was lighter than I'd expected. I took another sip.

"For the last time, Owen, you're not intruding. I want you to be able to come to me if something's wrong. I'm good at this. Fixing people's problems."

I snorted and stopped avoiding his gaze then. "I noticed you like fixing people's problems," I answered. "But you can't fix this."

"Maybe. Let me hear it."

I was silent for a while as I tried to sort through all the information to decide where to begin. He didn't push, but patiently waited, something that didn't miss me. From the night of his father's bachelor's party, I had observed him as someone with a take-charge attitude who listened, then acted.

"I've been a single father for over fifteen years," I started, dipping a finger in the drink to swirl the ice around. "I raised my kids on my own after my wife left me. I came home one night from work and she was gone, leaving the sitter in charge. I shouldn't have been surprised, but I was."

He reached across the counter and took one of my hands in his. He didn't say anything, just held onto my fingers with a tight grip. I never knew before how much I needed something… someone to hold onto. For years I had done life alone, and in such a short time Declan was calling my bullshit to this super dad image I'd enshrined myself in. I hadn't been a super dad. Parenting three kids had been hard work. I would have done it over and over again, but it had been hard, exhausting at times.

I held onto his hand because this was the first time someone was offering to be there for me since Jenna left. Everyone just assumed that, because I went through the routine without complaining, I had my shit together. No one knew the tears I had sometimes cried when I eventually got to bed some nights. Like the time Oscar snuck out, and I couldn't leave the other kids alone to go look for him. I'd been up half the night worrying, and even when he had come home that night, it had been a long time before I had been able to sleep, too distraught over all the things I had imagined could have been wrong. I would have been glad for someone to talk to back then about my fears of not being good enough to raise my kids on my own.

"Imagine having a best friend since you were both in middle school, then being bailed on by that person," I said, hearing the bitterness in my tone, but unable to help it. I hadn't talked about this with anyone since Jenna left. Not even with my family. "She didn't have to leave like that. She could have talked to me. Why didn't she? We'd always been close even before we got romantically involved. We had three kids together. Wasn't that worth something for her to pause and think about what she was going to subject us to?"

He linked our fingers and squeezed. "She never got in touch?"

My laugh was raw and hoarse. "Never. I couldn't find her. Our divorce happened without her because nobody knew where the hell she was. Do you know how embarrassing it was having to publicize in the paper that I was looking for my missing wife? It was as if she ceased to exist. I didn't know if she was dead or alive. I blamed myself for years that I had done something to drive her away. I raised those kids by myself, Declan. I was there for Oscar's soccer games, Auggie's science fairs, Summer's shows. I was there through the rebellious years, and Oscar was the worst. I stayed up nights worrying when they were sick, lost two jobs, because I couldn't leave them alone at one point or another. And what does she do? She fucking reached out to *my* kids behind *my* back." My voice broke and I had to struggle to get the rest of the words out. "They've been keeping it from me. How could they do that? For almost a fucking year, Declan, they've known where their mother is and they've said nothing."

"Shit." Declan released my hand, and I heard the scrape of his stool against the floor. He rounded the counter and was beside me in the next second, cupping the back of my head and pulling me in for a hug. I stiffened up for a while to protest his cuddling. Nobody cuddled me. I always did the cuddling, but it felt so damn good to be on the receiving end for once. I barely contained the tears that threatened to fall.

"My sons both broke the news to me tonight," I said, burrowing my face into his chest. He smelled so good, felt so solid against me, a tower of strength. I, who always had to be the glue that kept everything together, finally, was being allowed to fall apart, knowing Declan wouldn't let me slip through the cracks. He'd keep all the pieces and fix them all together again. I hadn't known him very long, but it was the kind of man he was. And for some reason, I had caught his attention. For once, I wasn't fighting it, because he was exactly what I needed.

I stopped fighting his advances, stopped pushing him away since I could no longer afford to. He was the dock my ship had been on the lookout for all this time. Now after years of being a lone sailor, ship weathering storm after turbulent storm, I was finally allowed to moor.

"You feel like they've betrayed you," he whispered softly, his nose buried in my hair. "You've been there for them. Now they seem to be on her side. That's how you feel, isn't it?"

"Yes." He'd summed up everything pretty well. "But I also feel like I've failed them. If they were truly happy, they wouldn't need her. She walked out on them. Why do they feel like they need her now?"

His grip tightened on me. "That's not true, Owen. I know you're hurt by them keeping it from you, but I don't think it has to do with you at all."

"What do you mean? How can it not be about me? It's been just the four of us all this time."

"Maybe they just want to get to know their mother, Owen."

"Why? Would you want to get to know someone who's not given a shit about you for fifteen years?"

16

DECLAN

Would you want to get to know someone who's not given a shit about you for fifteen years?

Owen's innocent question fueled by his frustration echoed in my head. Why indeed? I had asked myself the same question often as I grew up, and at twenty-five years old, I was still no closer to coming up with an answer.

"It's not as cut and dried as you think," I said softly into his hair. It felt good to hold him, and although he was calming down, I didn't want to let go.

"I think it's pretty simple enough," he argued. "I've been there for them. She wasn't. Why should it matter to them now to have a relationship with her?"

"Because, she's still their mother," I replied calmly. *He's still your father, no matter how he tries to act otherwise.* "There's a bond that will always be there whether she's in their lives or not."

Owen stiffened in my arms and yanked himself away from me. "Are you taking her side too?"

"This is not about taking sides. It's not, Owen, so don't give me that look like I'm betraying you too. They didn't and neither am I. I'm helping you to think rationally because you're too overwhelmed by emotions right now."

Owen clambered to his feet, and if looks could kill I would have been burned to ash already. "I'm not overwhelmed by emotions!"

His voice thundered in the room, and I winced, apprehensive that even though Ridge should be completely out for the night, Owen might wake him.

"Come." I crooked a finger at Owen, then turned my back to him, expecting him to follow me. I could have manhandled him into it, but I always left the choice to him. In this way, when he carried out my commands, he could not later argue that I had forced him into anything. He was simply following his natural instincts to be guided. To be led.

I heard his heavy sigh, but he followed, and that made me fucking light on my feet. The more time he spent in my presence, the more he was learning about the dynamic of our relationship. He was coming to accept who I was, but more importantly, he was recognizing who *he* was and that he needed this. He needed me to be in control as much as I craved it, and this was what I had sensed the night we had met. We were what the other needed.

I led him through the double doors to the other

bedroom I had offered him. When he entered, I closed the doors behind us and spun the lock. His eyes found mine, and I didn't try to hide my intentions from him. He wasn't going anywhere tonight. Not in the state he was in. The last thing I wanted him to do was experience a fallout with his kids. He would only grow to regret it, and I didn't want him to go through that. The malice usually fostered into bitterness that became harder to fix with every passing day.

I had lived for too long without the emotional support of a father to allow that to happen between him and his children.

"Owen, love is not finite," I told him. "Your kids won't love you any less just because they have discovered a new relationship with their mother. It's okay to feel hurt about the whole thing, but give yourself some time to get over it. You'll find that the feeling of betrayal will lessen with time."

"They are mine, not hers," he said stubbornly as he marched over to the bed to sit on one edge.

I followed him, nudging my way between his thighs. I cupped his face and tilted his head upward so he couldn't avoid my gaze. My heart ached for him and the pain in his eyes. He really was hurt by what his kids had done. I had been able to identify with his children's perspective, because as old as I was, I would give anything to have a proper relationship with Charles. Now I tried to see things from his perspective.

"It's okay to be upset," I murmured, and placed a kiss in the center of his forehead. "What happened when they told you about their mother?"

"They hadn't told Summer either," he said on a

groan. "She got as upset as me and wouldn't talk to anyone. Oscar left with her to ensure she got home okay. Instead of going back home, I decided to walk here." His eyes turned apologetic. "Sorry, I didn't know where else to go."

"I'm glad you came to me."

He sighed heavily and let his forehead droop forward. "But nothing's solved. I know they want me to say that it's alright if they want to get to know their mom. Hell, they don't even need my permission. They've been seeing her already behind my back. They'll just do whatever they want to anyway, and they're adults. It's not like I can ground them or anything. I can't, can I?"

He was getting riled up again, the tension in him mounting. His talk of grounding his children placed an idea in my head. There was no getting him to listen to me while he was this way. I needed to distract him, to calm him down. Maybe then he would be more open to understanding what his children were going through as well.

"Get off the bed," I instructed him.

He blinked at me. "What?"

"Don't question me, Owen. Just do as I say, and I won't punish you any more than necessary."

He choked on his words. "Is-is this some kind of joke, Declan? I'm having a crisis with my kids and you want to *punish* me?"

"Trust me," I implored him, hoping he would understand why I was doing this. I hadn't been kidding when I had told Ridge I didn't enjoy the punishment side of being a Daddy. It had its place though, like now.

He rose off the bed. "Now what?"

"Undress. Take everything off."

"Declan—"

"*Take everything off, Owen. Now!*"

His eyes widened at the tone of my voice. It was the first time I was giving him the full effect of my commanding voice, which Ridge called my Daddy Call. I was pleased to see it didn't work any less on Owen as he reached for his shirt.

"What are you going to do?" he asked me, sounding breathless.

"I'm going to make you forget for just a little while," I told him. "I'm going to spank you so hard, Owen, your sore ass will be the only thing you can think of. Then I'm going to fuck you into exhaustion, run you a bath, and then we sleep. How does that sound?"

He made a choking sound, but I didn't wait for him to respond. I left him to finish undressing as I slipped back through the double doors. Ridge was still fast asleep on the bed, and hadn't turned from where we had placed him. He should sleep through whatever I was about to do to Owen, and if he didn't, then it would serve him right.

I grabbed the supplies I needed from my bag and snagged a towel from the bathroom, stamping down my excitement. This was hardly about me, but getting him to focus on something else. When he calmed down, then we could discuss what we would do about his children.

When I returned to the room, I locked the double doors behind me. I paused inside and took in the sight of Owen who had taken every stitch of clothing off except for his gray boxer shorts that clung to his body and showed off his assets. Despite his hesitancy earlier, he must have liked the thought of my punishment because he wasn't entirely flaccid.

Owen was built bigger, hairier, stronger, and that didn't turn me off in the least. If anything, I was more excited at the thought of overpowering this man, making him mine and hearing him call me Daddy as he came all over the gold-colored bedsheets.

He wasn't muscled all over. His pecs were huge, and so were his nipples which were half-hidden by smooth chest hair. The line of hair continued down to his pubis. I was stimulated by the hot rugged look of his body. He didn't have a six-pack, but he looked damn good, not just for a man his age but for any man overall.

"You didn't completely undress," I told him on a frown. "'Fess up, Owen. You're hankering to get your ass spanked again like this morning, aren't you?"

"Anything you want, Sir."

I blinked at him in surprise because in the little time it had taken me to grab the supplies from the drawer, he seemed to have an understanding of what was about to take place. I would have expected him to protest and for me to coax him into the role, but for some reason he had adopted it all on his own, even if his face had gone red, and his head hung. As much as I wanted to ask him why, I didn't want to interrupt the flow.

"And what I wanted was you completely naked," I replied. "You're not completely naked, Owen. I can't let that slide."

"What are you going to do to me?" he asked so softly

I almost didn't hear him. His breathing filled the room, heavy and fast.

"What do you want me to do to you?"

He dropped his gaze to the floor and squirmed, mumbling something under his breath.

"I can't hear you," I told him.

"I want you t-to do what you did earlier," he replied, his lips barely moving.

I walked up to him and cupped his chin, jerking up until he couldn't avoid looking at me. I threw the supplies on the bed and kept my eyes on him. "You want me to spank you?"

He inhaled sharply and when he let it out, a tremor went through his body. "Yes," he said on a gasp. "Do it. Please. Get me out of my head, Declan. Let me forget everything but you tonight. Tomorrow I'll figure all the other shit out."

That was exactly what I had in mind for him—to have a means to escape the turmoil he was going through right now. Instead of immediately giving him what he wanted, I tugged him forward and kissed him, because I was so hungry for another taste of him, and I wanted him to know what was about to happen between us was about understanding his needs and fulfilling them.

His mouth became pliant under mine, and I almost ignored the spanking and bore him down on the bed to sink into his body's heat. I tugged my lips away from his before I was completely sucked into him.

"Kneel at the edge of the bed," I instructed him. "Knees apart, torso planted on the mattress with your ass in the air."

His eyes widened as though he was scandalized by the position. When he took too long to move, I narrowed my eyes at him, and he turned to do my bidding. He climbed onto the bed, settling himself on his knees and forearms with his chest on the mattress, offering his ass up to me like a sacrifice.

My heart quickened at the sight he made on his hands and knees. I imagined his face, that he had tucked into his arms, had to be red, but he had given in to the inevitable of what we had become—what we both needed.

"The only reason I haven't started to paddle your ass already, is because you're new to this," I told him, walking over to him. I cupped his tight end and squeezed, temporarily forgetting what I was about to say at the feeling of him in my hands. He was just the right amount of pliant as I palmed him through the cotton material of his boxers.

"I'll break you into it gently," I murmured hoarsely as I reached for the waistband of his boxers, and slowly teased them down over his ass. He lay still, not emitting a sound. If his back wasn't moving with each breath he inhaled, I would have thought him inanimate. "While spanking for punishment isn't necessarily what I want our relationship to be about, it can be that intense feeling of pain you need in a moment to ground you—distract you from everything else."

I finally got his boxers all the way down from his ass. Instead of removing them, I left them to hang about his hard thighs. Kneeling as he was, his cheeks naturally spread so I could see his pretty pink hole all manscaped and ready for me. He hadn't been fully clean-shaven earlier when I'd spanked his ass in the kitchen, which meant he had done this for me. Did that mean he had been thinking about this happening again? Whatever had motivated him into doing it, to say I was pleased didn't begin to describe the way I felt.

"I'll never forget what you look like kneeling before me like this," I told him and leaned forward to kiss the dimples in his lower back. "It's almost a shame my hands are about to mar your perfect skin."

17

OWEN

This was wrong. So wrong. So, *so* wrong. *Then why the hell does it feel so good to be spread open like this for Declan?* Every word he spoke heightened my anticipation until I had to work seriously hard to stifle my deep breathing into the sheets. It was bad enough that I wanted this, craved it. I didn't have to let him know just how much I had started anticipating this once he'd told me to undress.

The perfect distraction, I told myself. That was all this was. Nothing more. Nothing less. I would go ahead with the forbidden, allowing him to treat me like a naughty boy who deserved to get his ass spanked for misbehaving. I'd let him fuck me like I hadn't been penetrated in over fifteen years. Then I'd wake up in the morning and worry again about what I would do about my children. And Declan.

For now though, all I needed was Declan's hands all over me. I was no longer interested in questioning the why's of it. Why was he attracted to me? Why did he like an older man? Why didn't it bother him how much bigger than him I was? Those answers had no bearing on tonight. They wouldn't change the fact that I desperately wanted Declan Moore's hands all over my body. The more I thought about it, the more desperate I was for him to deliver what his words promised.

Declan had made it clear what he planned to do with me, but still, when his hand crashed into my left cheek, I cried out in surprise. I should have been prepared, but I wasn't. I welcomed the physical pain which served to dull the one in my heart. A harder slap landed on my other ass cheek this time, and I was better prepared.

"You fucking love this, don't you, Owen?" he asked, his tone full of amusement. "Now what kind of punishment is this if you're loving it like I know you are? Hmm?"

I responded with a groan as he aimed two more sharp slaps to my ass. I couldn't explain it. His hands fucking stung wherever they fell on my skin. There was no mistake what this was. He was spanking the crap out of me, hurting me, bringing me pain, but it was as though every sting veered into a territory I had never charted before—a world where the pain and pleasure co-existed, both making the other even more intense.

I wasn't completely dead to the world, so of course I knew all about spanking. Jenna had even spanked me a couple of times while we were having sex and she mounted me, but it had never been anything of this sort. Nothing this intense and punitive. Hers had been more playful.

I couldn't help my grunt of pain as I lost count of how many times Owen slapped my ass, but it was enough for me to squirm. It was enough for me to grab hold of clumps of the sheet in my hands and bury my face into the bed to muffle my groans. My ass was on fire, flames licking my skin wherever he touched. I lost thought of everything else except the sensation crawling over my flesh.

"Please," I cried out at the next slap. I wasn't sure I could physically take anymore. My cheeks hurt so badly that I was about to embarrass myself any moment now by dissolving into tears.

How the hell is my dick so hard when my ass hurts so bad?

"Not done with you yet, Owen," Declan remarked, but instead of delivering another slap, leaned forward to kiss my ass cheeks. The wetness of his lips soothed my skin somewhat. I whimpered and moaned pitifully as he took his time, trailing kisses over my glutes.

"Declan," I moaned when he teased me, fishing his tongue between my cheeks, but moving too quickly for me to savor the moment he swept over my hole. "Please," I begged him. "More. Need to feel you."

He took pity on me and let the broadness of his tongue stroke me over and over. Suddenly, being spanked so hard I was close to tears no longer mattered. All that did was me experiencing this magic of his tongue probing and stroking. I became a whimpering mess all over again, my cock so hard I inched a hand between my legs to grasp it and make myself come.

Declan's hand wrapped around my wrist before I

reached my goal. I made a sound of protest when he withdrew his tongue from my body.

"You don't get to touch yourself until I say when," he growled at me. "You don't want me to spank you again, do you?"

"But I want—"

I yelped from his hand greeting my backside hard. "You going to argue with me all night, Owen?" he asked. "Or are you going to trust that I know what's best for you?"

I was forty six years old. I knew what was best for me. But I didn't tell him this. I stopped fussing about how hard I was, or how it almost hurt to be so aroused and not touching myself.

Owen trailed his thumb between my cheeks and teased at my opening. "I did want to fuck you bareback, but that's going to have to wait for another time."

"Oh God," I groaned, a shiver running down my spine when his finger popped inside the tight ring of muscles, pushing deeper. Despite not having been penetrated in years by a living breathing man, I'd used my dildo that I kept boxed and locked away. With three kids in the house, I hadn't used it nearly enough, but since meeting Declan, I'd brought out my favorite toy to play with again.

"So fucking tight," Declan murmured, and reached for lube. His finger slid inside me easier this time, pushing past the knuckle. "Tell me, Owen. When was the last time you fucked?"

"Too long," I answered vaguely, because he would likely not believe me otherwise.

"A year?"

"Depends," I gasped as he twisted two fingers inside my body, plunging harder, faster.

"On what?"

"There was a woman a couple years ago." I swore when his finger scraped my prostate, gasping at the shiver that blanketed my skin in goosebumps.

"I'm talking about with a guy. How long since you were fucked in the ass?"

I grabbed for a pillow and stuffed my face in it to hide my embarrassment. This was not the kind of conversation I wanted to have, when all I wanted was for him to remove his fingers and fill me up with his cock instead. I mumbled my answer into the pillow.

"I can't hear you, Owen," he said, and yanked the pillow from under my head. "How long?"

I groaned. "Only once."

His fingers stopped moving, though they were still buried inside me. "What?"

"I've only been fucked by a guy once," I replied. "That was back in high school before I got married." I let out a sigh, eased my ass up from his finger, then slid right back down to give myself the movement he had stalled. "Look, can we finish this conversation afterward?"

"No, I need to know what to expect. How much experience you've had with anal. Are you opposed to it?"

Frustrated, I rose up to my knees so my back was vertical to his and twisted my head to stare at him. "I'm practically begging you to fuck me," I pointed out. "Does that sound like I'm opposed to anal?"

He pulled out his fingers and stepped back from me. I

thought he was changing his mind about what we were doing and almost sighed with relief when he reached for his shirt and quickly shed it. His shoes and pants followed. I tried not to be obvious about checking out his junk, but I failed miserably. My eyes dropped to his crotch, and I was pleased by what he packed. His cock was begging to be released from the confines of his tight boxers.

"Like what you see, huh?" he asked, reaching for the waistband of his boxers and pulled them down his thighs.

"What's there not to like?" I croaked out, my ass twitching in need at the sight of him completely nude. He wasn't all that long, but packed girth. My heart thudded in my chest as I stared at him, unable to look away. I'd never thought of a man's dick as sexy before. It was just there, another part of our anatomy which could give pleasure.

But Declan had a sexy dick. A sexy, fat, uncut dick.

"How bad do you want it, boy?"

I was too far gone to even care that he called me boy. Too far gone to think how ridiculous it was. There was nothing ridiculous about the way he was watching me, or how he lazily stroked his dick as though committed to torturing me. I would willingly be anything he wanted just for him to breach me.

"I want it now," I told him. "It's been so long."

He reached for the lube once more, and I watched him slip on the condom and prep himself. He stepped into the space behind me, his eyes never leaving my face as he guided his cock to my entrance.

"Kiss me," he ordered.

I didn't hesitate, twisting my head sideways. With his free hand, he held me to him, and his lips came down on mine. It wasn't the most comfortable kiss, but getting a damn crick in my neck was worth it when he plunged his tongue into my mouth at the same time his crown pressed inside my body, stretching me with just his tip. When I would have pulled away to moan, he didn't release me, so I ended up emitting the sound inside his mouth. He kissed me harder, pressing his lips to mine in a bruising manner as he made several shallow thrusts inside me, fucking me with just the tip of his cock.

"Declan!" I tore my lips away from his and cried in frustration, because I wanted so much more. "Give me everything."

He kissed the side of my face, my neck, my shoulder and ignored me. "Who calls the shots here?" he asked, tightening his hold on me.

"You," I answered readily. I didn't mind him calling the shots. That was exactly what I preferred—him taking charge and using me. I never quite got enough of this in the past, but Declan could give me all.

"Who's in charge?" he demanded again.

And I knew what he wanted to hear. I was blushing before the words even came out. "You, Daddy."

Declan stilled behind me, and my heart jackhammered in my chest as I wondered if now he was hearing the word, he was put off by the idea of a grown man calling him that.

"Fuck!" he exploded, and gripped my hips as he surged inside me hard. "Owen, baby…"

I wasn't the only one at a loss for words as he finally

gave me what I craved. It was almost like me calling him Daddy was the aphrodisiac he had been waiting on, so I pressed for more.

"Fuck me harder, Daddy," I begged him. "Please. It's been so long."

Owen pulled out of me and gave my ass a slap that rang out in the room. "Turn over. I want to see your face when I'm grinding you."

I shuffled over to the center of the bed, and he was over me in a flash. His lips found mine as he reached between our bodies to grasp his cock and guide it right where we both wanted it. I moaned as he filled me up and nudged my legs even wider to accommodate himself between my thighs.

"You never stood a chance," he smirked at me. "From the first night I saw you, I was determined that you would be mine."

I smiled at him, feeling ridiculously happy. At the back of my mind, I remembered the night's events which had upset me, but I couldn't summon the energy to focus on it right now. Not when I had such a gorgeous guy—and he was fucking gorgeous—going gung-ho over me.

"I still have no fucking clue why you're so obsessed with me," I moaned.

He bracketed both arms on either side of me and started that grinding he had mentioned just before. "Can't you tell? When you call me Daddy it's the sexiest thing ever. If I hadn't pulled out I'd have come right then."

"Daddy," I said, teasing him. His hips fell off the rhythm, and I laughed softly. "Damn, this is fun."

"Fun, huh?" He eased back so he knelt between my legs which he grasped and pressed forward. He pumped inside me, never leaving an inch to spare. His hips were fucking hypnotic, drawing me into his spell. He didn't fuck me fast, or hard. He moved with a fluidity he made look so easy, stroking in and out, deep and bold.

"Please, can I touch my dick now?" I begged him, as my hips picked up his rhythm, and I met each thrust of his.

"Not yet."

I groaned and subjected myself to the torture. My cock was a weeping mess on my stomach. Just a little tug and I'd be coming in streams.

"Fuck, your ass is good!" Declan groaned, biting into his bottom lip. The expression on his face was priceless, eyes haunted with the pleasure he was chasing.

"Don't stop," I begged him, as his movements intensified. The bed shifted under our bodies as he laid into me, fucking me like he had promised.

"I couldn't even if I wanted to," he hissed at me. "Too fucking good. Your tight ass clenching my cock, so good, boy."

He pushed my right leg back down to the bed, kept my left over his shoulder and leaned forward on his forearms. *Slap! Slap!* He grunted, I groaned and gasped every time he thrust.

"Oh God, I'm not gonna last," he moaned. "Touch yourself for me, boy. I want to watch you jerk that beautiful cock."

I didn't need further encouragement. I wrapped my hand around my dick and couldn't have gone slow if my life depended on it. My rapid jerks matched the rhythm of his cock pounding me.

"Oh fuck!" I grabbed a handful of sheet with my free hand as I felt my climax approaching.

"That's it. That's it, boy. Now, let me see that cum. Let me see how much I can make you fucking come."

One hard thrust later, and I was choking on my cry of release as he continued thrusting through my climax. He didn't ease up one bit, only pounding harder, deeper, faster, dragging out the series of mini-climaxes that wracked my body, before culminating into a combustion of pleasure so intense it was almost as if I passed out from it.

"Fuck!" I heard Declan's groan above me. His hands trembled as he surged inside me once, twice, and a third time before he stilled. His body went rigid, his mouth slightly open, head thrown back as he emptied himself, and I understood then what he meant by fucking me bareback. I would have loved for him to finish inside me without a barrier.

18

DECLAN

To say I was surprised when I woke up the next morning beside Owen was an understatement. I stared at the man burrowed into my side and racked my brain trying to remember if at some point in that night, which I didn't remember, I had gotten up. It was so long since I had slept through a night that I wasn't certain, but I felt rested.

The usual exhaustion from fighting with my inner demons throughout the night was noticeably absent. I wasn't dying for a cup of coffee to feel better, and I hadn't swallowed any pills to combat the stomach pains I usually got. I was rested, ready to start the day, and it was all because of the man snoring gently beside me. I hated snoring, so why did I find his so soothing? It was a reassurance that I wasn't alone.

For all his objections to being thought of as boy and calling me Daddy, he had sure gotten into it last night.

I smiled, watching him sleep while my heart did all

kinds of gymnastics in my chest. His face was relaxed in sleep, the usual frown lines not as dramatic. His hair was an untidy mess sticking up from his head, but he seemed happy.

I was always attracted to older guys as I grew up, my first crush being a high school teacher. I chuckled quietly remembering some of the thoughts I'd had back then, of bending my geography teacher over the desk and spanking him with a ruler. Growing up I'd kept those fantasies a secret, ashamed of myself. Mr. Palmer was older than Charles, was married and had kids, but that hadn't stopped me getting a stiffy right there in his class. I had thought something was wrong with me for so long and made a habit of sticking to boys my age to rid myself of the unwelcomed fantasies.

It hadn't been hard finding boys to fool around with at the boarding school I had been sent to. There had always been willing guys either gay, or simply wanting to experiment. They had loved my take-charge attitude, but I didn't get off as hard as when I imagined they were an older man begging me to fuck them. The former didn't do much for me. The latter made me feel powerful, in control.

That was the way I had felt last night with Owen. Hopefully, he had realized it too, that he was a natural submissive. He had basked in me taking control of him and using him for my pleasure. He had even seemed to crave it. My dick throbbed, making my desire known as I remembered the way his body had felt under mine—bigger, more muscular, more powerful physically, but psychologically subdued to mine.

The bed covers were down to his waist, showing off just a hint of pubic hair. I found it a bit humorous that he'd shaved his ass but not the hair around his cock. Not that I minded either. In fact, hairy could turn me on, and I was definitely not turned off by Owen's hairy chest and legs. Everything about him was exactly what I wanted in a man. Owen made me as excited as my sixteen-year-old self spanking Riley Jacob's ass while thinking of our principal sprawled across my thighs.

Owen stirred beside me, emitting a half-groan, half-moan that rumbled from deep inside his chest. He shuffled around like an oversized kitten looking to be scratched, so I leaned forward and kissed his shoulder, licking an interesting-looking mole I had been too busy last night to observe.

A lazy smile spread about his lips as his eyelids fluttered open. He frowned when he saw me, the worry lines becoming more pronounced than when he was sleeping.

"Good morning, Daddy's boy," I couldn't help but tease him. "How did you sleep?"

After having sex last night, we had shared a long bath. If Owen had thought I'd be Daddy in the bedroom only, I had driven that from his mind when I had taken him in my arms. Although his stiff posture had given away his discomfort at first, he had slowly relaxed against me. He had been lolling off to sleep when I'd roused him and tucked him into bed.

I never planned to get in with him, knowing my insomnia would drive me insane, but he'd blinked sleepy eyes up at me.

"Don't go. Sleep with me." I was struck by his vulnerability as

he tried to stay awake. "I've not slept beside anyone in fifteen years. My bed's been lonely before you."

I was touched at his request and honesty. He had the same hunger in him that I recognized in myself.

"Ask me properly," I encouraged, combing my fingers through the silver strands at his temple. "Say it. Admit it. You're my boy, Owen. You just need to ask Daddy nicely, and I'll give you the world."

His eyes opened. Blue eyes met mine, alert, serious. There was little trace of the humor which he had been using to get accustomed to the word. "Tonight I don't want the world. I just want you to sleep next to me, Daddy."

Each time he said it, I fell in love with him a little more. Insomnia be damned, I crawled into bed with him and cuddled my boy.

I snapped out of last night's memory to find Owen's face flushed red, and I would bet he was remembering our conversation before I had joined him between the sheets and tucked him against me. I would never forget his sigh of contentment, the bulk of his body fitting against mine.

Owen groaned, rolled over onto his stomach and pulled a pillow over his head, but not before I glimpsed the smile on his lips.

"Oh God, last night really happened?" he asked, his words muffled, so I barely was able to make out what he was saying. "I thought it was a dream. A nice, sexy dream, but nevertheless a dream."

I laughed out so loud the unusual sound almost scared me. Leaning over him, I ripped the pillow from his head, although he made a half-hearted attempt to grab for it.

"Oh no you don't." I kissed his neck and followed a trail down his spine, grinning against his skin at the shivers that ran down his body. He grabbed a hold of the sheet, clutching it tightly to cover his ass before I could get to my prize. "You can't take back what happened last night, Owen," I told him, crouching between his thighs and yanking down the sheet. His sexy hard ass was naked to the eye. I trailed a finger from the top of his ass and between his cheeks. "It's a done deal," I told him, circling his asshole with my thumb. "You are wholly and fully my boy. I'm your Daddy. Got that?"

"Yes," he gasped the word, spreading his thighs as my finger pushed into his hole.

"Yes, what?" I asked him, taking note of his hiss.

"Yes, Daddy," he moaned. "Ugh. I'm too sore for that right now. It's been a while."

He had been so eager last night I had forgotten he hadn't been fucked like that in years. I pulled out my thumb then spread his cheeks and soothed him with gentle licks. He almost reared off the bed, but I held him down and continued to caress his hole with my tongue .

"Oh fuck," he moaned, humping the bed.

Having worked him up, I retreated, kissing his cheeks before letting him go. "There'll be more of that later," I assured him, "if you're a good boy for the day, which means no questioning this thing that's happening between us."

"But... I'm so hard," Owen protested, raising his

head and twisting his neck to look back at me. He even had a sexy pout on.

I couldn't resist. I slapped his ass hard once. I was never much for punishment, but spanking Owen's ass was becoming addictive. He clenched, then released and groaned. I stared at the red imprint I had left behind.

"I'll save the rest for later," I told him.

He rolled onto his side, grabbing the pillow I had taken from him and hugging it to his chest. "Fine. No sex. Can I at least sleep for another hour then?"

I smiled because he had asked permission without even realizing it. Yes, Owen was indeed a natural submissive. Now I had to find a way to reward him. I kissed his forehead. "Sleep. I've some business to take care of." I hadn't forgotten Ridge in the other room.

"Okay," he murmured, his eyes already closing. Under my watchful eyes, he drifted back to sleep. If my hand didn't still sting, I'd have questioned whether the last ten minutes had happened or not. He was out like a light.

I carefully got out of bed, pulling the sheet up to Owen's waist before I strolled naked into the next room where my things were. I didn't expect to see Ridge already up, but he was. He looked better than I would have expected, considering his inebriated state last night. He was sitting at the table in the sitting room, drinking coffee.

"You're up early," I commented, and he winced.

"Keep it down," he said on a groan. "My head's still going through the beating drums stage. Everything is extra loud."

"And yet you still manage to get drunk so often." Ignoring him, I marched into the closet where I had hung my clothes yesterday. I picked out underwear, grabbed a pair of designer jeans and a gray shirt.

"Yeah, I know I'm a shitty person," Ridge mumbled. "I'm surprised you didn't just leave my ass at the party last night."

I frowned at him as I walked out of the closet half-dressed. "You were drunk, man. Why would I leave you hanging?"

"Because you had ass back here at the hotel waiting for you," he replied, then gulped on his coffee before he stood. "I wouldn't have blamed you for leaving me behind."

"I wouldn't." I didn't bother to deny Owen was with me. "You're my friend, and friends help each other out. Owen understands that."

He shrugged. "Still. Didn't mean to ruin your night."

I paused with my arms half through the sleeves in my shirt and smirked. "Actually, you didn't ruin the night. It was perfect."

"No kidding. Your boy's loud. I really didn't need to hear how deep you were, or how hard he wanted it."

"You heard?" I asked in surprise.

"Our neighbors two doors down probably heard," Ridge said, clearly amused.

"Sorry. I didn't think it would affect you since you were quite drunk and knocked out."

"Well, when you got into Daddy mode in the bedroom on your guy, I became wide awake." He laughed, mimicking a spanking motion with his hand. "Made my ass sore just listening to it."

I rolled my eyes at him. "Real mature of you, Ridge."

"Don't worry, I did the immature thing," he snickered. "The really inappropriate immature thing of listening to you fucking your boy and jerking off."

I shook my head at him. "You're a fucking liar."

"Okay, I wanted to," he admitted. "But my drunk dick wouldn't cooperate."

I stifled a laugh. "Ridge, please don't be this inappropriate around Owen. He's still getting used to things."

He waved a hand dismissively at me. "Don't worry, Daddy, I'll be on my best behavior when I next run into your boy. I can see how much he means to you."

"Don't call me *Daddy* for fuck's sake." I straightened my shirt. "By the way, we'll have to get you another suite. I'm not comfortable with the idea of you jerking off to the sounds of Owen and me having sex."

He laughed. "Don't worry. I'm leaving, so you can get all the time with your new bedmate."

I frowned at him. "You don't have to go. I'm sure Owen wouldn't mind."

"Nah, it's time I stopped running from my fears and faced them." He walked over to me and kissed my cheek. "You've been a good friend, Owen. I'll see you back in Cincy."

19

OWEN

For the first time in years I woke up in bed and wasn't rushing to get out. There was no kid to wake up and get out of the house for school. There was no breakfast to prepare. There was no job to get to. I felt lazy, drifting in and out of consciousness until I finally had to talk myself into staying awake.

I didn't need to see the time to tell me I had over-slept. I rolled over in bed, wondering why Declan hadn't woken me up sooner. I vaguely recalled begging for more sleep, but I had meant a few minutes, an hour at most. From the bright sunshine peeking out from the drapes leading to the balcony, morning had already passed.

Peering at the alarm clock on the bedside table, I discovered it was already past noon, but not yet quite one. My gaze was pulled away from the clock to a single red rose which rested beside my phone. The first time he had given me flowers, I had been wary. Now I reached over to caress the petals and wondered at my good luck.

Red rose. Was he trying to tell me something, or was I thinking too deeply about the meaning?

"Dec?"

I received no response. The hotel suite seemed empty. I frowned, wondering where he had gone, before remembering he had mentioned something about taking care of business while I slept. I grasped my phone only to find it was off. The battery couldn't have died overnight given it was fully charged when we went to bed last night which meant Declan had been thoughtful enough to turn it off while I was sleeping.

My stomach grumbled a protest from lack of food as I waited for the phone to power on. I was ravenous, and my muscles ached. My arms and legs hadn't gotten a workout like that in a long time. I couldn't take credit for keeping in such good shape at my age.

With all the sitting I did as a driver, just about the only thing I did was to try and eat healthy. I didn't do much by way of exercise, and the good genes responsible for my physique had come from my father's side of the family. The last time I had seen my father, he had looked a decade younger than his seventy-six years.

The phone was barely on before the messages started to flood in. I had advised my children that I would be staying with a friend, but they had still called me several times throughout the night and this morning. I read through the messages quickly.

Oscar: Dad, we're sorry we kept this from you. We just didn't want you to be upset.

Oscar: Okay, I admit we were wrong to keep it a secret from you, but we didn't want you to feel bad that we were in touch with her.

Oscar: Dad, will you please pick up the phone? You're freaking us out.

Auggie: Oscar says you're not picking up. I get it that you're angry, but please answer his call. We're freaking out. We haven't done anything wrong.

Auggie: Maybe we did something wrong by keeping it from you, but we had the best of intentions. Shouldn't intent count for something?

Auggie: Great, now Summer's not picking up the phone either. At least we know she's okay, because Penny says she is, but we have no idea where you are. Please, answer the phone!

Summer: Hi, Dad. How are you? Did you hear from Auggie and Oscar? They say she wants to meet us tonight. The nerve she has. As far as I'm concerned, she doesn't exist.

Summer: But then again, maybe I should go so I can tell her that to her face… what a shitty sorry-excuse-for-a-mother she has been. I'm not going if you're not.

Groaning at the messages that had come in while I was asleep, I started on the voicemails. There were more hysterical messages from the children that had me feeling awful about not contacting them sooner. I activated the loudspeaker and rolled out of bed, stretching the kinks and soreness out of my muscles, half-listening, half-wondering how I would explain to my grown children where I had spent the night. They would have questions, but this relationship with Declan was too fresh for me to tell them anything.

I was lost in thought until the automated machine

announced a voice message from a number that didn't
ring a bell.

"Owen, you probably don't recognize my voice after
all these years." Nervous laughter came over the speaker
and made me stiffen. "Our kids told me today they spoke
to you about me. Please don't punish them for what I did.
I begged and cajoled my way back into their lives. I know
what I did was wrong, but I missed them so much. You
probably won't believe me, but I've missed you too. I'd
like to clear up everything that happened and apologize
face to face. I'd like to see you tonight and the kids. I'm
making reservations for us at the following restaurant."
Still trying to decide why she sounded so different, I
finished listening as she proceeded to give the name of
the restaurant and address before finally adding, "I hope
you'll show up. It's been a long time coming."

Before the voice message from Jenna, I had the intention of calling my kids, but now I was too angry to talk to
them. The last thing I wanted was to do something I
would later regret, and because I was fuming, I sent off a
message in a group text to the three of them that I was
fine and would get in touch soon. As soon as the message
was delivered, I saw the squiggly lines that all three were
writing back to me. I closed the app and tossed the phone
on the bed before I headed to the bathroom to take a
shower.

Last night had been wonderful with Declan, but now
I had to deal with my kids bringing back their mother
into my life. I would have preferred if Jenna had stayed
hidden. I would have preferred if they had continued to
see her behind my back for the rest of my life without me

knowing. Instead, I harbored this intense resentment—not for them, but their lie. They had lied to me all this time by not telling me the truth.

Twenty minutes later, I walked out of the shower in no better of a mood. The first thing I noticed when I walked into the suite, towel wrapped around my waist was Declan, looking way too damn good and chirpy. He was relaxed, like a man who had already accomplished much for the day.

"What's wrong?" he asked, as though sensing my mood.

"Nothing," I mumbled, glancing away from him and around for my clothes from last night, but I couldn't find them.

"Somehow I don't believe that. Did something happen while I was gone?"

"It's nothing you need to worry about," I said, getting more frustrated by the minute since I couldn't find my clothes. "Where the hell are my things?"

"Owen—"

"What?" I shouted, turning to face him again.

The heavy weight of silence hung in the air between us at my outburst. My mouth went dry at the look that crossed Declan's features. I wanted to apologize, but the words wouldn't come. Declan's eyes took on a hard glint, and his chiseled jaw clenched.

Without a word, Declan walked over to the bed and sat. My heart pounded in my chest as I tried to figure out what he was up to. No, he couldn't. He wouldn't.

"Over my lap. Now."

I sucked in a deep breath and exhaled slowly. Unlike

me, Declan didn't need to shout. His meaning carried clear in his soft commanding tone. I glanced from his face down to my bare toes, catching a glimpse of my flaccid cock.

"Is that really necessary?" I had enjoyed his spanking previously, but this was a different situation. This morning he had been playful when he slapped my ass. Even when he had spanked me the first time in my kitchen there had been a playful air to it, but there was nothing jolly about him commanding me to position myself over his knees.

"Get over my knees now, or get the fuck out."

I almost staggered beneath the weight of his ultimatum. My heart pounded even harder, and the blood rushed through my head making me dizzy. I should go, take the easy way out. What could really come of this relationship with Declan?

I should clear the fuck out.

I didn't. Declan had become almost an obsession, and I'd rather be spanked than kicked out, though I wasn't certain if he really meant it. I draped myself over his lap just as he had indicated, the side of the bed supporting my body's weight. I buried my face into my folded arms and waited.

I clenched my teeth together at the first sharp slap that connected with my ass. Closing my eyes, I tried not to cry out or make a sound, but it was difficult when he hit me so hard. To distract myself, I counted each spank, but I eventually lost count at my ass stinging in displeasure. My silence turned into grunts of pain until I started to squirm and prayed that tears didn't fall. My ass stung like a bitch. I wanted to cuss, but was afraid that would only set him off some more, so I endured.

When I was at the point of breaking, he paused, his hand fanning across my burning cheeks as though soothing the pain. Sweat was trickling down my spine, and I stopped trying to disguise my moans of pain.

"I hate punishing you," Declan said, his tone truly anguished. "I'd rather give you the fucking world, but I can't have you raising your voice at me. That's not how we solve our problems."

"I'm sorry," I mumbled.

"Is that all?" he asked. "How about promising you'll never do it again."

I hesitated, thinking about making such a promise that I might not be able to keep. Shit happened. I might get upset again, and shouting did let off steam.

"I'll try," I answered honestly, moaning when he squeezed my ass. He continued fondling me and the slight discomfort mingled with the pleasure of being touched soon had my cock straining beneath my body. Surely he could feel it digging into his thigh. I squirmed, and he widened his legs to give me room to adjust.

"That's a good, boy," Declan cooed. "Now come up here and kiss me."

I managed to unbend myself from his thighs. His hands around my waist, he guided me where he wanted me, straddling his lap, my knees cushioned into the mattress on either side of his hips. I'd never felt as vulnerable as I did in that moment, completely naked while he was fully clothed. My ass smarted from being spanked, and yet when I dared to look at him, I discovered the anger gone, replaced by softness. All the tension released from my shoulders because I'd rather be spanked if that meant he was no longer upset.

He held my chin and brought my mouth to his. I hesitated, but he kissed me soft and sweet, his tongue sweeping into my mouth. It was like a kiss of apology, begging me to forgive him for the punishment he had generously doled out. Even if I wanted to be mad at him, I couldn't when our lips parted, and he kissed the tip of my nose.

He had me weak.

"Are you ready to tell me now why you got so upset?" he asked, kissing the corner of my mouth. "Or do I need to put you over my knees again?"

It wasn't the threat... promise—whatever— that made me give in. It was the way his arms came around me and the gentle press of his lips fluttering like a heartbeat over my face.

20

OWEN

"Here we are."

I stared straight ahead at the restaurant as Declan drove into the parking area to find a spot. The Ocean was a fine dining establishment which made me feel better about the clothes Declan had provided me with earlier today. After asking him where my clothes from last night were, he had told me that he'd gotten me new ones. I would have been upset with him except I had been so exhausted from all the emotion of dealing with my children. Plus, when he'd explained he had picked me up the outfits while I slept so I didn't have to rush back to my sons' if I still needed some time, I could hardly be mad at him.

He got the fit right which was a little weird, but I wasn't going to complain about clothes that fit me too well. I'd kissed him my thanks, and apparently that had pleased him. We had spent the day together at the hotel, ordering room service and watching detective shows that we discovered was an interest we shared.

"I have a bad feeling this will go south," I told Declan. I shouldn't have allowed him to talk me out of my refusal to have dinner with my children and their mother, but Declan could be quite persuasive. *I've started calling him Daddy, haven't I, despite feeling strongly about it at first?*

"You need the closure," Declan replied, expertly parking the vehicle. He had opted to drive us instead of using his chauffeur who also had a room at our hotel. Apparently, Declan treated his staff well. He was unlike all the other rich folks I had encountered in my time as a chauffeur.

"I *had* closure," I remarked. "Until the kids brought her back into our lives."

"At least now you get to ask all the questions that were never answered over the years," he replied, using rationale to make his point. "I'm not saying you have to forgive her or anything, but do it to get some peace of mind. You know you'll regret it if you don't, Owen."

"Why should I regret it? She left us."

He sighed and reached across the console to take my hand. His grip was firm. "Listen, remember you asking me last night who would still want to have a relationship with a parent who neglected them for fifteen years?"

"Yes, and I still stand by that question."

"Well, I sort of understand what your kids are going through because I'm in a similar predicament."

I frowned at him. "What are you talking about?"

"My relationship with Charles," he said.

"Charles?"

"Yes, you met him. My father."

"Oh." I didn't know what else to say, because talking about his father had me squirming. I wasn't even certain I wanted him to tell me about his fucked-up relationship with his dad. What if that had contributed to him wanting me to call him Daddy?

"Charles and I are not on good terms," he replied. "We never were. He was more of a child than a father. My grandfather raised me and, well, he was busy tending to the business, so I was left in the care of staff. I grew up independent because I had no choice. Charles was never a father to me. Never. But, if he was willing, I'd try to bridge the gap in a heartbeat, Owen. He just doesn't want a son. What he wants is someone who can clean up his mess."

His words caught me as full of anguish. He truly was hurting over the bad relationship he had with his father. The regret and hope were clear in his words. This time, I clung to his hand to give him some of the comfort he had been dishing out since he had learned about what my children had hidden from me.

"I'm so sorry about your father," I said softly. "I hope you can repair things."

"Charles," he answered, clearing his throat and releasing my hand. He cupped my face and leaned forward to kiss me hard. "I didn't tell you that story to solicit sympathy from you. I told you so you could be more understanding of your sons' plight. Listen to them."

"What are you going to do while I'm having dinner

with them?" I asked, wishing I had the courage to ask him to accompany me. The situation was already tense, though, and bringing him would only add to the confusion and possible disaster I already predicted would come of this night.

"I'll hang around in case you need me," he told me.

I frowned at him. "You don't have to do that. I can get a cab back to the hotel."

He kissed me again. "No cab. I'm sticking around. Now be a good boy and tell me who's your Daddy?"

Fuck if he didn't make me instantly hard by his words. "You are," I answered, my agreement no longer being a hardship. I craved this. I basked in the attention he gave me, and if it meant being his boy and accepting him as my Daddy, so be it.

Plus, seeing his eyes light up when I called him Daddy was worth it all. I kissed him hard, holding on to the lapels of his shirt. I could taste the amusement on his lips as he allowed me to take charge of the kiss, but then he had me against the door, and his hand was around my throat with just the slightest pressure as he took over, dominating the kiss, dominating me. I whimpered in his mouth, hot and ready to be fucked already.

Disappointment unfurled in my gut when he pulled back. "I think you'll need some comforting later. When we're back in our suite, you can show me how well you can ride Daddy's beautiful dick."

I groaned as my cock tightened. "You're killing me."

"Good. Now go make as much of this dinner as you can."

I pouted at him, a move that should have felt ridiculous coming from me, but made me feel powerful at the way his nostrils flared. I gave him a demure look from beneath my lashes and unlocked the car door.

"Okay, Daddy. I'll call you if I need you."

I could still hear his harsh breathing filling the car as I hurried up the steps of the restaurant. Just inside the building, I plastered a smile on my face as I tried to calm down from Declan's kisses. If his intent had been to distract me, he had succeeded. I was less upset when the hostess announced my party was already seated.

"Dad," Oscar said, getting to his feet when he saw me approaching. I followed the hostess, scanning the seating arrangements and discovered Summer was missing despite her assurance she would be here once I showed up. Beside Oscar, Auggie also rose to his feet, eager and nervous as he tugged at his tie. They were both dressed to the nines, something they didn't usually take kindly to, and for that reason I was inclined to believe this restaurant hadn't been their pick.

"Thank you," I told the hostess when she wished me a pleasant evening. When she left, I turned to my sons, nodding at them.

"Hey, where's Summer? I thought she was showing."

"She just texted ten minutes ago that something came up," Auggie replied as we all took our seats. It didn't miss my attention that there had been no hugs between us. We had always been close, and this thing with their mother had driven a wedge between us.

"And your mother?" I asked.

Auggie and Oscar shared a look I refused to beg them to explain. It hurt that they were still keeping secrets from me, and suddenly being here tonight didn't seem like such a good idea anymore. My hand itched to fish into my jacket for my phone to call Declan.

"She's running late," Oscar answered.

"Actually, she wanted to give us a chance to work out our misunderstanding before she arrives."

"What misunderstanding?" I asked, grabbing a menu from the table. If they didn't believe anything was wrong, why was there a need to work out anything?

"You're mad," Auggie replied.

"More like seriously pissed," Oscar clarified. "Before we do this, can we order first? I'm kind of starved."

And that was how we ended up with a mountain of food between the three of us, stuffing our faces without working out our *non-misunderstanding.* Halfway through the meal that I was picking at anyway, Auggie put down his fork and wiped his mouth before directing his attention to me.

"Where have you been staying? I didn't know you had friends here in Columbus."

"I'm staying at the Hilton," I replied, omitting that I was with a lover. That tidbit about Declan and I would have to wait until we had sorted out our family matter.

"That place is crazy expensive," Auggie remarked. "Did you get a raise or something? First the phone, the hotel, and new clothes. You've been splurging."

I frowned at him. "Is there a reason I can't have nice things?"

Oscar jumped in to defend his twin. "That's not what we're saying at all. You've just never cared before. Dad, you usually shop at the thrift store for yourself even though you insisted in us not wearing second-hands."

"There's nothing wrong with wanting better for your kids," I said on a grunt. "I had three kids to take care of. I wasn't going to spend good money on frivolous things for me." *I still won't. This is all Declan.*

"Ah, so now you can," Oscar concluded. "Just don't dip too much into your retirement funds."

I glared at him and decided enough was enough. "Why don't we stop nitpicking at me and talk about the real issue here? I'm disappointed in both of you."

"I know," Auggie replied. "You keep telling us that, but it's complicated. She... uh... didn't want us to tell you."

His words only made me angrier. "After being the only parent involved in your upbringing, I would have thought your loyalty would have been to me, not her."

"It's not about loyalty," Auggie refuted.

"Then what was it about?"

"We wanted to get to know our other parent." Auggie looked like he wanted to cry. "You raised us to forgive and put the past behind us. Well, that's what we did, and we hope you can do the same. You have to believe that we never meant to hurt you over this. We just thought it was the right thing to do at the time."

"The right thing to do would have been to tell me!" I cringed as my raised voice reminded me of being spanked earlier for allowing my anger to get the best of me. I rose to my feet abruptly to go to the bathroom and calm down.

"Dad," Oscar groaned. "Don't run out on us again. We're trying to make amends."

"I'm not running away," I replied. "I'm simply going to use the restroom."

I turned to find myself face to face with a shorter man with short blond hair, sporting a well-trimmed beard.

"Uh sorry," I murmured and started to move around the man but he remained in my path. I frowned at him, our eyes meeting. I cocked my head to the side, contemplating his features. Did I know him? He was looking back at me intensely.

"Do I know you?" I asked, my tone a little sharp at the way he was staring at me.

"Hello, Owen," he said, pushing his hands inside his pockets. "It's me."

And then it hit me. The eyes were basically the only thing that remained, but he had been my wife. He looked completely different, and I wouldn't have recognized him anywhere. The blond hair was a texture darker and thicker than I was used to, and there was the beard and moustache. He filled out the jacket he was wearing quite well, his shoulders broader than I remembered. I would not have recognized him except for the eyes. I had been gazing into those eyes since we were thirteen, and the longer our eyes held, the more I was catapulted back into time.

"Jenna?" I said uncertainly, sweeping him with my gaze, because I was having a hard time reconciling this man with my wife.

"I go by the name James now," he replied. "I'm sorry

I'm late. I could make up some lame excuse, but the truth is that I almost ran scared."

"Hey, Dad," Oscar said, getting to his feet, Auggie right behind him. I glanced at him, thinking he was speaking to me, only to find him moving toward James, embracing the other man.

"Hey, son, how have you been?" James's face lit up with a genuine smile as he hugged *my* sons one after the other. "Did something different with your hair?" he asked, running his fingers through Auggie's hair.

My son smiled at his other father. "Bethany thinks it's cute."

Bethany? How the hell didn't I know about this Bethany? I stared from James to my boys and felt a deep sense of loss and sadness. Had I lost them? Now they were telling him things they usually told me?

"I-I-uh… need to use the restroom," I croaked and fled. I knocked into a waiter, mumbling my apologies and grateful he carried nothing in his hands apart from a menu. I almost careened into a table as I glanced back at my former wife and sons smiling at each other. I avoided it just in the nick of time as I hurried to the bathroom before I caused an accident.

I managed to find the bathroom following signs on the wall. Once inside, I slammed the door shut behind me and made my way over to the sink, bracing on the marble while I took deep gulps of air. Now I understood why the boys had kept it from me. Another betrayal. Another secret. Did I even know them?

I splashed water onto my face, trying to calm my breathing as I assessed my feelings on the change James would have gone through. That had to be the reason he had left, but why? We were both open-minded individuals? Our relationship had stemmed from sharing our deepest feelings and needs, knowing we would never judge the other. Had he come clean to me about his preference, I would have supported him. Instead, they had all sprung this surprise on me.

The bathroom door burst open, and I glanced up, expecting to see the twins or worse, James, since he now used my public bathroom.

"Owen, are you okay?"

"Daddy." The word came out as a whimper as Declan entered the bathroom. I had no idea what he was doing here, but I was grateful for him. He came up to me, arms outstretched, and I had no choice except to seek comfort in them. I shuddered against him, my arms wrapped around his waist. "I shouldn't have come," I mumbled into his neck.

"Hey, it's okay." He rubbed the hair at the nape of my neck, soothing me. "Calm down and tell me what's wrong."

"What are you doing here?" I asked instead.

"I told you I would be close," he said, kissing my temple. "Didn't you believe me? I got a table where I could keep an eye on you in case you needed me."

"Oh thank God," I moaned. "It's a fucking disaster. I feel like I have no relationship with the twins anymore, like they substituted me for him."

"What are you talking about?"

I took a deep breath and stepped back from his embrace. "Did you see the man who joined our table?"

He nodded. "Yeah."

"That's her-him. My ex. All this time he's been transitioning."

"So, that's the reason he left you?"

I sighed. "I wish I knew. I guess. I excused myself before I could find out."

"Do you want to leave?" he asked.

"You think I should?"

"Honestly? No. I think there's a lot more that needs to be said, but if you do want to leave, then yes, I'll take you back to the hotel."

I sighed, running my fingers through my hair. "I suppose you're right. I'm already here, and the cat's out of the bag."

He grabbed me gently by the neck and pulled me in for a hard kiss. "You've got this."

I kissed him back. "Thank you. I don't know what I would have done without you this weekend."

"It's my greatest pleasure to be here for you, Owen."

We kissed again, parting when the bathroom door opened. A young man close to Declan's age took one look at us, mumbled something and tumbled back out the bathroom.

"I guess he thinks I'm gonna hump you in here," Declan said, amused, and I laughed.

"Any chance of that happening?"

"When we get to the hotel."

We parted, and I returned to my party of three while Declan returned to his seat. I trailed him to find he was sitting in clear view of me, watching me all this time, making sure I was all right and that he was there if I needed him. Emotions so thick clenched my insides, giving me a warmer feeling as I approached the table to find only James remained.

"Where are the boys?" I asked, resuming my seat.

"They told me to relay their good night to you," he answered, plucking at a napkin on the table nervously. "They wanted to give us some privacy to speak."

I placed my hands on the top of the table and stared at him. "Then let's speak. Tell me why, James? Why did you leave us the way you did?"

He lowered his gaze to the tabletop. "You know. We'd talked about it. I wasn't feeling my usual self. I wasn't happy."

"So you just walked out on us?"

"You weren't happy with our marriage either," he replied. "You just remained in it because of a sense of duty, and I loved you for that, Owen, but we were making ourselves miserable. I couldn't take the children from you. I couldn't, although I desired to, but I was messed up mentally and not sure of who I was. I needed the time to get to know myself."

"And it took you fifteen years?"

"It took long enough for it to be too late to get in touch. I didn't want to interfere."

"Interfere?" I cried. "They are your kids. Our kids."

"But, after what I did, what right did I have to walk back into their lives, Owen?"

"You seem quite fine doing it now," I snapped. "How dare you conspire with them behind my back and get them to keep this a secret from me?"

"I didn't plan to," he answered. "Our meeting was

completely accidental, but I thought it was fate giving me another chance. They had grown up, but I was able to recognize them. I was able to see you in them, and I knew they were ours. I had a split second to tell Auggie who I was, and I took that chance. I wasn't thinking of how you would be affected. I just wanted the opportunity to know the fine boys that you raised. I don't want to take away anything from you and them, Owen. I'm not here to threaten your closeness."

I stared at James, my anger dissipating, but leaving disappointment in its wake that was just as bad. "You were the closest person to me," I told him. "I loved you. I would have done anything for you. I thought we had a bond that went deeper than being lovers. We were partners in everything. You knew my deepest secrets. I knew yours. Or at least I thought I did."

"I didn't know how you'd react at finding out I wanted to be who I always felt I was inside," he answered. "In fact, I wasn't even certain if this change I wanted was a temporary idea I had, or if this was truly what I wanted. That's why I needed to get away. I needed to understand me. Owen, we had become each other's bad habit. You'd use me to satisfy your curiosity and need to be dominated, when we both knew you really wanted to be with another man."

I blushed, glancing away from him as he reminded me of our sex life. He was right. I couldn't refute that, but still, this could have been dealt with better on so many levels had he been honest with me.

"I would have given you the time you needed," I told him. "All you had to do was explain."

"How could I explain something I didn't even understand, Owen? Please." He reached across the table to touch my hand. "Can't you find it in your heart to forgive me? The boys tell me there hasn't been anyone since I left. I was thinking perhaps we could give it another go."

21

DECLAN

"He what?"

I stiffened as Owen repeated what his ex had proposed to him last night over dinner. Last night I had sensed he needed space, so I hadn't pressed him about it. After dinner ended with James, I had taken him back to our hotel, where as soon as we entered our suite, he'd whispered that he had been a good boy and deserved a treat. Understanding what he needed, I hadn't questioned him. I had brought him over to the sofa and given him the opportunity to show me how well he could ride my cock.

He'd almost unraveled me. He'd been eager, needy, greedy, and I had loved every second of his vulnerability. He had twisted me up inside so much that for a brief minute, I had been confused as to who was in control. What if he realized just how much he could get away with because of how much I needed him?

"Please, don't make me repeat it," Owen said on a

sigh, as he stared out the car window. We were halfway through the journey back to Cincinnati and much of the miles we had already travelled had been done in silence.

"What did you say to him?" I asked calmly, although I was anything but. Owen had been needy last night. What if his actions had stemmed from him thinking about his ex and contemplating the pros and cons of them getting back together. I wanted to believe he would choose me after how much we had connected over the weekend, but he'd had years with James. They had three children together. That was three times the reason he had for choosing James over me.

"I told him that we'd be repeating our mistake of twenty four years ago when we took our marriage vows."

"I see." I tried to hide the disappointment from my tone that his refusal had nothing to do with me. *That is a good thing, isn't it?* It meant he was making the right decision for him.

"I'm not sure I can completely forgive him," he continued. "At least not yet, but we've decided to keep in touch for the kids' sake. We're meeting up again next month."

New opportunities to rekindle their love? I was under no illusions whatsoever. Owen had loved his ex. They had been friends for years before they got married.

"I'm still pissed the twins didn't say anything to me before this," he said, his tone frustrated. "And according to James, Auggie's girlfriend is also transgender, which is the reason he hadn't told me about it, because he wasn't sure what I would think. That makes me sad."

"Well, there are gay people who don't support trans-gender rights," I reminded him.

"But he should know I'm not one of those people."

"Hmm." I glanced over at him, my heart skipping a beat. He had no idea just how much of a catch he was. No wonder James wanted him back. I could have taken my private jet to Columbus if I had wanted to, but I had opted for us to drive because the journey lasted longer. I wanted every single minute to get to know him.

"Owen, tell me about your marriage."

His head whipped around as he frowned at me. "What?"

"Your marriage," I repeated. "It's a little confusing. I understand you two were friends for a long time before you started dating, but you're a submissive by nature. How did you manage intimately with a woman?"

"Uh, we had an open marriage," he replied.

"So you took another lover?" That didn't seem right when he had told me he had only slept with a guy once. Why would he have taken another female lover when it was obvious what he craved was a man? Owen might have been bisexual, but his preference was evident.

"Actually, I didn't take a lover," he answered. "That was more for James's benefit at the time. I could tell he was restless and wanted to step out."

"So you gave him the option to do so without it being cheating."

"Yeah, if I didn't, I believed he would have anyway, and I didn't want our marriage ruined. He was right that we'd been having problems before he left."

"And your sex life?" I prodded, wanting to know all. "How did you get off?"

"I'm not opposed to sleeping with a woman," he said in protest. "We managed fine, and if there were times I wanted... uh, um... to be the one bottoming, he indulged me."

His face was averted, but I still saw how red he got. "You mean, you allowed him to peg you?" Now that made sense. Owen was a hungry bottom. There was no way he would have lasted for long in a heterosexual relationship where he wasn't having his bottoming needs fulfilled.

"Yes, or I kept a dildo handy."

"And now, will you go back to him?" I asked, wanting to hear him confirm again.

"Maybe if I hadn't met you," he replied, turning to face me once more. "I was quite fine with a lot of things before I came to know you, Dec."

My earlier disgruntlement vanished as he had damn near melted my insides. I was plunging fast and needed to know this wasn't an illusion. He wasn't taking this—us —for a game.

"Owen, I've one last question," I told him.

"What is it?"

I shifted on the seat so we were facing each other. As calm as I appeared on the outside, I was anything but. His answer could define what our relationship would turn out to be when we got back to Cincy.

"What do you make of us?" I asked him, taking his hand nearest to me and overturning his palm before placing mine on top. "Is this something you can do permanently or… is it a game to you that will one day lose its appeal? Because I'll never get tired of hearing you call me Daddy."

"And when I get too old for you?" he asked, and his fingers shook a little beneath mine.

"You'll never be too old for me. And besides, you know I enjoy taking care of you. Plus, there's a little matter of the possibility of me kicking the bucket first." It could totally happen given the strange sensations I had been experiencing lately.

He scowled at me. "I hope that doesn't happen." He flipped our hands so our fingers intertwined. "Listen, when I first called you Daddy, I did it out of humor. I knew the effect it had on you, and that it would please you. You could say it started off as a game, but it's become so much more. I may not get why you chose me, but given the past twenty-four hours, I can honestly say that I've enjoyed being your boy." He glanced up at me, looking more serious than I had intended for our conversation. "I like the way you take care of me, how you seem to know exactly what I need, even if it's a spanking. I just hope I continue to please you in the same way you please me."

A part of me harbored guilt for pulling him into a relationship without being completely honest with him about my health, but I couldn't initiate conversation not knowing what was going on. I had been avoiding my doctor who had appealed to me to return if the pains continued so he could perform further tests, but since the feelings were few and far between, and rarely lasted long, I preferred to forget.

Promising myself that I'd bring up the subject after I saw a medical expert and had something factual to report, I pushed the thought of not being completely well from my mind.

Besides sex and spanking, which were high on our list of interesting things to do, I enjoyed talking to Owen. He listened and asked questions. He wasn't afraid to talk about his childhood and his family's rejection. At least Charles was okay with me being gay, which didn't necessarily mean anything other than his lack of concern over what I did with my life.

We were finally in Cincy and driving Owen home when the topic of Pride came up. Pride was probably the only huge event I kept abreast of. Last month in May, I had traveled to England to take part in the Birmingham Pride Parade. I hadn't been on the ground per se since Pride events could be crammed with people, but I had been able to bask in the gay atmosphere from the private balcony of my hotel room. There was always a lighter, happier ambiance during Pride events.

"Sounds fun," Owen remarked when I told him about my experience in England. "I've never been to a Pride event."

"Never been to Pride?" I inquired in disbelief. "I think every person alive should experience Pride at least once."

"It wasn't exactly priority given the children," he explained with a shrug.

"But now you have no excuse," I told him.

"I doubt Pride's the kind of place I'll want to be. Too

much noise and crowds. I'd rather grab a beer and watch it in front of the television."

When we eventually dropped Owen off, and I kissed him so hard he melted against the door of his house, I had an idea. I would take Owen to his first Pride event. There were several ways to enjoy Pride, and if he preferred a private viewing, we could always get accommodations around the location where we could watch the entire thing from our hotel room.

And I had an idea exactly where I would take him.

22

OWEN

"Harder, Daddy!"

"You love Daddy's dick, don't you, boy? Tell me how much."

"I love the way you fuck me," I growled at him, a heat surging through me unexpectedly. Declan had one of my legs pinned into the mattress and the other held vertical in a position I never thought I would ever be able to find myself. He was good at that, commanding my body to position the way he desired. Like the tune to his melody, my body followed wherever he played.

Gripping the headboard sweat dripping down my face, I moved my lower body in tandem to Declan's ferociously pumping hips, helping myself to more generous servings of him. His cock stretched my ass, filling me in the most delicious sensation before he pulled out, leaving me wanting, then filling me up again. I was already so close to the brink, but I needed his permission. Always his permission, which made my release so much better. So much sweeter.

My grunts filled the room, and I made no effort to sensor the cuss words that tripped from my lips each time he thrust harder. There was no one else around to hear anyway. Another beautiful advantage to having my home all to myself. For the past two weeks, Declan had dropped in whenever he liked, once I was home from work. More often than not we ended up in bed, or the floor, the kitchen counter, and once on the couch.

Declan pulled out and released my leg. "On your knees," he instructed.

Keening at the absence of him inside me, I turned over just as quickly as he had said the words, dropping onto my knees and gifting him with my ass.

"Eager for Daddy's cock, aren't you?" I heard the smirk in his voice as he crammed me full once more. Instead of moving, he slapped my ass hard, and I groaned. I'd developed a real fetish for his spankings and sometimes pushed his buttons when I wanted my ass to sting from his palm connecting with my flesh.

"Help yourself, boy," he growled at me. "You want that cock, you better work for it."

I didn't need to be told twice. I moved forward then backward, my rhythm starting out slow as I did exactly what he had commanded. He hissed above me, and when I glanced back and saw the look of awe on his face, my heart blossomed. I moved faster, pushing my torso forward into the bed to give myself leverage as my ass slapped into his pelvis over and over.

I was just getting into the ride when Declan grabbed

me by the hair and pushed my head into the bed. With his other hand, he jerked my ass upright even more and crouched over me while he pounded me. I gripped the bed sheets, my grunts louder as he encouraged me in that sexy voice of his to take more of his cock.

I loved our sex from our first time together in my living room. If ever I doubted that I was a bottom, Declan had taught me for certainty that I was.

"Touch yourself for me, Owen," he grunted, his hands running down my back, touching everywhere he could reach.

"Thank you, Daddy," I moaned, reaching beneath my body to grasp my cock. I was already coiled so hard that all it took was one jerk of my shaft before I was spewing all over the bed sheets.

Declan slowed the motion of his hips as I skyrocketed through my climax. I slumped on my upraised arms, trying to catch my breath. Declan pulled out of me and pushed me over onto my back on the other side of the bed away from my cum.

"Tell me where you want me to come," he hissed, condom removed as he straddled my abdomen.

"Everywhere," I answered.

He moaned, and the look on his face fascinated me. His pupils dilated, his body jerked, his muscles contracted, and he seemed almost transported to another dimension.

"Open up," he rasped at me, and I opened my mouth as his cock erupted cum all over my face. I caught but a few droplets on my tongue. A shudder rippled through him before he stilled. "Fuck, Owen!"

We blew hard as we tried to recover. With a groan, Declan rubbed at his abs and rolled off me.

"Why do I have a feeling I have cum in my hair?" I moaned.

Beside me he chuckled. "I'm pretty much certain you do. Here let me help."

He rose up on his arms and dipped his hand in the sticky mess on my cheek. When his finger traveled to my lips, I didn't hesitate to open up and allow him to feed me. He repeated the process until most had been cleared from my face.

"Good?" he teased.

I made a face. "Not particularly, but I'm acquiring the taste."

He laughed, a sound I was getting used to every week that went by. I couldn't believe two weeks had already passed since we came back from Columbus. Two of the best weeks of my love life. Declan continued to be attentive and caring in every aspect. Sometimes he had business which demanded his attention for most of the day, but there was always a text or a call, or I'd get home to find more roses delivered on my doorstep. The last time they had been accompanied by theater tickets, and that was to be our destination tonight.

While my relationship with Declan thrived, I worked on repairing the trust broken with my kids. Summer still refused to visit her other father, and the last time I had spoken to James, he had implored me to speak to Summer on his behalf. I had reminded him that Summer was an adult who could make her own decisions. Our family had changed, and we were all finding ways of reconciling with that fact. I would have felt lost, without purpose and direction, if not for Declan.

He rolled off the bed and grabbed hold of my arm. "Come on, lazy boy. Let's get you in the shower. Our show is in an hour and a half."

I groaned, but complied. "We're still going?"

"Of course," he announced. "Why wouldn't we?"

He actually asked it with a straight face, and I directed it right back at him. "Hmm, I don't know. Perhaps the fact that I *was* dressed and everything, but *someone* saw fit to rip my clothes off and fuck me stupid."

"I didn't rip them," he denied, jerking the sheet from the bed. "You're turning into a mouthy brat. Get in the shower, Owen, or do I have to make you stand in the corner again?"

The one and only time he had made me stand in the corner, I had thought it would be amusing. It turned out that I hated being in the corner a hundred times more than being spanked. Too bad he realized that, so when he really wanted to punish me, that was where he sent me. When he had coupled it with the silent treatment last week, I had transformed into the perfect boy. I hated the silent treatment the worst.

I ducked into the shower and got started on my hair, wishing someone had told me before that cum in the hair was nearly as hard to get out as glitter. As soon as Declan hopped into the shower with me, I turned to him.

"Is it all washed out?"

"Hang on. It spread right here." I could hear the laughter in his voice as he got the rest of the gooey stuff out.

"That's the last time I let you give me a facial," I threatened half-heartedly.

"If we didn't have a show to get to, I would call you out on that," he replied.

Declan lived for finding out things I had never done before, and then surprising me with doing that activity together. I had never been to the Aronoff before for a live show, and he had gone ahead and secured us tickets to watch a popular musical live.

Despite the serious side of him, I loved when Declan turned downright playful as he did in the shower. Each time I washed off the soap from my body, he would only apply more. The shower turned out to be a long affair, with both of us snickering as we finally managed to get out.

"Sit on the bed and let me dry your hair," Declan offered, and I took him up on it.

I sat at the edge of the bed, and he stepped between my legs, rubbing at my hair. His hands were gentle, yet firm. He was as completely naked as I was, yet there was no embarrassment between us. Being with him was as natural as breathing.

"Do you have a passport?" he asked, pulling me out of my thoughts.

"Wait, what?"

"A passport," he repeated, scrubbing at my hair harder. "Do you have one?"

"Uh yeah. I had to get one when one of our clients wanted a chauffeur on a business trip overseas. At the last minute I had to pull out when I couldn't get anyone to mind the kids."

"Great, I'm going to need it when we get back from the theater."

I reached up to grab his wrists and stall his motions so I could look up at him. "What for?"

"It's a surprise."

I groaned. "I hate surprises."

"Liar. No, you don't."

"You won't even give me a hint?"

"Nope. But you'll need to take a few days off work. Like five. Or maybe make it the whole week." He paused and ran his fingers through my hair, checking the dampness before he continued rubbing. "Can you get a few days off work?"

"I'm not sure my boss will grant me the time off," I told him. "Not after missing that weekend we were in Columbus, plus you had me call in sick on Tuesday."

"And wasn't it worth it?"

It was.

I'd been met with breakfast in bed, and the day had continued in that direction.

"I can't keep taking a day off," I replied, chewing on my bottom lip. I wanted to go wherever he had in mind, because he was right. His surprises were always good, but at the same time I had to be a responsible adult. "I can't afford to be fired from my job."

"What if I promise to take care of you for life?"

I stiffened. "Don't even joke about that."

"I am not, but that's a conversation for another day."

I frowned because I had an idea where he was going, and as much as I was getting used to him buying me things, I would never be comfortable not having the means to get my own. I had been working since I was fifteen, and I wasn't about to stop just because I had a younger wealthy boyfriend, who could decide on any given day that our relationship had gotten stale for him.

"Listen, don't worry about it," he said, as if he could sense my disturbed thoughts. "I'll take care of everything, including your time off."

His money of course. He thought he could control situations because he had the money to get people to do whatever he wanted. I was a bit disquieted that I was adapting to his lifestyle when I used to view rich people as snobs and manipulators.

"Just don't get me fired from my job," I told him quietly.

He tugged at my hair. "Have a little faith in me, Owen. Daddy makes things happen, and you best believe this is going to happen."

23

DECLAN

"You're taking him to Brazil?"

I winced at Ridge's loud voice so early in the morning. I hadn't slept well last night. In fact, I hadn't been sleeping well for the past week, because I hadn't been able to spend as much time with Owen. Giving him all that time the first couple of weeks that we had returned to Cincy hadn't been without a price and now I was trying to catch up with the pileup of work on my desk.

To be fair to me, the majority of the work on my desk belonged to my father and the disastrous job he had been doing. Not only did I have to undertake his tasks, but I also had to undo several of what he had done wrong in the first place. I hadn't slept over at my boy's place in three days, and it was beginning to show. I slept better when I was in his bed, his body stretched out next to me. Whether I woke up to him crowded at my back, me spooning him, or his head on my shoulder, I didn't care.

Just being with him was a calm in the otherwise turbulence of business.

"Yes, that's exactly what I said," I answered Ridge, then thanked our maid Molly who brought us coffee, inquiring if I needed anything else before retreating.

"This is becoming really serious, isn't it?" he asked, pouring a generous amount of creamer into his coffee. By the time he was finished, I was convinced there was more cream than coffee in the cup. Both Owen and I took ours black with just a pinch of salt. I was surprised he did this too, because so many people acted appalled whenever they witnessed my coffee-making ritual.

"You already know this," I replied on a sigh. "Everything is perfect." At least when I was with him and not immersed in work.

"But why Brazil?"

"Pride. He's never been."

"Let me get this straight. He's never been to a Pride event, so you plan to take him to the freaking largest Pride event on the planet? Shouldn't you have kind of initiated him into something smaller first?"

"You know me, Ridge. It's either go big or go home. He'll love Brazil."

"And you know this because…"

"Because, I know him," I answered, then scowled at him. "Why are you here so early in the morning? Just to antagonize me and question my relationship?"

He put down his coffee. "I'd never question your relationship. You may know this guy, but I know *you*. You've made your mind up about him, and he obviously suits your needs well, so I know better than to question it."

The tension eased from my shoulders. "Good." I didn't care about the looks Owen and I received sometimes in public, but I preferred knowing the people in my life were supportive of our relationship.

Ridge still hadn't said why he was here so early in the morning, so I decided he was feeling left out and a tad lonely. I had meant to drop in on Owen since he wasn't on duty until later this evening. I hated the times I was free and he would be working, but it couldn't be helped. I had sensed him gearing up for a fight about quitting his job, so I hadn't brought it up again. What kind of Daddy would I be if I didn't allow him his independence within the boundaries of our relationship?

I only half-listened to Ridge chatting away about his recent exploits as we made our way to my bedroom where I dressed for work while he watched. I paused in the act of pulling the final loop in my tie and wondered if Owen was around whether he would have a problem with Ridge being in my bedroom like this. I never even thought how Ridge being here might seem wrong, because this was how we had grown up. He had seen me naked more times than anyone else I knew, but perhaps Owen wouldn't be comfortable with the idea.

"Ridge," I said his name, interrupting his incessant chatter. "Do you think we're too familiar?"

"What do you mean?"

I nodded at him sitting on my bed casually. "I mean you being here right now and chattering away while I get dressed. Doesn't it seem too familiar to you?"

"Of course not. Why would it? We're friends."

"But maybe we make our partners uncomfortable

with the idea," I stated with a frown. "That last Daddy you had for reference. I honestly think he may have not been comfortable with you kissing me at times, and to be honest, I don't think Owen would be down for that either."

He rose from the bed. "What are you saying?"

"I'm saying that we need to set some boundaries going forward," I replied gently, because I didn't want him to take my words the wrong way. "Eventually, you'll find someone else who will be into you, but if you continue to be so familiar with me, it might cause problems. Again. If you're honest, it's happened several times before."

"You sure you're not just saying that to get rid of me so you can spend more time with Owen?"

"Why would I want to get rid of you, Ridge? You're my best friend and nothing will change that— not me being in a relationship."

"So no kissing," he stated.

"Yes, that's the most extreme one I can think of." Thankfully, we hadn't spent any time around Owen for him to witness Ridge kissing me. It clearly meant nothing, but remembering Owen's reaction the night Ridge had kissed me, it wouldn't go down so well with him. Our relationship was still on a fragile balance of building up trust, and the last thing I wanted was to make him doubt us.

"Are there any other rules I should know about?"

I winced at the bite in his question. "I don't want our friendship to be affected. In the same way I would want Owen to respect our friendship, I want us to respect my relationship with him. That's all. Don't go getting all weird on me now because I mentioned this stuff. Besides, when you find a Daddy you want to keep, you'll not even be interested in rubbing on me anymore."

"If I find a Daddy."

Before I could respond, a wave of dizziness came over me, stealing my breath.

"Declan!"

I heard Ridge's cry of alarm from far off as I waded through the gray shroud. I had no idea how long I was out for, but came to lying on the bed on my back, my feet dangling over the edge. A frantic Ridge was peering at me in concern.

"What the fuck, Declan!" he shouted. "You scared the crap out of me. Are you okay? Should I call the ambulance?"

I shook my head, groaning as I struggled to sit up. "No, no ambulance. I'm fine."

Ridge started to pace in front of the bed. "You're not fine," he objected. "You keeled over and would have kissed the floor had I not caught you. Do you know how bloody heavy you are?"

"Payback for carrying you that night in Columbus," I said, trying to make light of the situation.

"But you're not drunk," he retorted, coming to a stop before me. "Something's wrong, I can tell. What aren't you telling me? A perfectly young healthy man just doesn't faint at my feet."

"I thought you would be flattered. Now stop your yammering."

His shoulders drooped, and he came over to sit beside me. "Please, tell me. What's wrong?"

"I don't know," I answered honestly.

"What do you mean you don't know?"

"It's just stress and not sleeping well," I replied, getting to my feet, determined to go about my usual day. "I saw the doc a couple months ago about it."

"And?"

"And I just need to get over all this mess Charles created, then I can take some time off."

He frowned at me. "Maybe it's about time you have Charles assume more responsibilities. He's your *father*, Declan. He has a responsibility toward you and the business. You shouldn't have to do everything."

"It will get better," I assured him. "I've just inherited his desk, so it's tough right now managing his workload. I still need to find someone to replace me so I can fully immerse myself in the new portfolio, but for now, I have to juggle both."

I turned away from him, but he got up and grabbed my arm. "Declan, are you certain it's just stress?"

He had hit a nerve. Stress, the doctor had said. I wanted it to be stress which I could more or less control, rather than some medical condition that all the money I had in the world couldn't cure.

"I'm certain," I lied.

He knew me too well. His eyes narrowed. "Does Owen know?"

"No, there's nothing to tell." *Not yet anyway.*

He swallowed hard. "Declan, your mom—"

I pushed his hand away. "Ridge, don't. I don't have time for this. I'm already late for work."

Thinking about my mother was too terrifying. I had buried her memory deep inside me, not wanting to remember her as she had been in her last moments, nor the frightened boy I had been, watching my mother wither away day by day.

24

OWEN

"Dec—"

Declan's lips crushing mine stole my words as he slammed the door shut then pushed me back against it. I had no complaints about where his mouth was, or what his hands were doing to me. He had them in the back of my jeans, cupping and squeezing my ass as he ground his pelvis into mine. I threw an arm around his shoulder and let myself get carried away on his kiss, trusting him wholeheartedly with where he would lead me.

"I missed you," he mumbled, raising his head and giving me a couple of seconds to catch my breath before he was kissing me again. I liquified against the door and only his arms kept me upright. As busy as he was, we had talked every day, but it wasn't as before. He'd been busy, clearing his desk he had said, in addition to finding a replacement for him since he was assuming Charles's now vacant role.

One second I was kissing Declan and the next I was all puckered up, but he was several feet away. I blinked my eyes open and frowned at him. I was so wired that this wasn't the time for him to deny me an orgasm.

"We need to go," he remarked.

I stared blankly at him. "What? Go where? The bedroom?"

He chuckled. "No, get dressed."

Without waiting for me to respond, he was heading for the stairs. I strode after him. "My question still stands. Why?"

"It's a surprise. Now come on. You're free for the week."

I scowled at his back, following him into the bedroom as he reminded me of the phone call I had received from my boss yesterday. I had been hired out for a week by none other than Declan Moore. I had heard the question in my boss's voice that he hadn't asked, and it had been hell stammering through the call while pretending Declan hadn't just bought me time off work.

"I don't have work for the week, because you went behind my back and interfered with my job," I said, entering the bedroom behind him.

"I told you I would take care of things," he answered. "It'll be worth it. Now are you going to trust me to do the right thing for us, or argue all day just so I can punish you later?"

I watched him move toward my closet which temporarily distracted me. What he was doing was so deliberate that I believed he was keeping something from me.

"What are you doing in my closet?" I asked him.

"Picking out something for you to wear, obviously."

I bristled at his *obviously*. "I can pick out my own clothes, *Daddy*," I said sarcastically. "I'm a big boy."

He shot me a look over his shoulder. "Cute." He backed out of the closet, my best jeans and a nice shirt in hand. He tossed them on the bed and pointed at me. "We're running late thanks to a last minute hiccup at work. Get dressed, Owen. Now." He softened his tone. "I'll explain everything soon."

I opened my mouth to argue and damn being placed in a corner, or being given the silent treatment, but before I could speak I noticed something different about him. His eyes were exhausted, the corners of his mouth a little pinched.

"You okay?" I asked him.

His eyes widened as if he was surprised at the question which brought on another revelation. I didn't ask him nearly enough how he was doing. Even when he was swamped at work and called me, he asked how I was doing, not the other way around. I might have answered right back at him, but never gave it real thought. *How could I be such a selfish bastard?*

"I'm fine," he replied, but he couldn't meet my eyes, which worried me even more.

"Are you sure?"

"Stop procrastinating and get dressed," he commanded, ignoring the question.

"I won't make a fuss anymore about where we're going if you answer my question, Daddy," I said, knowing the effect that would have on him. "Are you positive you're okay?"

His features softened, and he walked over to me, cupping my chin. "I told you, I'm fine. Just a little over-worked which is why this is important to me. I need to get away for a few days, and I'm taking you with me. Now will you please get dressed?"

I nodded. "Okay."

I didn't question him after that as he watched me put my clothes on. "Do I need to take anything?" I asked, uncertain.

"No. You're ready. I got your passport."

"My passport?" So many questions flew around in my mind, but I had agreed to go along meekly if he answered my question which he had. He only smiled at me, not explaining and with a groan, I tagged along.

"Trust me," was all he said, and since he had yet to fail me, I decided I would.

His car was parked in the driveway, Silas smiling when he saw us. After transporting us around so many times, I was more at ease with him. He was friendly enough, and we had struck up conversations before since our job was a common factor between us. I had figured with as much as he knew about those days and nights spent making out in the backseat of the car with Declan, I might as well get friendly with him for things to not be awkward.

"Hey, Silas. Your granddaughter feeling better?" I asked him as I walked toward the car beside Declan whose hand was casually draped about my hip. I liked that he was an affectionate Daddy. In the past, I always thought of daddies as getting off on punishment and making their boys feel little. I couldn't have been more wrong in my misconception, and I had Declan to thank for opening my eyes. I was grateful enough to have found a younger Daddy who was everything I never even dreamed of.

"Doing better, but now my grandson has the flu," he replied on a sigh.

"Ah man, sorry about that. Hope he gets better soon." I stopped at the door he had opened for us and asked. "Where are we off to today?"

Declan swatted my ass, the first time he had done that in public. "Get in the car and stop trying to sneak answers out of our driver."

Silas hid his chuckle behind a cough, and face burning, I ducked inside the vehicle. Declan entered after me, and we were off, driving to an unknown location. The only thing he had allowed me to bring was my phone, so I figured we wouldn't be gone for long or far.

"You know, this might equate to kidnapping," I told him, trying to figure out where we were going based on our direction.

"If it is, you'll enjoy it."

I settled back against the seat and shrugged, deciding to let whatever was about to happen unfold, but I became suspicious when we were on Eastern Avenue. We were heading in the direction of Wilmer Avenue where the airport was. I glanced at him suspiciously, and he only smiled at me. *He wouldn't. Not like this. If we're going out of the country, he would have given me more notice to prepare.* But he had mentioned passports.

He could, and he did. I stared, at a loss for words as Silas drove us onto the airport grounds.

"Declan," I groaned, palms sweating. Apart from the brief business flight I had almost taken, I had never flown out of the country before. "Why are we here?"

"I promised to take you to a Pride event," he said, his face the most relaxed I had seen him since he picked me up. "This is it."

"Where are we going?" I asked him as Silas parked and came around to get the door.

"Brazil."

Brazil? I was speechless as Declan took charge and guided me from the vehicle toward a private area for us to be screened before our flight. We didn't join the usual queues, he explained, because we were not taking a commercial flight. We were traveling to Brazil by a private jet.

My brain did shut down a bit then. I always knew Declan was wealthy, but this was the first time I was seeing his money in full effect. I had been on inter-state flights before, and the treatment we received was completely different from what I had experienced before. Bright smiles greeted us as Declan was easily identified. If he didn't keep a hold of my hand, I would have probably felt too intimidated to move along with the whole process. Our passports were checked, but the agent barely glanced to ensure everything was in order before wishing us a pleasant trip.

"This is unbelievable," I heard myself mutter, only

for Declan to lean over and kiss me briefly before guiding me toward the checkpoint where our private jet awaited. I tried to be cool then, to act like this was the norm and he hadn't impressed the heck out of me with this trip. I couldn't stop staring at the jet while my heart thumped in my chest.

Declan's wealthy. Like filthy rich. The thoughts echoed through my brain as I coaxed my wax cheeks into a smile while we met our pilots. The jet wasn't even rented. He owned it, and I found out because I asked. He answered with such nonchalance that one would have believed it was the norm to own a jet.

"Sometimes I do a lot of traveling," he explained, hand lightly grazing my ass as we ascended the bridge. "It seemed smarter to invest in one."

"The only things I've ever invested in are my kids," I remarked in a daze.

He chuckled. "That's a pretty damn good investment if you ask me. You're a good father, Owen. I like that."

I couldn't respond as we finally entered the jet, and I was struck by all the beauty and luxury before me. I'd had no idea what to expect from the outside, but the interior was decorated well.

"I usually have a hostess, but figured we could do with the privacy on the long flight," Declan stated, nuzzling my neck. "How about I show you around before takeoff? We're good for another half an hour before we're scheduled to depart."

"Okay," I strangled out the word, still trying to keep in my awe.

The first zone was a seating area consisting of eight

seats lined up two behind each other on the right and left, leaving a spacious aisle for walking. I tried to take everything in from fold-out tables to reclined seats that converted into full flat beds. An iPad device was used to control everything from lighting to the blinds at the windows.

"I mostly use this area for business related purposes or dining," he said, exposing laptops that were accessible from beneath the seats. "There's less of a distraction for conducting business." He touched my elbow and nudged me forward. "Let's go to the next zone where I usually relax."

As if I wasn't already impressed, we moved deeper inside the jet into another sitting area. L-couches, recliners, and plush sofas added to the luxurious feel. He even had a wet bar, which he strolled toward as I took in the television that made mine seem like a toy. Soft music played in the background, although I couldn't identify what song was playing, because it was too low.

"It's like a mini-hotel," I remarked, as he returned to my side with two champagne flutes and a bottle in his hand.

"Wait until we get to my private bedroom and the bathroom," he stated, handing me the two flutes. "You'll be begging me to take you with me on all my business trips which I wouldn't be entirely opposed to."

He popped the champagne, the sound causing me to jump because of how skittery I was. I tried not to show my embarrassment as he raised his eyebrows in question at me.

"This doesn't feel real," I told him. "One minute I'm home waiting for you to drop by so we can hit the sack and the next minute I'm on a private jet. I'm about to ask you to slap me to see if this is just a dream I'll wake up from."

"I won't slap you," he said, laughing softly. "I have no desire for punishment on this trip, but I do intend to spoil you rotten, so be forewarned."

Insecurities hit me hard again, and my hands were shaking so badly he had to take the flutes from me so he could pour the champagne.

"Why?" I asked him hoarsely. "You have all this. You could have any man you want on this jet with you—men who would be happy to be anything you want just to experience all these things you want to do for me. Why would you choose someone like me?"

He frowned at me. "Someone like you? What does that mean?"

"Someone old. All my good years are behind me. I spent them all raising three kids. What do I have to give you?"

His eyes met and held mine. "You underestimate yourself, Owen, and maybe that's what I like about you. Trust me, if anyone else had been here in your place, it wouldn't have been the same. It had to be *you*." Before I had time to process what he was not exactly saying, he was moving ahead. He came to a halt at a brown wall and slid it back. I approached him and discovered what he meant about his private quarters.

He stepped aside to allow me ahead of him into a

cozy room decorated in cream, black, and ivory. Sunlight streamed inside from the three oval windows next to the inviting queen-sized bed, providing us with sufficient lighting. The bedspread matched the half a dozen or so ivory and white throw pillows that adorned the bed. To complete the room was a personal TV, a small bedside table with a stylish ivory lamp and a reclining chair.

"You were not kidding," I told him, downing the champagne and handing him the glass. "Can I move here permanently?"

As I kicked off my shoes, Declan chuckled. "No, but I've a penthouse suite in New York I have a feeling you'll like."

I groaned as I allowed myself to drop onto the bed. It was as soft as it looked, but I didn't feel like I was going to sink through the mattress either. "Too far from my kids."

I watched him as he finished his drink and placed both flutes onto the bedside table. He walked over to the bed and stopped to stare down at me. I smiled up at him, hoping he could read my mind so I didn't have to spell out for him what I needed.

"Distance is nothing," he remarked, removing his shoes while he checked his watch. "Daddy owns a private jet. You can be in Columbus anytime you want."

"That's too much hassle, babe. Now are you going to kiss me or what?"

His answer was to straddle me and reach for my arms to stretch them above my head. "Just a kiss?" he asked, gazing down hungrily at me. "We have another fifteen minutes before takeoff. Think you can come in that short of a time?"

"Yes, please."

I was good at being polite when I wanted his loving because his reward in that department was always great. I wasn't wrong. He had me gripping the sheets and shouting my release into the bed in less than ten minutes.

DECLAN

"Holy fuck, we're in Brazil." Owen's attempt at enthusiasm fell flat as we piled into the private chartered vehicle I had requested to meet us at the Guarulhos International Airport in São Paulo. I chuckled in amusement and closed the car door firmly behind us. Our driver, Joao, secured the safety locks and turned to address me with a smirk on his face.

If I'd had a choice about the situation, I would have requested another driver, but it was almost 3AM, and I needed to find Owen a bed. The poor thing was exhausted from the twelve hour flight.

"Você está pronto, senhor?" Joao asked, smiling invitingly at me. This wasn't my first time in Brazil, and I was aware how some of the younger men made extra cash on the side. He had been checking me out since I introduced myself and Owen as my partner. The question in his eyes as he had looked from Owen, who had been leaning heavily on me, didn't need translation, and I was grateful Owen was too sleepy to notice the interest.

"Sim, estamos prontos," I answered, assuring him that yes, we were ready.

He gave a shrug then adjusted himself in his seat and backed out of the airport's parking lot. A loud thud drew my attention beside me to where Owen had crashed into the door still fast asleep.

"Shit." I reached for him and pulled him into my arms, cursing my stupidity in not insisting that he sleep when we were up in the air. He had asserted that he wasn't tired, and I'd enjoyed his company so much on the long flight that I hadn't pushed. He had fallen asleep half an hour before we landed in São Paulo, and it had taken me several minutes to wake him up. He was a damn heavy sleeper.

Later when he woke up, Owen would regret missing the nocturnal view of São Paulo. Although Pride was still two days away, the city was pulsing with excitement. São Paulo was always a busy city, but during Pride everything magnified. Rainbow flags were already flapping in the cool night wind, hinting at the excitement that was to come.

"You here for Pride, senhor?" Joao asked in English, attempting to make conversation.

"Yes," I replied. "I wanted my boy to experience the Pride of who we are."

I glanced away from his look of confusion and down at Owen with affection. His mouth was slightly opened, and he was snoring lightly. I closed my eyes and allowed the feelings that I was developing for him to wash over me. It was hard to fathom I cared about him so much in the little time we had spent together. Approximately a month ago, I hadn't known this man, and now I couldn't envision my life without him in it.

The drive from the airport to L'hotel Porto Bello took us longer than it should have because of the traffic of both people and vehicles. By the time we arrived, I had the urge to crash as well. With all the work I had done lately to give myself enough berth to take the days off like this to spend with Owen, I had only grabbed a few hours of sleep for the past week.

There was also the worrying about what the possible cause could be of me fainting the other day. I had promised Ridge I would see my doctor, and I would. After Pride with Owen. I didn't want a gloomy diagnosis to ruin Owen's first Pride that I got to spend with him. If something was wrong, I wanted to have memories of this moment with him.

At the hotel, I paid the driver and tipped him generously. I had asked for a private bell assistant, and the man was prompt to grab our bags from the vehicle while I woke Owen to get him inside. He grumbled about me waking him, even mentioned me leaving him on the sidewalk to sleep. I would have found it funny if I wasn't as dog-tired myself.

Our check-in was expedited, and I was relieved when we entered our suite. I meant for our stay to be one Owen wouldn't forget anytime soon, so I had booked their most prestigious suite. I wasn't disappointed at all.

The suite had an expensive, but homey feel with its wooden paneling.

"I'll be back in a minute," I told Owen as I supported him inside to our private sleeping quarters and guided him to the king-size bed to sit. "Can you get your clothes off? I'm just going to tip the bellhop."

"Yeah, I can manage," he said on a frown, looking so damn adorable even though he was grumpy when sleepy, but who wouldn't be? All he wanted to do was sleep, and I kept waking him up.

I kissed his forehead. "Sorry I keep waking you. We're here, so you can sleep as long as you want now."

"Sleep with me?" he pleaded. "You haven't slept in my bed for days."

"I will. Get your clothes off."

I left him wrestling with his shoes while I re-entered the main room where the bell assistant waited with our bags.

"Where do you want me to put the bags, senhor?" he asked, his English good, but halting as if he had to give thought to each word before he voiced it.

"Right here is fine," I responded. "We'll pick them up later. Right now, we both desire a nice long sleep."

He smiled, and I had the impression he didn't understand spoken English so well. I fished my wallet from my pocket and tipped him. His eyes lit up at the amount I handed him.

"Obrigado pela sua ajuda." I thanked him for his assistance before I let him out and closed the door. Finally.

I left our bags right there in the main room while I returned to our bedroom. I groaned when I found Owen lying on the bed with his jeans half-on. It was as though he had decided he couldn't be bothered before grabbing the pillow and going back to sleep.

I worked his jeans down his legs, knowing from experience how uncomfortable sleeping in them was. I unbuttoned his rumpled shirt and had most of the challenge getting his arms through the sleeves. He eventually cooperated, though, he mumbled protests.

Once he was undressed, I coaxed him under the covers before I attacked my own clothing. I made a quick stop in the bathroom to pee before returning to the bedroom and joining him under the covers. We were here in Brazil for Pride. There was nowhere else that I would have preferred to be, and no one else I would have rather come with.

Usually I tossed and turned, a million thoughts going through my head before I was able to sleep. Tonight I had no such problem. As soon as my head hit the pillow I found myself drifting. Before I slipped away into nothingness, I felt the bulk of Owen's body settling closer to me, his arm thrown over my hip.

My heart pounds in my chest as I glance around to check that nobody saw me. Everyone is inside the house, and for the first time, I'm happy to be the unforgotten child. I grip my shovel harder in my fist, digging into the soft earth since it had rained the night before.

When the root of the plant breaks away from the soil, I am excited that I have another flower.

I pause, wiping my sweaty forehead with my dirty hand and counting the number of flowers on the ground. Four. Are they enough? I have no idea, but if I stay out much longer and Papa catches me, he will send me to my room and forbid me to see Mama. I can't let that happen, so I decide that four stalks of roses will do.

The first time I had brought flowers to Mama from her garden, I had thought she would be furious at me for digging up her rose bush. She hadn't. She had smiled at me for the first time in a long while and told me that the rose made her feel better. I think maybe if I give her enough roses, then she will get all better, and everything will be like before she got sick.

I hide my shovel in the overgrown weeds and grab the roses. In my haste, I'm careless and several thorns prick my skin. Tears gather in my eyes, but I refuse to cry as I pull the thorns out. Papa had scolded me for crying the first time I had seen Mama sick. Now I don't cry any at all, even if I want to. He says crying makes her sad, and I need to be strong for her.

I slip into the house through the back door and hurry along the corridor. I check right and left before darting into the hall and clambering up the stairs. I run to Mama's bedroom door, but come to a halt when the maid Anna spots me.

"Declan, what happened?" she asks, her voice rising. "Were you in the rose bushes again? Your father will be furious."

I show her the flowers and turn pleading eyes to her. "I picked them for Mama. She says they make her feel better. Please, don't tell Papa. I won't disturb her."

She frowns at me, and I'm not sure if it's the tears that gather in my eyes that I was trying so hard not to cry which finally makes *her nod. "Okay, fine. Hurry up, but straight to the shower with you afterward before your father finds you looking like this mess."*

I smile at her and slip into Mama's bedroom. I close the door behind me and pause just inside the room, finding Mama's frame on the bed. She's sleeping, but as if she senses I'm there, she opens her eyes.

"Declan, honey, is that you?"

"Yes, Mama," I answer, suddenly unsure if I should go any closer. I'm close to tears, and I don't want her to see me cry and get upset. Papa will be mad.

"Come closer, son," she urges me, and I can't say no to her.

I approach the bed and show her the flowers. "I bring more flowers for you. Do you feel better today?"

She smiles at me and reaches out to touch me, but I'm scared of the skin and bones of her hand and step away. She tucks her hand back beneath the covers and turns away from me.

"Mama."

"It's okay, baby. It's okay."

But it's not okay. I can hear her crying, and I feel bad that it's all because of me.

Before I can say anything, the door opens. I drop the flowers as I face my father who terrifies me. Mama isn't the only one who has changed. He no longer smiles, no longer ruffles my hair or plays with me.

"What are you doing here, boy?" he snaps, and I tremble so hard my skinny knees knock together.

"Charles, leave him be," Mama says weakly.

"I told him not to disturb you!" he shouts, stalking over to where I'm standing. I cry out as his hand clamps around my shoulder, and his fingers dig into my six-year-old tender flesh.

"Charles," Mama protests. "You're hurting him. I need you to be there for him when I'm gone."

That only seems to make Papa angrier as he drags me across the room and tosses me out of the bedroom. He points a finger at me. "If I ever catch you in this room again, I'll send you away."

GASPING, I jerked awake, my chest heaving with every effort it took me to inhale. My heart pounded in my chest, and I glanced around wildly, trying to figure out where I was. That I was no longer the six-year-old boy from my nightmares was very evident, but it took me a while to remember I was in Brazil. I was nowhere near my mother's death bed.

Someone stirred beside me, pulling my attention away from the recurring nightmare and to Owen who peeked at me from one eye. "You okay?" he asked, his words slurred by sleep.

"Yes, yes, I'm fine," I said, but he frowned at me as if he didn't believe me. "I just need to use the bathroom," I lied, then climbed out of bed. "Go back to sleep."

"It's not morning yet?"

"It is, but we've no place to be yet, so go back to sleep, Owen."

He nestled back down beneath the covers before he raised his head and peered at me again. "You sure you're okay?"

"Positive. Go to sleep."

I didn't wait for him to question me anymore, but made

my way to the bathroom. From the lethargic movements of my body, I hadn't gotten enough sleep, but I knew better than to think I would be able to get more rest after that nightmare. I took a shower, hoping that would buy me some time to regain my composure before facing Owen again.

I didn't need to worry as he had fallen asleep again by the time I exited the bathroom.

26

OWEN

"What the fuck, Declan, you want me to wear that out in public?"

I stared in horror at the expensive collar and leash Declan placed on the bed. The words *Daddy's Boy* was spelled out with rhinestones on the collar, and there was no mistaking what it meant, especially when Declan meant to keep the leash to my collar.

"It's Pride, Owen. Nobody gives a damn. It's also a way to ensure I don't lose you in the crowd."

"Couldn't you have found another means?" I still eyed the collar, apprehensive of that thing being around my neck.

"It's just a collar you'll wear for an hour or two," he answered. "Now be a good boy and sit on the bed so I can get it on. Consider this makeup for yesterday."

I groaned and sat on the bed. "I already apologized for sleeping through the entire day. That's what you get for having a middle-aged boyfriend. We get tired and take longer naps."

He laughed at me while he scooped the collar from the bed. "Hmm, you keep up well enough when we have sex."

I smirked at him. "Because I let you do all the work."

That had him laughing harder. "Well, that's true enough."

I smacked him in the gut. "Hey, you're not supposed to agree. I deserve some credit for riding you last week. I damn near slipped out my knee too, doing it."

When he laughed even harder, I felt better and pleased that he no longer looked tired and brooding. He didn't like me querying if he was okay, so I had scaled back asking, but I was observant, and he looked more wan than usual. Something was up with him. I could feel it in my bones. Maybe it was from the years of being sensitive to my kids' needs as they were growing up, but Declan was keeping back something from me.

I had feared that something was him wanting to end our relationship, but trying to figure out how to go about it. As much as I argued about the collar, seeing it had dispelled that notion. It wasn't about ending what we had. He could hardly be so cruel as to have me wear a collar that basically spelled out the kind of relationship we had to the public, then called us quits. It was some-thing else, and I intended to find out what it was, but for now I would let it be so we could enjoy Pride.

We had lost half a day yesterday because it had taken me a while to get over my jetlag. I had only resurfaced in the afternoon, so we had missed our helicopter tour of the city which he had booked for us. As bummed as I was about that, we'd still had a wonderful evening shopping at the Praça Benedito Calixto outdoor market. It had been crowded, but given so many people were in the city for Pride, it was expected.

I had bought trinkets for the kids, although I hadn't figured out just yet how to tell them how I had come to be in Brazil. They had no idea I was out of the country, and since Declan had activated roaming on my phone, I was able to receive their calls and texts without them knowing I wasn't in Cincy.

Later when I arrived home, I could feel bad about not telling them, but I didn't want anything to ruin Pride for Declan and me. Besides, if he had given me time in advance to prepare, I would have found a way to tell them, but he had basically kidnapped me and taken me to Brazil. Not that I was complaining. I didn't mind this kind of kidnapping.

"You look great," Declan announced when he had the collar secured around my neck. He leaned forward and tugged a little on the leash. "I'll have to fuck you wearing this when we get back."

As if I was going to protest. "Yes, please."

"Hah! Always so polite when it comes to you getting your ass filled, aren't you, boy?"

"Only for you, Daddy," I replied, initially meaning it as a tease, but it came out serious. Like the words on the collar around my neck, I was completely his for however long he wanted me.

He kissed me hard. "Fuck, hearing you call me Daddy makes me hard every time."

I smiled because I was aware, and I tended to use it to my advantage. Whether or not it was because of my years of little to no sex, I was insatiable when it came to Declan. *He* knew that too and could use that knowledge to get me to behave.

"Leave your phone," he told me. "Unfortunately, Pride is a huge event which can attract those with less than good intentions. I'll keep a copy of our room key and you keep the other. We don't need much cash on us since we can use our cards almost anywhere."

I had discovered that yesterday. As ridiculous as it sounded, even the street ice cream seller we had stopped at yesterday had accepted card payment.

The streets were already filling with people when we left our hotel. Although the leash was connected to my collar, Declan reached for my hand instead, and I hid my smile, not wanting to make more of it than I should, but how could I help it? The man had collared me, then held my hand. The message I got was that he owned me, my body, but I owned his heart.

Does Declan Moore love me?

The thought was electrifying. Thrilling. Satisfying.

He caught me looking at him and frowned at me. "Why that look?"

I answered by cupping the back of his head and kissing him, pouring out my heart to him, and hoping he understood what I couldn't say out loud until I knew for sure he felt the same.

Someone shouted something in Portuguese that seemed directed at us. Loud laughter and more shouts came our way. I didn't speak Portuguese, but I understood the tone well enough.

"What are they saying?" I asked Declan, our lips still touching.

"They say to kiss my boy like I mean it."

I grinned up at him. "I agree. Kiss me, Da—"

Before I could get the word out, he was kissing me harder, deeper, tongue sweeping into my mouth. I gasped at his hands creeping down my back to grab my ass. He ground his crotch against mine, and my knees almost gave out. Declan was practically humping me right there in plain sight of everyone, and I was allowing it.

"Love is love!" a woman cried in English. She sounded surprisingly British.

"Declan, I've got a hardon," I moaned when he eventually released my lips.

"So do I," he answered. "And we're going to walk with pride about it too, aren't we?"

Finally, I understood why he had brought me here. I had never felt such an acceptance before of who we were. Even back home while we weren't bothered much, we were still mindful of doing certain things together depending on our location. Things weren't so bad being with Declan, because he was wealthy, and even homophobic people knew the power of his dollar, but here, we had nothing to fear. Nothing to be ashamed of. If a man could walk down the street ahead of us in nothing but a jock strap, a tank top and heels, I could damn well do the same with a hard-on caused by the man I loved.

It took us only five minutes to get to the long stretch of

avenue where the parade would begin. The avenue was already so crowded with people that I automatically drew closer to Declan, not wanting to get caught up in the crowd.

"This is the one pass you get," Declan leaned over to whisper in my ear, but I heard the laughter in his voice. "I won't deck anyone who gropes your ass, but if your ass gets too sore from all the pinching, let me know, and we'll go back to the hotel."

I stared up at him, wondering if he was joking. "*I'm gonna get my ass pinched?*"

"Even I'll get my ass pinched," he told me. "It's the only day that it's allowed."

I grinned at him mischievously, stretched a hand behind him and groped his ass. "I call dibs."

He peered at me with a curious look on his face. "You want me to bottom for you?"

My heart skipped a beat before racing as I considered which answer to give him. The selfish truth or the one who wanted to be considerate of him. "Hmm. I really don't feel inclined to top," I answered, measuring my words carefully. "I could bottom for you forever. However, I don't mind if you want me to be an occasional top. A highly occasional top."

He chuckled, his arm tightening around my waist. "I don't think we'll have a problem. I'm an exclusive top. Tried bottoming once and didn't like it. I'm glad you do."

I didn't realize I was holding my breath until I let it out in a loud whoosh that made him chuckle harder.

"You don't find it strange I don't want to top?" I

asked, wanting to be positive. "I know being versatile is more popular than most people think."

"Believe me, Owen. I'm quite pleased with you being my enthusiastic bottom."

Our attention was drawn to a huge crowd that descended on the avenue then. I had already thought it was crowded, but I had no idea what I was in for. The last few minutes before the parade started, more and more people kept pouring out into the avenue. People were even on top of buildings, balconies of apartments and hotels, looking down on the spectacle.

It didn't take much for the spirit of Pride to spill over. Swept up in the moment by the music, the people, the infectious spirit, and the togetherness, Declan and I drifted along with the crowd. He was right about getting my ass groped, and although I liked that part the least, it didn't dampen my mood at all. The move was slow, but it allowed us to stop at different points to be covered in Pride stickers with positive messages and collect cheap plastic wristbands with the colors of the Pride flag.

At one point, I tried to figure out all the country flags that were represented at the event, but there were too many. It felt like everyone had descended upon São Paulo. Declan was even more affectionate than usual, kissing me and groping me wherever he chose. It was hot and had my cock aching throughout the march.

Two hours into the march, I was ready to drop out of the parade and head back to our hotel, but I didn't want to drag Declan away if he wanted to last the entire march, so I tried to endure it. I got distracted every now and then by an outrageous costume that you would only dare to wear to a Pride event. The only thing I didn't see was someone completely naked, although that was moot given some of the more transparent costumes. It was definitely an enriching experience I was glad for.

A group of male belly dancers caught my attention, and I paused checking out the sight of men balancing on heels that were so high I winced thinking about my poor ankles. They were beautiful and skillful. I was immersed and couldn't take my eyes off them even when I felt a tug on my leash. I kept watching them while I tried to catch up with Declan ahead of me who tugged at the leash.

I almost tripped over someone which had me turning to apologize to a man in his sixties wearing a dress and a wig that suspiciously resembled Dolly Parton's. I mumbled sorry, but the man only smiled at me and rattled off Portuguese I didn't understand. I turned to ask Declan what he was saying when I noticed the man tugging at my leash and grinning at me was not in fact Declan.

With hand gestures, I got him to let go of the leash, and I reeled it in, trying to pick Declan out of the crowd. There were too many people, and I had no idea how far I had walked off with the idiot who had been pulling on my leash.

"Declan!" I called his name over the crowd but there was too much chattering, laughing, and music. "Declan!"

There was no response. I was jostled from the left, my ass groped again, but I didn't even care to glare at the person who had done it. More than likely they had disappeared into the crowd already anyway.

The sea of faces swam before my eyes, but none

belonged to the man who had claimed my heart. I stood, rooted to the spot, trying to figure out what to do. Move on with the crowd and hope to pick Declan out of the millions of people engaged in the march or return to the hotel? I wasn't sure which would cause Declan the least stress when he discovered we had been separated.

27

DECLAN

One minute I was walking slightly ahead of Owen as he checked out the various costumes attendees were wearing, and the next, I was descended upon by a group of people wearing skimpy dresses and various types of heels, wanting to take a photo with me. There were too many of them for my protest to be heard, so I decided to be good-natured about it and snap a few photos with them. I didn't realize I had let go of Owen's leash, or how far their bodies had pushed mine until it was too late.

As the group of people hurried away to attack their next victim, I turned, trying to pick out Owen where I had last seen him, but he was no longer there. Frightened at the thought of losing him, I told myself he had to be close by. I hadn't spent even a minute taking the photo with the group, but the truth was that it was easy to get swallowed up by this crowd.

I retraced my footsteps, pushing past bodies to find Owen. He didn't know anything about São Paulo. Would he even think to return to the hotel to wait for me if he got lost? What if he couldn't find his way back with this crowd? Logically, I knew he was old enough to handle being lost. It wasn't like he was a kid, but still I worried.

"Owen!" I yelled his name, but other than a few curious glances, nobody paid me any mind. Fuck, there was no use yelling his name in this crowd. He wasn't going to hear me above the noise. The music alone distorted my shout.

I searched the faces that streamed by me, but there were so many people. Millions of people were in attendance at the march. Trying to spot Owen in this crowd was madness. I would never find him, and I couldn't report him missing either. For all I knew he was already headed back to the hotel.

I tried to figure out if Owen would continue with the march or return to the hotel. As much as he had been enjoying the event, I couldn't see him getting into it without me. He had the spare key, and although we had been out for two hours, in reality, the hotel was just a few minutes away.

Feeling torn between going back to the hotel and potentially leaving him to weather this crowd alone, I had to make a tough decision. Owen was smart, and he didn't particularly enjoy the crowd. There was no way he would continue this parade when he discovered we had gotten separated.

Hoping I was right, I hurried in the opposite direction of the parade back the way we had come. The way seemed longer than I remembered, and by the time I arrived at our hotel, my heart was lodged in my throat. I bypassed the pleasantries of the front desk staff and headed for the elevator.

"Fuck!" I cried, slapping my hand against the wall. How the hell had I lost him? For the past couple of days I felt myself slipping up, losing control and now this. A responsible man didn't lose the partner he had taken to Pride with him. I had even taken the extra precaution of leashing him, something I would have never done otherwise. I should have bloody well handcuffed him to me.

I barely waited for the elevator doors to part before I dashed out to our room. I closed my eyes, praying to a god I no longer believed in since my mother passed away, and I was left with a cold-hearted man who no longer desired me to call him father. I just wanted Owen to be safe inside our suite, waiting for me. I needed to hold him a minute before even trying to find out what had happened.

"Owen?" I called, entering our suite. "Owen, honey, are you here?"

When I was met with silence, my gut twisted with nausea. I didn't mistake this for the stress-induced nausea I sometimes got. This was different. This was fear that I had lost him and he could be anywhere. He could be drugged and the devil knew where. Pride was a beautiful event, the most glorious freeing event I had ever participated in, but wherever there was a crowd, unscrupulous people always lay in wait, ready to prey.

I paced the length of the room, trying to figure out

how to proceed. I had to get him back. My life would be empty without Owen and not because I wouldn't be able to forgive myself if anything happened to him, but because I loved him. I had fallen hard for Owen Long, and I hadn't even told him that.

The front door opened, and I spun around, relieved when Owen entered, looking sheepish. He still had the collar around his neck, but had removed the leash which he carried in his hand.

"Oh thank god." We met in the center of the room, and I held him as tightly as he clung to me. "I was terrified something had happened to you."

"I'm sorry," he said, hands going around my waist. "As soon as I realized what had happened, I headed back here to the hotel, but I took a wrong turn and had to find my way back."

I shivered at the thought of him going the wrong way. "It's all my fault," I said on a groan. "I released the leash by accident, and by the time I realized, you had vanished."

"I got distracted watching a group of dancers," he admitted. "I didn't realize you weren't the one at the end of the leash leading me along. I was just following blindly."

"What the fuck!" I exploded, a chill traversing my spine when I realized how wrong this could have gone. I crushed him to me, and he snuggled into me, seeking comfort.

"For a minute there I was terrified when I realized you weren't the one holding the leash," he said softly.

"But then I figured I should come back here instead of getting further lost in the crowd."

I squeezed my eyes shut and bit back the words to tell him how much I loved him. I had no desire to blurt it out during a crisis moment that might breed doubt with it.

"You want to go back out there?" I asked him, though I couldn't muster up the desire anymore. I just wanted to keep him close for the next hour or so.

"Can't we watch from our private balcony? It's all wonderful, but I think I'll be just as fine staying here and viewing it. There's just so much energy, and I'm not sure how much I have left in me to keep up."

That eased some of the tension out of me. "Yes, let's do it. I'll get us a drink."

He followed me to the wet bar instead of going out to the balcony to wait for me. I got the feeling he didn't want to be apart just as much as I had no desire to have him out of my sight yet. He brought the wine glasses, and I grabbed the bottle of expensive wine I had been chilling for our last night here in São Paulo. There was no better time to drink it than now.

I led the way to the balcony, and our view was perfect to watch the parade below us. He walked over to the balustrade, resting on his forearms while he looked over the crowd.

"It's beautiful, isn't it?" I approached and handed him a glass of the wine.

"Thanks." He took a sip before he answered. "Yes, it is probably the most magnificent thing I've ever seen. I can't believe how many people made the trip here, and I get to be a part of it because of you."

I crowded behind him and kissed the space between his neck and shoulder. He moaned and leaned back into me, baring his neck to my mouth.

"You scared the crap out of me today, Owen," I told him, licking his ear. "When I came here and didn't find you, I was beyond pissed with myself for dropping the leash."

He reached back his left hand to grip my hip. "It all worked out okay. That's all that matters."

We continued drinking our wine in silence, me kissing him, letting him know my intention. He tucked his ass right into my groin, silently giving me his permission. I plucked the empty glass from his hand and placed it with mine on the table out on the balcony, slipping inside to grab the bottle of lube from the nightstand. On my way back out, I snagged the leash he had dropped to the sofa in the sitting room. He glanced over his shoulder at me as I returned to his side.

"Here?" he asked, gesturing to the crowd below. "We're in full view of anyone who bothers to look this way."

"Who cares? We're too high up for anyone to make out who we are. All they will see are a couple of dudes getting off while watching Pride. Tell me, Owen. What's better than that?"

His moan was answer enough as he moved toward me. Arms placed on his narrow hips, I met his kiss half-way, deepening our connection. As eager as ever, Owen's body curved into my own. I would never get tired of this, of the solid more muscular build of him against me. He was more than my equal, which made his submission that much more sweet.

Although he preferred being led, he was by no means passive in our sexual interactions. With every moan, every grope of his hands, every thrust of his hips, he begged for what he wanted. He knew all the right buttons of mine to push for me to give him what he wanted. I should have been terrified, but I was too pleased that I could satisfy his needs.

I worked my shorts down my hips, peeling my boxers down with them. The music blaring through the city traveled up to us, but I barely heard it, distracted by our own music. The whisper of need, the grunt of satisfaction, the sigh of pleasure.

I wrapped the leash around my arm as Owen knelt before me, his hands on my thighs. I kept a tight hold on him as I teased his lips with the tip of my cock, but not instructing him to open up and take me in until he glanced up at me, eyes tortured with need.

Only then did I give my permission.

"Open up for me, boy. Please Daddy the way he likes it."

He sucked the tip of my cock between his lips greedily, circling his tongue over the head, teasing the slit.

"Spit on it. Get it wet."

He released my cock and followed instructions, head raised so he could stare into my eyes while he sucked me off. Plenty of eye contact, just the way I liked it. The best thing about Owen sucking me off wasn't how amazing it felt, like he was massaging the climax from my very soul. No, the best part was seeing how much he enjoyed pleasing me, how well he took instructions.

I braced my hands on the balustrade to give myself leverage as I fucked his mouth, slow and deep. The back of his throat tickled my cock, shooting sensations of delight down my spine as he gagged. I pulled on the leash so his head tilted back some more and fucked his face.

"Fuck!" I growled, and pulled back from him. "Come here. Kiss me."

I helped him to his feet, and we kissed while I shoved his shorts down his hips. I cupped his balls and ignored his cock which hardened between our bodies. I squeezed and released him, teasing his sensitive scrotum. I paid keen attention to him while we made love and knew where I could push his buttons. I released his cock and reached behind him to grasp his cheeks, spreading him before all of São Paulo who dared to look. I didn't give a damn. He was mine. Mine alone.

"Turn around and show me that sweet ass."

I had him whimpering by the time he faced the parade, bending at the waist and spreading his thick hairy legs. I didn't need to ask. He even went so far as to reach behind him and spread his cheeks to award me the sight of his budding flesh.

"Did I tell you to spread 'em for me?" I asked.

"Sorry, Daddy," he said, impatience tainting his apology. "I just want you so much."

I would have scowled at him any other time, but decided to forgive him now. I was just as impatient as well to be inside him, but first, I needed to taste him.

While he held his cheeks apart for me, I planted a kiss

right over his hole rather than to tease us both. Spreading my lips apart, I tongued him, stroking over the ribbed edges, exploring him with bold licks as the wind snatched his moans and scandalized us to anyone within hearing. I could hear patrons on either side of us on their own balconies, taking in the Pride event as well.

If Owen had heard them, he gave no indication. I reached for the lube and dribbled it into my hands getting both of us prepped. Rising to my feet, I grasped his busy hips to keep him steady as I teased his hole with the tip of my cock.

"I'm going to fuck you raw, Owen," I cautioned him, because it was long overdue. We had both done the necessary tests, and given our exclusivity, there was no reason not to.

He glanced over his shoulder at me, but the look in his eyes wasn't one of protest.

"Do it," he growled at me. "I want you to come inside my ass, Daddy. To feel you running down my legs when you're done."

He purred in such a sexy way that I could no longer hold back. Without the rubber, I slid inside him, feeling every inch of his hot hole tightening around me. I bottomed out in one thrust but had to pause, tightening my hold on the leash and pulling. He eased upward, head turned to kiss me as he arched his back. He was beautiful. This older boy of mine never ceased to amaze me.

"Touch yourself for me," I moaned into his mouth as I started moving inside him, deep strokes that echoed the sound of my pelvis slapping his ass. My balls swung upward with each movement slapping against his in such eroticism that made me almost weep. This was more than just a fetish, more than him calling me Daddy and him being my boy. I felt it between us. This connection I had never experienced before in my adult life. This wasn't pretend. He truly was mine the way he gave himself up to me in abandonment, trusting me to make it good for the both of us.

"Baby boy," I moaned, running my hands along his sides and up his chest to smooth into the mat of hair there. I found his nipples and teased them.

"Yes, Daddy," he groaned, his hips working backward to meet each of my thrusts. He kept his head turned to glance back at me taking his ass over and over. The silver in his hair glinted in the sunlight, but the joyous expression on his face made him look so much more youthful.

I couldn't have given him permission to come if I wanted to. At a loss for words, I hoped he was able to interpret the look I gave him. His hand fished between his legs to take a hold of his cock. He became even more intense, his groans and hisses growing louder.

"Owen!" I gasped his name and grasped his hips to pump hard into him. I pushed as deep inside him as I could, pressing him to me as my climax drove me onto the tips of my toes. Owen grunted, his breathing shallow as he continued to jerk off. I pulled out of him, spreading his cheeks as, with gentle pushes, he dispelled my cum to run out and down his taint.

Unable to resist, I pressed my dick which was still hard back inside him, finished as far as my climax was concerned, but I could fuck him for hours more if it was physically possible.

"Please, don't stop," he moaned. "Almost there."

I found his nipples again and twisted them hard. "Fuck!" he cried, his body jerked as he spat his cum onto the tile. When he was spent, I pulled his shaking body back into my arms. My cock was going soft inside him, and any minute it would slip out, but for now I was content holding him, basking in the aftermath of our sex while our hearts interlocked with pride.

28

OWEN

I didn't want to leave São Paulo, but the idyllic five days in the heart of the beautiful city had come to an end. As much as we had bonded being so far away from our responsibilities, we could avoid our realities only for so long.

Since we had become separated during the parade, Declan remained fastened to my side for the remaining two days we were in the city, more often than not holding my hand. I would have found it offensive if I didn't enjoy the attention so much. It had taken me forty-six years to discover that I could be an attention whore for the right man.

Declan seemed to be *him* in every way.

I should have been appalled at my behavior and how eager I was to bottom for Owen. I'd had brief hookups with other guys before who had made me feel awkward and embarrassed. Most people didn't expect a guy who had my size to be a submissive, but the opposite was the case with Declan. There were moments I felt powerful for wringing emotions out of him that seemed just as new to him as to me. Other times I would feel vulnerable and small, but regardless of which, it had always felt right. He made me feel right, and he always knew what I needed, whether it was his gentleness, or his tough love cracking down on my ass.

As if he didn't already spoil me rotten with his attentive lovemaking, he was as equally considerate outside the bedroom. I still blushed every time I thought about how I had allowed him to have sex with me right there on the hotel balcony where I was quite positive at least the people from the neighboring suites had heard—maybe even seen us.

The night we had visited Drosophyla, a 1920s townhouse which served excellent food and liquor, we had run into our neighbors who had kept giving us funny looks all throughout the elevator ride. If the jazz night at the townhouse coupled with the delightful ambiance of wall art and classic furniture hadn't been so excellent, I would have spent the entire night feeling embarrassed.

Declan had insisted in giving me the full São Paulo experience, resulting in us having a packed day of activities to fill the days we spent in the city after Pride. From taking in the wall art on Batman Street and visiting the museums to having a picnic date in Ibirapuera Park, we'd also found time to book another aerial tour of the city by helicopter. We enjoyed the nocturnal side of São Paulo which was filled with parties and bar-hopped before we finally ended up at our favorite club, Panam, a helipad nightclub on top of the Maksoud Plaza Hotel.

In São Paulo, I discovered more about Declan than he probably realized. Despite his dominant side that craved being my Daddy, he had a youthful side to him as well. I would have been nervous at that side of him, wondering if it meant our relationship was temporary, but when he'd pulled me onto the dance floor with him, he'd had eyes only for me. He had ground against only me. He had kissed and made out with only me.

Unlike the day I had arrived in São Paulo too exhausted to keep my eyes open, I took Declan's advice this trip and slept on the flight home. Even if I didn't want to, I couldn't have avoided it. Declan backed me up into his private room and after slowly making love to me, I hadn't been able to do more than to roll over and tuck my head into the crook of his neck before I fell asleep.

It was with reluctance that I climbed into the back of the car when Silas picked us up at the airport.

"The next time we go on vacation, I'm going to need a whole month with you," Declan remarked, nuzzling my neck. "Five days was way too short."

I squeezed his knee. "I still find it hard to believe you took me to Brazil." I turned my head to graze his lips with mine.

"Brazil's just the beginning, Owen," he said, his voice low. "Maybe the next time I'll take you to France with me. We could travel all over Europe before coming back. Would you like that?"

My brain was spinning with too much information for me to respond. I gave a shaky laugh and tried to downplay how sincere his words were. "What are you going to do? Keep paying Cush for my services so I can go off on random vacations with you?"

"If that's what I need to do to take you with me, then yes."

I narrowed my eyes at him to check if he was serious. He wasn't smiling. I swallowed hard and shifted so I was facing the front of the car and didn't have to look into those compelling dark brown eyes of his.

"You don't have to do any of that, you know."

His hand brushed the five o'clock shadow already showing on my face. "I know, but I want to."

We traveled in silence, me deep in thought and Declan allowing me to wrap my head around everything he had just said to me. By the time I realized we weren't on the route to my home, I had figured out where he was taking me. His home.

"Declan, why are we here?" I asked, nervously glancing around as Silas drove up the long driveway. I had thought the house imposing when I had first driven there to pick him and his father up for the bachelor party. Now that we were together, it seemed even more daunting. Declan lived *here*. The house was magnificent. What could he have possibly thought of my small house and sleeping in my cramped bed? He hadn't complained once, but I could just imagine the luxury he had here in his home.

"We're just stopping by for an hour at the most," he answered, without directly answering my question. "I'll take you home afterward."

"You staying the night?" I cringed at my question, and my face flamed as I wondered if he was contemplating what a greedy lover I was. Not that I just wanted him over for sex. In fact, I was pretty sure after our five days of sex including the last episode up in the air, my ass needed a break. Having him over, however, meant I didn't have to sleep through the night alone. Plus, I enjoyed the way cuddling was so natural to him and the way he went to great pains to take care of me. His rose-giving had become a tradition of ours, and for a man so wealthy, he didn't mind doing little things for me such as foot rubs, a massage, running me a bath, or bringing me food.

"Do you want me to stay the night?" he asked, flipping the question on me.

"I don't mind," I answered. "But I understand after the last five days you may need some time to get away from all my neediness. Sorry about that. I've never been a clingy guy before. Don't know what's gotten into me."

"I know what's gotten into you, and that's me." I scowled at the smirk he aimed at me. He sobered up but still smiled at me. "I like you the way you are, Owen."

"I like you too," I confessed, feeling like thirteen-year-old me who had whispered to Scotty, a student a year ahead of me, that I *liked him liked him.* Scotty had punched me square in the eye before he ran off calling me names and telling me to stay away from him.

"One day you may even confess that you love me," he remarked with a wink, and his words slammed into my gut because he had seen into my heart. I was falling in love with him. How could I not? It was a combination of everything—the powerful attraction between us, the nice things he did for me, the new world he exposed me to, but most of all the way he cared.

He climbed out of the car, and I followed him. He reached for my hand, just as he had done in São Paulo, and together we went up the steps of the wide porch.

"This is your father's home?" I asked him, uneasy at the thought of entering the other man's home.

"No, this is *my* home," he answered, as we cleared the steps. "Charles didn't wish to continue living here after my mother passed away. My grandfather willed it to me, instead of him."

"Your mother died?" I had wondered about his family life, but I never pried especially since I knew the memories weren't all pleasant.

"Yes." His answer was straightforward and didn't invite questions, but I still pushed.

"How did she die?"

Before he could respond, the door opened from the inside. My attention shifted to the tall, formally dressed man who stood at the door.

"Mr. Moore, welcome home," the man's eyes swept over me, brows raised slightly from curiosity before shifting away back to Declan.

"Thanks, David," Declan responded, then stepped aside, gesturing for me to move ahead. "Owen, this is my butler, David. David, we'll be here just for a short time."

"It's good to meet you, sir," David said with a little bow.

I couldn't decide whether or not this was a joke. Who had their own butler in the twenty-first century? Well, maybe the POTUS and definitely the Queen of England. I swallowed hard.

"Nice to meet you too, David," I replied, acting like I met butlers on regular occasions.

"Do you need me for anything, sir?" David asked. "Perhaps refreshments?"

Declan was already walking along the long hall, and because he still had my arm, I had no choice but to follow him.

"We're fine, David," he told the butler. "I'm just giving Owen a tour of the house. We'll start on the exterior."

"Very well, sir."

I lengthened my strides to catch up to Declan's side. "You have a butler?" I whispered.

"I have two butlers. One's part-time for when David has a day off."

"Geez, you make that sound like the norm."

I ground to a halt as portraits hanging on the wall of the hall caught my attention. Declan stopped to look back at what I had discovered.

"That's you," I stated, pointing at a picture of Declan when he was around four years old. He was peeking out from behind the skirt of a beautiful laughing woman. She was breathtaking. No wonder Declan was so handsome. There were other more formal pictures taken separately before the final picture was of all three: Charles, Declan, and his mother. In that last photo and his solo, Declan's expression was quite the grownup's.

"Yes," he answered.

"And your mother," I added. "She was quite lovely, Declan."

"Thank you," he replied, and because he sounded funny, I turned to find him observing me. "Shall we continue?"

"Okay."

I didn't get to see much besides a chandelier and a curved staircase before Declan took a right turn. He bypassed the biggest kitchen I had ever seen in my life, and when I thought that would be our destination, he continued. The hall got smaller.

"Am I going to be locked in a dungeon or something and kept for your amusement?" I teased him.

He shot me a grin over my shoulder. "Don't go telling me your deepest fantasies, Owen. You know I'm compelled to make your dreams come true."

"Then where are you taking me?"

"You'll see."

We finally came upon an unlocked glass door. I stepped outside with Owen and found that we were in the backyard.

"Declan," I gasped his name, moving down the twin steps to get a closer view. The backyard had been touched by loving hands which had created a beautiful rose garden. Within the garden, there were arches run through with vines and stone benches that beckoned for me to sit and enjoy the view all afternoon.

"This is amazing," I said softly, in order not to disturb the peaceful landscape.

I watched as Owen moved over to a thorny bush. He removed a pocket knife and cut one of the stalks. My heart skipped when he moved toward me, his intent clear. How could I not be head over boots in love with a man who picked me a rose from his garden? My eyes widened.

"All this time you've been getting them here?" I asked, taking the flower he extended toward me. I had grown quite fond of collecting the flowers he gave me.

"Yes, they are quite special."

"It must cost a fortune to set up and maintain this garden," I remarked, still in awe.

"I do all the caretaking that's necessary to keep the garden healthy."

My jaw went slack. "You did all this? I don't believe you. You don't have to try and impress me, Dec. You already did that with São Paulo."

"It was my mother's favorite part of the entire property," he answered, face taking on a wistful expression. "She used to bring me here when I was quite small and show me things. I keep it together in honor of her memory. Now I have someone else to share that with."

"How old were you when she died?" I moved closer to him because his shoulders had drooped. The tired look was back on his face, and I just wanted to reach out and comfort him.

"I was six going on seven," he answered. "By then you could hardly recognize her as the beautiful woman you saw in the portrait."

I reached out for his hand and squeezed. "How did she die?"

"Pancreatic cancer. Do you know what it's like to watch the mother who kept your family together deteriorate before your eyes?"

A shiver ran down my spine from the anguish I heard in his tone. My heart tugged with his pain, and I was overcome with the urge to comfort him.

"Declan, I'm so sorry. That must have been hard."

I tried to pull him into my arms, but my movement brought him out of the trancelike state he was in. He shook off my arms, captured and held them to the sides of my body.

"It was a long time ago," he stated, glancing away from me, but not before I saw the pain reflected in his eyes.

"It still affects you," I said firmly.

His eyes hardened, his jaw clenched. "It was a long time ago," he repeated, and I couldn't tell if he was trying to convince me or himself.

"She was your mother. It's understandable you'd still be hurt over it, especially when you were at such an impressionable age."

Declan released my left hand and gripped the back of my head. His mouth smashed on mine, and as much as I knew he was deflecting, I couldn't resist the familiarity of his lips. If he wouldn't allow me to console him then maybe I could do it in another way. I wrapped my arm around his back, rubbing between his shoulder blades. I was just getting into the kiss when he pulled back and dropped my hand.

He blew hard even though we hadn't been kissing for even more than half a minute. It had nothing to do with the kiss. He was hurting, but he didn't want to admit it.

"Declan, let me—"

"I just remembered there's a lot that I have to do now

that I'm back," he remarked, more emotionally closed off than I had ever seen him. He had me locked out tight of his emotions. Usually I could read the desire and happiness in his eyes, but now he gave me a blank stare that made my heart ache. This wasn't the man who I had gotten to know over the past five days. This was a side of Declan I had never seen before, and apparently I wasn't handling it well.

"Declan, don't shut me out," I pleaded.

"I'm not," he lied, turning away from me. "Stay here. I'll have David escort you back out to the car so Silas can take you home. I'll call you."

"Declan!" I called to him as he walked away from me, but I was too stunned by this change in him to go after him. I didn't know if it made sense for me to press, or to leave him alone for now. He didn't seem to appreciate my concern over him, but how could I not care?

If he still struggled with his mother's death after all these years, he must have witnessed her tragic demise.

"Ow." I pulled my hand away as a thorn from the rose pricked my thumb. I stared at the bright red bubble that surfaced on my skin, and I had an unsettling feeling in my stomach.

29

DECLAN

Stumbling from my private bathroom inside my office, I groaned as I made my way back to the chair and sank down into it gratefully. I closed my eyes, leaning my head against the neck rest as I waited for the nauseating sensation in my stomach to disappear. Fear twisted my gut, and I tried to push it away, but it remained. What if it was... *No, I wouldn't allow myself to think it, but how would I know if I didn't get myself checked out?*

An image of Owen smiling at me, cuddling me in bed while we were in São Paulo popped up in my mind. Along with it came the guilt of pushing him away the day we had arrived back in Cincy. I hadn't planned for that to happen, but I had been a fool to think bringing him to the rose garden wouldn't have dredged up old memories better left buried.

For years I had laid all thoughts of my mother in the deepest sepulchre of my mind. I lived life as best as I could without remembering her, but with the dread I now carried that I had inherited her illness, I couldn't stop thinking about her. She crowded my thoughts, making it impossible for me to function except for immersing myself in work. I wished they were thoughts of her before the diagnosis, but that image of her had been wiped out, and the emaciated woman left behind in her wake was what lingered in my mind all these years.

I winced at the thought of me neglecting Owen. That day I had Silas drop him home without accompanying him, I'd had every intention of spending the night with Owen as promised, but I'd called him to take a rain check. I hadn't been in the best of moods thanks to his insightful comments and questions. For years, I had pretended that I wasn't affected by the loss of my mother at such a young age, and in one day Owen had revealed otherwise.

Just a night to compose myself, then I'd jump back into our relationship, I had thought, but that same night I had been so ill I hadn't slept a wink. Since that night, the feelings had been off and on. Not knowing what was wrong, now I spent all the time being distracted with memories of my childhood and the deterioration of my mother while summoning the strength to do what was needed.

Still, how long could I avoid Owen? Even though I hadn't seen him in four days, we spoke every single day. He was the last person I called before I settled into bed at night, waiting for a sleep I knew beforehand would never come. On several occasions, when he'd asked me to come over, I almost said yes. I turned him down gently every time out of the concern of having the nausea and dizziness around him. Then he would know for sure that something was wrong.

I didn't want him to see my weakness.

But, how long could I avoid him? I missed being around my boy. I had fallen harder for him than I had thought, and the separation proved it. It wasn't just the longing to have him spread out beneath me, his ass in the air as I mounted him like the world's most prized stallion, it was being in his presence, enduring his teasing and the ways in which he tested his limits of pushing my buttons just to be punished.

My cell phone beeped, and I popped my eyelids open, willing myself to ignore the text even for a few minutes to prove to myself I still had some semblance of control when it came to Owen. Since meeting him, I had known I wanted him, but now I had him, I was uncertain what to do with him. I had wanted a lover who satisfied me the way I wanted, but I hadn't been necessarily looking for love. It was frightening to care about someone so much, especially when life was uncertain given my suspected condition.

I should let him go. I should ignore his texts and calls until he gets the hint and finds someone else. At least until I confirmed with my doctor what was happening to me.

Instead of taking my own advice, I reached for the phone and stared at the screen. I didn't need to unlock the phone, because the message could be read behind the locked screen.

Owen: Are you coming over tonight?

He had asked that question every day for the past

four days, and I always found an excuse not to go, but tonight I desperately wanted to see him.

Unlocking my phone with my fingerprint, I ignored the text and found my doctor's number. I needed to know what was going on with me so I could guide my relationship accordingly. I needed to know if I was living on borrowed time, or if I was simply being paranoid because of my fear of the debilitating illness that had claimed my mother's life.

"Dr. Reid," the man answered his cell phone. Most patients of his would have gotten his receptionist, but he was always on call for me. I paid a small fortune to maintain that privilege.

Such a pity money couldn't take care of all illnesses. I knew. Charles had tried everything for my mother. Nothing had worked despite all the money he had pumped into her recovery to ensure she had the best of everything. In the end, she had ordered an end to the treatment and returned home for nature to take its course.

"It's Declan Moore," I identified myself although he would have known my number by now. "I'd like to make an appointment to see you."

"Mr. Moore, of course. Let me check on my calendar for you." About a minute passed before he returned. "I'm booked solid for the rest of this week, but I can bump someone to fit you in today or tomorrow. How does that sound?"

"Tomorrow is better," I replied. "Time?"

"At eleven. Is this in relation to the last time we spoke?"

"Somewhat. I'd rather speak in person." I would have some explaining to do to account for why I had left my mother's information blank on my medical history report.

"Okay, got it. I'll see you tomorrow at eleven then."

"Great. See you then."

I hung up the phone and sighed with relief. For too long I had ignored the possibility of what could be a medical problem because I was afraid of no longer being in control. Staying on top of situations was my strength. Even Owen liked that side of me. If this illness, whatever it was, took over and controlled my life, I would no longer be the man I was.

I sent Ridge a text message to alert him of my upcoming medical appointment. I didn't wait to receive a response from him, but rang Owen. He answered on the third ring.

"Declan, hey."

"Hey, Owen, yes," I answered.

"Huh?" he asked.

"You asked if I was coming over tonight," I clarified. "The answer is yes. I'll make us a reservation at a restaurant, and we can have dinner together. Then we can go back to your place. I miss our sex, boy."

"Me too, Daddy," he answered, his voice dropping an octave lower with desire. "I don't want to eat out tonight. Why don't I make you dinner instead?"

"The restaurant would be less hassle."

"It's no hassle cooking for you. Please. My kitchen's closer to the bedroom, plus I can have you watch me cook. In nothing but my apron. I bet Daddy will like that."

Uh yes, this Daddy liked the sound of that very much. "I'll be there at seven," I confirmed.

"Clothing is optional," Owen teased.

I chuckled, feeling more light-hearted than I had been over the past few days. "For you, it is. I'm going to fuck you as soon as you open the door. You know that, right?"

"Trust me, I won't complain." Owen paused, and hummed at the back of his throat before he continued. "I wasn't sure if you were trying to avoid me. I hope I didn't say anything wrong about your mother that day, or that I didn't press too hard."

I closed my eyes and swallowed to get rid of the ache in my chest. I could come clean to him about the things bothering me, but that wasn't the kind of relationship Owen and I had. I took charge, helped him with his problems. I ensured he was happy, that he didn't need anything. That was my duty to him. I had always understood my role in the Daddy/boy dynamic I wanted for myself. In fact, I had chosen this lifestyle because this was exactly how I envisioned my life. Managing somebody else's happiness made me feel more in control than anything else I had ever done.

"It's fine, Owen," I told him. "I'll bring a bottle of wine."

"And lube," he replied. "I'm all out."

I chuckled. "Alright. I'll add lube. Anything else?"

"A rose."

"I'll always bring you a rose, my love." I inhaled

sharply at the last two words, then tried to quickly play it down, hoping he wouldn't take them seriously. It was hardly a declaration of love, but it came pretty damn close. Too close. I wasn't ready yet to tell him I loved him. "I should get back to work," I quickly added. "See you later, Owen."

"Can't wait."

I hung up, my hand enclosed tightly around my phone as I finally let out the long groan I had been holding in. Before I could gather myself, my phone rang. Charles. I stared at the incoming call, debating whether or not to answer it. I had every intention of ignoring the call, but my conscience wouldn't allow me to in case he needed me.

"Hello, Charles. How's your honeymoon going?" I asked, making no attempt to mask my heavy sigh.

"I want a divorce!" he yelled into the phone, and I winced at the way he dragged his words, evidence that he had been drinking.

"What's wrong, Charles?"

"I've been a fool," he hiccupped in my ear. "I was wrong for marrying Poppy. Listen, son, I've been an idiot."

I winced at him calling me son, something he had not done since I was six. "You've been drinking, Charles. You should go to bed and sleep it off," I told him. "Where's Poppy? Let me speak to her."

"I left her at the hotel," he answered. "It's the best damn thing I've done since we arrived in Honolulu. I was so wrong for marrying her, Declan. She's the wrong woman."

"They're always the wrong woman," I muttered sarcastically.

"Exactly. They're all wrong, because they're not your mother."

I would have been willing to listen to his drunken tirade so early in the day if he hadn't brought up my mother. I couldn't bear the thought of him speaking about her, given the life he had lived after her death.

"You need to sleep this off, Charles," I said, knowing him too well. "I promise when you wake up you'll feel much better."

"No, it's different this time. I need you to work on my divorce."

Irritated at him, I glared across the room and imagined staring daggers through him. Figuratively of course. As much as he had been an indifferent father to me, he was still family, and I didn't wish him any harm.

"Guess what, Charles?" I finally said into the phone. "I'm seeing someone right now who needs my attention more than you need me to babysit. Sleep it off. If when you wake up, you remember this conversation and still want a divorce, how about trying to file for one yourself? I'm done cleaning up your messes, Charles. This time you're on your own."

I hung up and turned off my phone for good measure. I had never felt such a calm before as I did in that minute. I had my own problems to deal with. Charles would have to learn how to handle his problems like every other grown man.

The only responsibility I had was to myself and my boy.

30

OWEN

Deep in thought with a silly smile on my face, I startled as arms snaked around my waist and a firm chest pressed to my back. Recognizing those arms, I tilted my head to the side as Declan nuzzled my neck. His sigh of contentment caressed my sensitive skin, and I rocked back into him, trusting him to support my weight even though I was bigger.

I had thought him coming over would have been awkward given he *had* been avoiding me. He didn't want to admit it, but I knew avoidance when it was directed my way. Given the reason though, I had opted to give him space to sort through whatever emotions he might have been experiencing about his mother's memory that I had dredged up.

There had been no need to worry though about things changing between us. Not even one minute after crossing the threshold of my home, Declan had me against the wall. I couldn't blame him either, since it had been a part of my plan. Otherwise, I wouldn't have answered the door wearing nothing but an apron. Then I'd made sure to turn so he got an eyeful of my bare ass.

"You should have woken me, boy," he rebuked me gently, and dragged his teeth down my neck.

"You were clearly exhausted, Daddy" I pointed out, buttering him up. "I didn't think it would hurt to let you sleep after the sex we had."

He released me. "But now I'm starving. What have you cooked me, boy?"

"Food," I answered with a grin, turning to find him dressed in a pair of my dark sweatpants. The waist was bigger, and he hadn't cinched the cords, so they rode low on his hips, showing me the bare line where his underwear would be if he had been wearing any. I glanced away back to the sautéed green beans in the pan, reminding myself that we'd had sex just an hour ago. I could go through dinner without yanking him back to the bedroom.

He snorted, running his fingers through his hair. He was peeved I had let him sleep, but I wasn't sorry in the least. He looked slightly better than when he had arrived, but he still had dark smudges under his eyes that made me conclude he wasn't sleeping well.

"You've developed into a saucy boy," Declan remarked, eyeing my backside. "Hmm, I'm having fun just thinking of new ways to punish you. New ways you won't enjoy so much."

I winked at him. "Looking forward to the challenge." I turned back to the green beans flavored with bacon and turned off the stove. "I think I'm done. Why don't you grab your bottle of wine from the freezer and pour us a drink?"

With my back to him once more, I removed the shepherd's pie from the oven, pleased at the way it had turned out. I shouldn't have been surprised since I had excellent culinary skills, but I had catered all my life to three teens who would eat anything placed before them. Declan was different. He was used to fine dining and chefs who had been to culinary school.

"You've been collecting them."

At Declan's voice, I froze, remembering too late that I shouldn't have sent him into the freezer. My cheeks burned in embarrassment, and I kept my head averted. I didn't need to peek to know what he was talking about. After returning home from Columbus to find the roses he had given me dead, I had made a conscious effort afterward to preserve every petal by following the instructions I had found about freezing them.

"They're just flowers," I said, shrugging as I placed the pie onto the counter and removed the mittens.

Before I could move, Declan had me by the chin and we were face to face. I couldn't avoid the knowing look in his eyes, and words stuck in my throat. I didn't want to be the first person to say it. I needed time to be certain, although I was convinced my feelings for Declan wouldn't change any time soon.

I loved him.

"If they were just flowers, you wouldn't mind watching them die," he murmured, spreading his hand about my cheek, stroking my stubble.

"I-I couldn't," I answered, frowning. "I didn't expect

it to mean so much when we came back from Columbus and I found they had wilted. I didn't want to watch them die and have to throw them out all the time."

"Me giving you the roses means that much to you?"

"More than you can imagine. That was the first act that defined our relationship. Me not *having* to be the giver for a change. You gave me something no one else has ever done before."

His lips ghosted mine before he let me go and dug his semi against my thigh. "In this instance, I don't mind being the giver at all."

I chuckled and swatted at his hip while I moved away from him. "Don't start that. We're about to eat."

He sighed. "I should show you who's in charge, but I'm hungry, so remind me later to put you in the corner."

I gasped. "The corner! Will I get anything to play with while I'm there?"

"Dinner first, boy. Feed me then you get to enjoy your punishment."

I grinned as I moved us to the dining room for dinner. We sat opposite each other at the small table still crammed with four chairs. In the beginning, there had been two when Jenna and I just started out. We had ended up with five, and after waiting the first year for Jenna to return in vain, I had eventually removed hers so the kids didn't always have to see the empty chair when I made us eat together as a family.

"I suppose you have a lot of practice cooking," Declan remarked, grunting in satisfaction at the green beans and bacon mix.

"You wouldn't be wrong." I made a face and shuddered. "Maybe I made things tough on myself for not taking the easy way out for parenting. I didn't want my kids to grow up on fast food, so even when we didn't get to eat together as a family, there was always a home-cooked meal waiting when they got home from school or wherever. I also insisted on family dinner at least twice per week."

He nodded in approval. "You sacrificed a lot of yourself for your kids, didn't you?"

I shrugged. "They kept me sane after James left. I wouldn't have done parenting any differently."

"How are things going with them now?"

"Better," I admitted. "Still sucks to feel like they betrayed me, but I'm beginning to understand their reason for doing what they did wasn't selfish. They had good intentions, so I can't hold it against them."

"Has Summer finally met him?"

"No. James has invited us all to his home, though, for July the fourth. Summer says she might show up, and James wants me to convince her, but I refuse to try to influence her. She's old enough to make her own decisions, and she'll meet her other dad when she's good and ready."

"I assume you're going?"

I glanced up at him, wondering if that was jealousy I heard in his tone. "Uh yeah. The last time we all met together didn't exactly go well. I'm hoping this time things will be better."

"Like a reunion? Think your sons have hopes of you two getting back together?"

I dropped my fork to the plate. "I don't think so. They're old enough not to harbor such foolish hopes."

"And if all three want that to happen, can't they persuade you to give the relationship another shot?"

"What? Declan, that's not going to happen."

"How can you be so certain?"

Because I love you. I tried to speak the words, but they refused to come out. The last person I had told I loved them had shattered my heart and left me to pick up the pieces.

"Because I don't love him anymore," I answered instead. "It's as simple as that."

"Is it though, Owen?" Declan persisted. "Let's be reasonable here. You're a man who lived your life before out of a sense of duty. You do things because it makes other people happy, and not necessarily what you really want. What's to stop you this time from caving in to create the perfect family image for your children's sake?"

Maybe he was right. My family meant the world to me, and I would do anything for them. I would have probably considered James's request for a relationship too, but not now that I had met and fallen in love with Declan. Not now that I understood this was my time to be a little bit selfish in being with whom I wanted. I had devoted twenty-three years of my life to raising my children, ignored my needs and put them first in everything. They were now adults, and surely they couldn't begrudge me being happy?

"I was hoping you would come along," I announced, pleased when his eyes widened.

"You were?"

"Yes. I'd like them to meet you. Unless you have objections?"

"We don't want to push too much at your children at once," he replied, reaching across the table to squeeze my hand. "Especially if your daughter goes that day to meet her moth-other father for the first time. It might be too much for her to deal with all at once."

He made a good argument, but disappointment bloomed where nervous excitement had perched only moments before. "I don't want to hide us from them anymore. It almost feels like them hiding James from me."

"I'll think about it."

I opened my mouth to argue about what he had to think about, but his eyes narrowed, and I swallowed the words. I wanted to push, ask the real reason he was against meeting my kids. Perhaps he'd have to face the reality of how much older than him I was.

Frustrated, I stabbed my fork into the shepherd's pie.

31

DECLAN

"*Mama, mama wake up, please. I brought you a rose. Wake up.*"

With a gulp like I was drowning, my eyes flew open, seeking out the darkness, trying to figure out where I was. Before my brain could register anything, I doubled over at the sharp pain in my stomach which blurred my vision in the dark. Beside me, someone stirred in bed. *Owen.*

Fuck, not now.

I had felt this kind of pain too often not to know what it meant. The burning sensation in my chest felt like something was eating through the cavities. My stomach roiled and dipped. If I didn't get to the bathroom soon, I would throw up all over Owen's bed sheets that we had changed just before we tumbled into them after dinner.

I moaned, managing to rise to my knees before another roil of nausea passed through me. My mouth was bitter as I swallowed back the bile. My mouth filled with fluid I forced back down. I needed to get to the bathroom ASAP.

"Dec?"

I clamped my eyes closed tighter, trying to uncoil my frame at Owen's sleepy voice beside me.

"Go back to sleep." I tried to use my stern Daddy voice which failed me since the words came out more of a pathetic whimper that made me feel so incredibly ashamed.

I felt Owen moving around, and I managed to sit at the edge of the bed by the time he had the bedside lamp on. I spotted his sweatpants on the floor and snagged them, forcing myself to stand. I swayed a little before I could even lift one leg to insert into the hole.

"Dec, what's wrong?" Owen asked, rushing to my side.

I loathed asking him for help, but I was naked which made me feel even more vulnerable.

"Help me get these on," I answered. "The room's spinning."

"But you didn't even drink that much," Owen protested as he helped me pull on the pants.

I kissed his bent head as a means of saying thanks. "Go back to bed, Owen," I said, my tone stronger, more forceful, the way it should be.

"I'm not going back to bed. You're obviously not fine."

"I'll keep you in the corner for hours if you don't do what I say," I threatened weakly.

"I don't care. Just tell me what's wrong and how I can help."

A rush of bile filled my throat again. "Bathroom," I croaked, because it was better to be helped there than falling flat on my face.

"'Kay. Come on."

An arm around my waist, we were able to get to the bathroom fairly quickly. Once inside, I paused and pushed at his hand. "You can go now."

"I'm not leaving you," Owen argued.

Summoning all the energy I had left, I turned to glare at him and pointed at the door. "If you don't get the hell out of here, Owen, so help me god!"

"B-but Declan p-please, let me help you."

"Now, Owen!" I snapped.

Reluctantly he stepped away, and I slammed the door shut, barely making it over to the bowl before my guts erupted. The metallic taste of blood filled my tongue before it gushed out. Alarmed, because I'd never vomited blood before, I closed my eyes at the sight and continued to retch. My stomach heaved and dipped as I tried not to choke but concentrated on breathing through it all.

I lost track of how long I remained in the bathroom. Moaning pitifully, I slumped against the toilet, my flushed forehead pressed to the coolness of the tank. At one point, I regained consciousness after blacking out, and I had no idea for how long. With a groan, I struggled to my feet and hauled myself over to the vanity to rinse my mouth. Staring into the mirror, I saw my pale face and the damp hair clinging to my forehead.

I tried to drown out the sound of Owen outside pacing. I had been quite aware of him on the other side of the door listening to everything happening inside the bathroom. There was no fooling him after this that everything was alright. There was no fooling myself either that everything was fine with me.

Owen's fist slammed into the door. "Dammit, Dec, I'm calling for an ambulance!"

I left the sink running and pulled the bathroom door open. "You're forgetting your place, aren't you?"

Owen faced off with me, and my heart reached out to him. His eyes were full of worry. His hair was sticking all over his head where he must have been running his fingers through the short locks.

"Are you okay?" he asked before he frowned. "Of course you're not okay."

"Must have been the food," I lied.

"That was not the food! Don't lie to me, Declan! Please."

He knew I hated it when he shouted. I took it personally, and I couldn't leave it unchecked, or it would break down our dynamic.

"Bring me my phone," I instructed him. "It's on the nightstand."

"Will you call the ambulance?" he asked, clutching the edge of the door as though afraid I would shut it in his face again.

"Just bring the phone, Owen."

He sighed, but left, and I allowed my body to sag while using the door to hold me up. The pain in my stomach was still there, and if it was anything like a few nights ago, it would continue throughout most of the night. I couldn't stay here like this. Owen had already seen more than I had wanted him to.

He returned with my phone and held it out to me. I took the phone from him gratefully. "Now go stand in the corner of your bedroom."

His face fell. "What? Declan, no."

"Are you disobeying me?"

"No. I-I'm worried about you. Don't push me away if I can help you."

"The only help you can give me right now, Owen, is the satisfaction of knowing you're standing in a corner just as I have instructed you."

Sweat broke out on my forehead as my stomach churned once more. Damn.

"Will you call me if you need me?" Owen whispered.

"I'll call you if I need you," I answered, softening at the accusatory look he aimed at me.

With a nod, he turned and dragged his feet as he walked away. I closed the door and rested my head on the cool surface, waiting until the nausea passed. I stabbed my finger at the button to dial Silas who answered on the fourth ring despite it being the middle of the night.

"Yes, boss?"

"I need a pick up," I answered, a shudder running through my spine. "I'm at Owen's. Honk the horn twice when you get here, and I'll come out."

"Uh, sure. Just let me get some clothes on, and I'll be there in ten."

I hung up and managed a few deep breaths before having to hang out over the toilet again. The blood alarmed me more than anything. It brought back flashes of memory of my mother coughing and watching the splatters of blood hit her hand or the bed covers.

I must have dozed where I sat on the bathroom floor, because I was startled awake by the blast of a car horn twice. I climbed to my feet, taking a deep breath. The pain in my chest and gut had reduced to an ache but hadn't disappeared.

Upon entering the bedroom, I found Owen exactly where I had sent him. He was standing in the corner, head bent, shoulders slumped. I had been cruel to send him away, but it was for his own good. He hadn't signed up for this. Owen had already been saddled down with responsibilities all his life. He had taken care of three kids. I couldn't expect him to be saddled down with another responsibility because of whatever illness I had.

His shoulders stiffened when he heard me come in. For now, I changed out of his sweatpants and into the clothes I had been dressed in when I arrived here. Once clothed, I walked over to him and placed a hand on his waist. His body was rigid, but he said nothing. I sighed and placed my head in the center of his back, wishing I could unload and let him understand, but the minute I explained, he would be adamant to see to his duty, because he loved me. He hadn't said it, but it showed. Because I loved him in return, I would not do this to him and saddle him with further responsibilities when he was now just free to live his life.

I kissed the back of his neck. "This is for your own good, Owen," I said softly. "You don't deserve to be in the corner, but I had to put you there."

"Why?" the word came out emotionless, defeated.

"Because you would have interfered," I replied. "I'm going. I'll call you when I'm ready. I won't answer your calls, so please don't."

He dragged in a deep breath which caught on a sob. "I don't understand why you won't let me take care of you when it's obvious you need help. Don't you know how much I love you?"

His confession shouldn't have felt so good, especially since I'd already figured out how much he cared.

"I love you too," I confessed. "Now I need you to trust Daddy to take care of things. Okay?"

He sighed as I stepped away from him. "Declan?"

"Hmm?"

"You know I won't think of you any less if you show me your weakness, right? That you'll always be Daddy regardless. We all have our own demons to fight."

I froze, not expecting that question, but he had hit a nerve. I *was* afraid showing him my uncertainty and exposing him to my fears would change the face of our relationship. How could he see me as the man in control, with his shit together, if I couldn't even work up the courage to seek medical attention?

"You can leave the corner in the next ten minutes," I told him, backing away and toward the door. "Silas is waiting for me."

"Declan, please, don't leave me like this."

My steps halted at the door as I turned to look at him. He had his forehead rested against the wall, shoulders slumped once more, waiting for me to give him permission to leave his corner. I couldn't. If I allowed him to leave while I was still here, I didn't trust myself not to spill everything to him. I didn't trust myself not to stay.

Without a word to him, I left my boy standing in the corner of his room, heart likely breaking as mine was, but I didn't have a choice. Sometimes, Daddy had to do what was best even if it meant his boy would turn around and hate him for it.

There was no way I was going to saddle Owen down with another person to care for. I had watched Charles grow bitter and angry at the world while caring for my mother, watching her suffering and not being able to do anything about it. I couldn't control whatever illness I had that was causing all these symptoms. I couldn't control how long I lived, but if there was one thing I could control, it was keeping Owen at a distance so he didn't have to suffer through this.

Respecting my mood, Silas was quiet on the drive back home. By the time we arrived, I was soaked in sweat and near the brink of passing out again. Or maybe I did. The last thing I remembered were the faces of my mother and Owen swimming before my eyes.

32

OWEN

"Take my bags inside."

My hackles rose at the command carelessly thrown at me by one of the wealthiest businessmen in Cincinnati. Apparently, he was too busy staring down the front of his companion's blouse to realize he was talking to another human being and not playing fetch with his dog.

"Excuse me?" Normally I would paste a fake smile on my face and do as I was told, but I was still too wounded by Declan's treatment last night that I didn't have it in me to fake anything at the moment.

The man dragged his eyes away from his companion to glare at me. "The instructions are simple enough," he snapped, looking down his nose at me. "Take the bags inside."

Without a word, I strolled around to the trunk of the car, but overheard him talking to his female companion.

"I swear it would be better if we didn't have to deal with imbeciles all the time."

That was the last straw. To hell with it all. I didn't care if all my anger wasn't exactly as a result of him. I had been keeping everything bottled up inside overnight, trying to pretend that I wasn't heartbroken. His comment was the straw that broke this camel's back.

I grabbed the two bags from the trunk of the car and threw them at his feet. He jumped out of the way to avoid one bag landing on his foot.

"What the hell!" he cried.

"It wouldn't kill you to say 'please' next time," I growled at him, pacing over to the driver's side of the car. "But if it's too much, then do us imbeciles a huge favor by carrying your bags yourself!"

Without another glance, I got into the car and buckled my seatbelt.

"You'll be fired for this!"

I shook my head at his audacity and stepped on the gas. I doubted he would want to call the office and complain, drawing attention to the fact that he was sneaking off with a woman who was clearly not his wife. That was the only reason he had for hiring out a chauffeur instead of using his regular driver. These wealthy types always had their own personal chauffeur. I had driven too many unfaithful husbands around to not know one when I saw one under my nose.

I took the long way back to the depot, giving myself some time to cool off. I should have taken the day off. I hadn't slept well last night after Declan had left. Caught in a limbo of fearing something was wrong with him and being angry at him, I had tossed and turned all night. I would have called in sick except that I had used so many days already, and Trevor was no fool. He had to have known there was more to it than Declan hiring me during the time we had spent in Brazil. He hadn't said anything today, but I had seen the way he looked at me when he thought I wasn't watching.

Back at the depot, I was no closer to feeling better about last night, or this afternoon's debacle of being upset at a paying customer. I had dealt with my fair share of wealthy douches in the past, and it had never bothered me before. I had taken this afternoon's incident way too personally, but I was sick and tired of these rich minority taking the rest of us for granted.

I was tired of Declan not treating me like he could trust me. I thought we had been building a future together. I was so stupid to believe he had come to care for me in the way I cared for him. If he did, he would have talked to me, shared whatever had happened to him last night, instead of shutting me out.

I couldn't help wondering if it was my fault. Maybe he thought I wasn't his equal because I had submitted so easily to him… because I was his boy. Used to be his boy. I wasn't his anything anymore, and he wasn't my anything either.

If Declan couldn't trust me, we had nothing.

"Owen, my office," Trevor announced as soon as I entered the depot. It was as though he had been waiting specially for me. From the look on his face, unsmiling, I knew he wasn't inviting me into his office to give me a pat on the back. I had screwed up today.

Without a word, I returned the key for the car I had driven today, then followed him to his office. He was already seated behind a cluttered desk, not minding the mess. It was his natural state, and it would take him but a minute to find anything he wanted.

"What's up, Trevor?" I asked.

He waved to the seat across from him. "Have a seat, and I should be asking you that question."

With a groan, I took the offer. "So I guess he really did call you?"

"I was willing to give you the benefit of the doubt that you'd never throw his suitcases at him," Trevor said on a frown. "That was the CEO of Nobles Co, Owen. What the hell were you thinking?"

"I was sick of being treated subhuman," I muttered, staring down at my knees.

"Jesus, Owen, you're in a customer service field. You're trained for this kind of thing. You've been doing it for over ten years. You have enough self-control not to let it get to you. At least you had. So, just what the hell is going on with you?"

I rubbed at my forehead. "I've had a rough night."

Silence ensued between us, and I dared to peek at him. He was staring at me, assessing me, like he was trying to find a way to ask me what was on his mind.

"What happened when you were away with Moore?"

I swallowed hard at his question. "Wh-what do you mean?"

"Don't bullshit me, Owen. That was no normal request of his to have you be his chauffeur for the days you were gone. Plus, the man has a personal driver. The only reason he had requested our service the first night was because of the fleet he needed."

I flushed under his knowing gaze, not certain what to say. "It doesn't matter," I ended lamely, unable to hold his gaze.

"Jesus, Owen. What the hell are you thinking getting involved with a client? Especially a man of Moore's caliber. They eat people for breakfast and spit them out by noon to move on to the next victim."

I groaned and covered my face with my hands, wishing I had heard this before I got involved with Declan. Who was I kidding? Declan had been forbidden fruit, and there had been no way I was going to walk away from that. I should have nipped it in the bud after we got back from Columbus, chalked it down to experience and moved on.

"I didn't mean for it to happen."

"I expected this from any of the other drivers, but you've always had your head screwed on properly, Owen. Why would you do this?"

Like I can control falling in love with someone. If I could, I wouldn't have fallen for Declan. He was good for a romp, but not to fall in love with. We were too different.

"It's over," I told him, forcing the words past my lips. "You don't have to worry about this."

Trevor's loud sigh filled the office. "Look, the only reason I'm not sacking you right now, is because I know you have a lot going on with Summer leaving and all. You went too far today, Owen, and I'm docking your pay as a result. Now go home, take the day off and sleep off whatever's going on with you, but when you get here tomorrow, you better have your shit together."

I didn't make a fuss or complaint. I deserved everything he threw at me and so much more. I hated having to be chided by my boss. It had happened to several of my co-workers before, but never me. I was aware of my position in life. I took my responsibilities seriously, and I never strayed from what I had to do. Since I had met Declan, I'd let him blindside me at every turn, becoming obsessed with him and the way he made me come alive. I got reckless and careless, shirking my duties.

When I arrived home, I found a bouquet of red roses on the porch. I left them there, ignoring the gesture. I didn't want roses. I wanted Declan to be straightforward with me about what was going on with him. Until I had that, we had nothing.

My house was a constant reminder of him, which did nothing to improve my mood. I took to cleaning everything to get his expensive scent out of my home. I changed the bed sheets, holding onto my anger so I didn't burst into tears thinking about how we'd bonded on my bed. If I could, I would have thrown out the mattress. I almost did, but concluded that would be admitting he had too much of a strong hold on me.

I was heating up leftovers from the dinner I had made last night when I heard the doorbell ring. Despite everything, my heart skipped a beat, and I had to fight the urge to run to the door to confront him. It had to be Declan, coming around to ask my forgiveness. I was adamant this time wouldn't be like what had happened in his rose garden. I wasn't going to pretend everything was fine.

I waited for the doorbell to ring a few times before I headed for the door, wiping my sweaty palms into the material of my shorts. I took a deep breath before pulling the door open.

"James?" I stared at my ex in a mixture of confusion and disappointment. I glanced over his shoulder as though expecting Declan to pop up from behind him and yell, "surprise."

"Uh, hey."

I focused on him and not the heaviness in my gut. "This is a surprise. What are you doing here?"

"I was in the neighborhood," he answered, with a shrug and a smile. "I thought I'd check out what the old place looked like."

I frowned at him. "And you never thought you could have done this years ago? Maybe pop in and let us know you were alright?"

His eyes widened at my sharp tone, and he stepped back from me. "I-I'm sorry for intruding. I-I had the wrong impression. I thought we had bypassed that. I should go."

"James!" I called to him before he could act. "Don't go. I'm sorry. I can't say that we have bypassed all that, but my anger isn't directed at you. It's just a stressful time right now. You can come in if you want. I was just preparing something to eat. Join me?"

James raised his eyes and smiled at me. "Thanks, that would be great."

I had a moment's pause when I saw the gleam flickering in his eyes. A light tremor ran through me, and I flushed because I knew that look all too well. I remembered him stating his interest in me and me turning him down. At the time, with Declan's kiss still fresh in my mind, there was no way I could have given much thought to his proposal.

I should send him away now to avoid him mistaking my generosity for anything else. My heart hurt. For some reason, seeing him standing there made me want to cry even more.

"Owen, are you okay?" James asked, finally picking up on my mood.

"Yes, I'm fine." Tears swam before my eyes, and his image blurred. I cleared my throat, fighting a losing battle.

"Oh, Owen, you're not fine," he remarked, placing a hand on my shoulder. "It might have been years, but I can still read you like a book. I'm still your friend if you want me to be."

I stared at James, and despite the changes he had been through, I could see the girl I had befriended and the woman I had fallen in love with. I saw the concern in his eyes. He still cared. Of course his presence didn't exonerate him from all the wrongs he had done in abandoning us, but I couldn't hold on to my anger at him anymore. I was too upset about Declan and needed someone who could give a listening ear.

Closing my eyes, I allowed my shoulders to slump and the tears to flow as he embraced me.

33

OWEN

Tears trickled down the sides of my face, into the hair at my temples, bringing back memories of Declan running his fingers through the gray hair. At first I had been self-conscious when he started doing it, but gradually I became fond of his attention and the way he loved the little signs of age difference between us.

I barely noticed how long I lay in bed staring up at the ceiling. I didn't have work until later that evening which was all the encouragement I needed to stay in bed and wallow in self-pity. I could see myself as though from afar, pining after Declan and knowing how stupid I was for giving him another thought, but I couldn't help it.

Last night before going to bed, I had tried ringing his phone even though he had advised me not to call him. The phone had rung without answer, and I didn't try to ring him again. I couldn't even be fully mad at him because I was also too busy worrying about what had taken place the last time he had been here in my home.

Frustrated, and no closer to finding out what was going on, I pushed the bed sheets off my frame and unfolded my limbs out of bed. Had Declan been here last night, I would have more than likely been throbbing in interesting places. This morning, I was empty, unused, untouched. I had been used to this state before Declan, but now that I was used to him in my bed, I didn't want to go back to the way things were before we met.

I didn't expect my mood to brighten without at least a cup of coffee, so I shuffled across the room to the door. Once I was outside my bedroom, I sniffed the air. Coffee and bacon. My stomach grumbled, but then went queasy.

I had quite forgotten that James had slept over last night. Embarrassed that my ex had witnessed me breaking down, which I hadn't even done when *he* had walked out on me, I lingered outside my bedroom.

James had seen the entire waterworks last night. I had barely started to cry when he had wrapped his arms around me and pulled me into a comforting embrace. He had allowed me to cry on his shoulder before we had entered the house. He hadn't pried about the reason for my tears, and I hadn't volunteered a response. We had ended up throwing out the leftovers, and James had cooked for us. We had eaten dinner together, mostly in awkward silence as he glanced around the house, noting the changes.

At some point we had moved on to the couch where we had enjoyed a few cans of beer. It was at that point I had asked James to stay over for the night, then he could go back this morning. He had slept in Summer's room. Now thinking about it, I cringed, hoping Summer wouldn't mind.

Shoulders squared to face whatever would greet me, I descended the stairs and took the turn into the kitchen and found James at the stove. He was wearing one of my oversized T-shirts he must have snagged from my laundry which still needed folding and putting away. The shirt ended above his knees. He was hairier than before and he had to have been lifting weights, because he was well filled out. His arms rippled with muscles.

He was an attractive man.

James turned and smiled when he saw me. "Hey, how are you? Did you sleep any at all? I was just about to wake you."

"Hey, yourself," I greeted him awkwardly as I took a seat around the table in the kitchen. "I slept fine."

"Liar, liar, pants on fire," he chanted, and I grinned, remembering when we were younger and I would always say that to him—her at the time.

"It's so nice to see you smile," James noted. "You've aged really well, Owen."

"So have you," I answered, then cleared my throat. "Uh, so, you umm got rid of your breasts. Was that hard to do?"

"You know, it's really insensitive to comment on things like that," he stated.

My eyes widened at the possibility of offending him which I hadn't meant. "I'm so sorry. Forgive me. I wasn't thinking."

He smiled at me. "You didn't know, but now you do. Why don't you talk to me about what's wrong instead? And I may talk about the little of my journey that I'm comfortable revealing."

It was on the tip of my tongue to let him know he would be the last person I would talk to, but he *was* basically that anyway. I didn't have any other friend I could discuss my life with. Keeping everything in was killing me.

"Fine," I agreed.

He dished out scrambled eggs and bacon with toast and coffee. As he settled down at the table before me, I couldn't stop thinking about when we had first started living together. This table was one of the first pieces of furniture we had bought for the apartment we had first lived in before the twins were even conceived. We'd sat at this table and eaten way before we had a dining room with its own table and chairs.

"It's like the more experienced we become with life, the more complicated it gets," I murmured, playing around with the eggs on my fork. James had remembered how I preferred my eggs done, scrambled with sweet pepper, green onions and sprinkled with cheese. That was really sweet of him.

"I think of life in terms of levels," James remarked. "And the more levels we climb, the harder it gets."

I stared wide-eyed at him. "You mean it's going to get harder?"

He laughed, the attractive sound surrounding me in familiarity. The more time we spent together, the more the years rolled away. "Yes." The laughter died down, and he sobered. "The people we have in our lives make it bearable."

That I believed. Declan had made life more than tolerable for me. Now what was I supposed to do without him?

"Was it very hard for you?" I asked. "I mean, I would have been there for you, if I'd known. You know that, right?"

"Now, I do," he answered, a faraway look in his eyes as he reminisced. "I admit at times I even wondered if I made the right decision, but then I realized that for what it was. The fear that people who knew me before would look at me differently. I am happier to let the real me out into the world."

"You look damn good," I told him, nodding my head in appreciation.

His beard wasn't enough to hide his blush. "Thanks. It's not so bad picking up chicks. And guys."

I wanted to pry a little and ask him how the transformation had changed his sex life, if any at all, but decided that it wasn't any of my business. He was right. These things were personal and had absolutely nothing to do with me or how I felt about him.

"You seem happy. I didn't understand before, but I'm beginning to get it."

His smile wobbled. "Sometimes I do wonder if the sacrifice was worth losing you and my kids, but if I hadn't left, Owen…"

He choked up with tears, and I reached across the table to place a hand over his and squeezed.

"It's okay. I think we did good without you."

"But you shouldn't have had to do it alone." He got up abruptly from the chair and walked over to the sink, his back to me and his head bowed. I put down my fork and moved toward him. I placed my hands on his shoulders as he breathed hard.

"James." I squeezed his shoulders. "We did alright. The boys forgave you."

He turned to face me, and I dropped my hands but didn't move.

"And Summer?"

"Give it some time. She was hurt the most I think, but she will come around. I'm sure of it. She's really a lovely girl."

His eyes brimmed with tears. "I know. You did a good job, Owen. Thank you for picking up my slack."

"Always."

He inhaled deeply. "What about you? Do you forgive me?"

I took my time in answering his question, wanting to be as honest as possible. I discovered I wasn't angry with James any more. A part of me was still disappointed that he hadn't trusted me enough to share his deepest thoughts and secrets, but I couldn't fault him when he hadn't been certain himself. If he hadn't left, we would have been miserable. We probably would have ended up resenting each other anyway. That would have been a worse environment for the kids to be raised in.

"Yes," I replied. "I forgive you."

His eyes lit up, and before I knew it, he had an arm on my shoulder and the other pulling my head down to his. My first thought was that his kiss was different. His beard tickled my skin as the warmth of his mouth settled on mine. It wasn't necessarily an unpleasant kiss, and I would have enjoyed it if I didn't remember Declan. The bastard. As much as I hated his guts and worried about him, kissing James didn't feel right.

I pulled away and took a step back. James's cheeks were flushed with desire.

"We can't do that," I told him, my chest heaving. "I'm sorry, I can't."

At the quizzical look he gave me, I blurted out everything about Declan. I even went so far as to tell him about the kind of relationship I had with him. When I finished, I took in a deep breath. James stared at me, his jaw slack.

"I had no idea you were seeing someone," he muttered. "I'm so sorry. I wouldn't have done that."

"It's okay. Now that you know…"

"Do the boys know?" he asked, still staring at me and shaking his head in bewilderment.

I lowered my eyes. "No, I haven't told them yet. I-I didn't know if it would get anywhere. I had planned to take him to your place for July the fourth, but now that's not going to happen."

"Are you in love with him?"

"Yes." I sighed, and returned to the kitchen chair to sit.

He gave a shaky laugh. "My god, I made a big mistake coming here, didn't I?"

I frowned at him. "What do you mean? Did you come here thinking that…" I trailed off as the color in his face was a telltale sign that I was right.

James made for the exit. "I'm sorry. I've been here long enough. I should get dressed and go." He paused by my chair and leaned forward to kiss the top of my head. "You're a good man, Owen. I hope your guy knows it and doesn't make the same mistake that I did."

I should stop him from leaving. I should forget all about Declan and pick up where I left off with James. We have history together. We have kids together.

But I couldn't. Not if there was even the slightest chance that Declan still wanted me.

34

DECLAN

"That's it, Declan! I'm not going to sit by and watch you commit suicide!"

I grimaced as soup plopped back into the bowl and splashed onto the back of my hand. As Ridge stormed into his guestroom, I carefully placed the tray with the half-eaten soup onto the table by the bed.

I had sensed Ridge wanted to say something to me earlier when he had brought me my first meal of the day. He had left without saying much, however, so now that he was back, I could only conclude that he had bolstered his courage to face me.

Two nights ago when I had passed out in the back of the car, Silas had freaked out. I had come around to find him driving me to the hospital. I had insisted on him taking me to Ridge's home instead. It was the first time we had disagreed since he started working for me, and he had only complied after I had threatened to fire him. His reluctance had been evident, but he had given in to my wishes.

"Your concern is touching," I said, sinking back into the pillows at my back. "But this is none of your business."

Ridge paused at the foot of my bed and planted his hands on his hips. "You're lying in my bed awaiting death, instead of getting medical attention!" he snapped. "That *is* my business, Declan Moore."

"I didn't come here for you to try to control this situation, Ridge," I told him. There was nothing I hated more than not feeling in control.

"Then why did you come here, Declan? For me to watch you die? Is that what you want? You'll spare Owen from witnessing that, but you can't spare me as well?"

I stared at Ridge in surprise. I never thought of how my presence here could be construed as a nightmare for him. He was right that I wanted to spare Owen having to witness how weak I had become. The vomiting hadn't stopped, and the blood was getting worse. Maybe death would come quicker than I had anticipated.

I didn't fear death. I had confronted it and stared it in the face when I was only six and lost my mother. I only had regret that I didn't have time to get to know more about Owen and to love him a little longer. I didn't want to let go just yet. If I had the option of giving away every dollar I had in exchange for more time with him, I would have done so without hesitation, but I was aware that some things could not even be helped with money.

Seeing the anguish in Ridge's eyes, I felt guilty for bringing this to his doorstep. I peeled back the comforter and shuffled to the edge of the bed, ignoring the gnawing in my gut. The pain had never really left me since that night I had taken sick at Owen's. At times, it reduced to a dull ache. Sometimes though, it intensified to the extent where it knocked me out.

"What do you think you're doing?" Ridge asked, his voice rising as he rushed over to my side and pushed me back onto the bed.

"I'm getting out of your hair," I answered, making an effort to sit up again, but he wouldn't let me. I glared at him, and he stopped.

"Did I say I wanted you out of my hair?"

"You implied it, and I can take a hint."

"That's not what I meant and you know it," he said softly, his shoulders slumped as if in defeat. His eyes welled up with tears, and I glanced away.

"Don't waste your tears on me," I told him.

"I swear when you get through this I'll punch you in the nuts for doing this to me," he said on a sniff. "And I'll offer Owen to do it too. You should call him and tell him. He cares about you."

"I know he does, which is exactly the reason I can't. He will insist I see the doctor."

Ridge sat at the edge of the bed. "And that's what you should do." He plucked at the bed sheets and lowered his eyes. "I called your doctor, Declan."

I stiffened. "You did what? Who gave you that right?"

"Fuck that," he replied, and I didn't care if I was his Daddy or not. My hand itched to have him doubled over, to spank him hard enough to make him cry. I had told him when Silas dropped me off at his house that I didn't want him to interfere. This was my battle. I didn't want to get anyone caught up in it. I didn't want anyone getting hurt like the string of broken hearts my mother had left behind. Hearts that never truly healed.

"I care about you," Ridge remarked. "Owen cares about you, and yes, even Charles cares about you. Why should you always take care of those around you and not expect us to do the same to you?"

"You have no idea what it was like to watch my mother die, Ridge."

He moved forward and placed his head on my chest. "I know, but it might not even be cancer. It could be something else, Declan. Have you thought about that? Plus, even if it is cancer, people have fought that fucking disease before, and how will you know if you don't try?"

I rubbed at his shoulder in comfort, allowing him this closeness for now, because he sounded so devastated. I felt a twinge of guilt that I was letting him comfort me somewhat, while I had shunned Owen's offer. At that thought, I pushed at his shoulder, and with a sigh, he got off.

"Even now, you're thinking about him," Ridge announced. "That says everything. He deserves not to have you hide this from him, and I deserve not to lose my best friend over this."

I didn't respond to Ridge, but internalized my desires. I wanted to talk to Owen about what was going on with me. I wanted him by my side. I wanted to tell him in vivid detail about how I had watched my mother waste away. Maybe then, he would be more inclined to understand my dilemma.

I had already seen it all. All the tests that would come. All the treatments they would recommend. Everything working and seeming fine before it got worse. Eventually, the result would be the same. Death, and not even in a dignified manner. I would rather Owen remember me as the man who had walked out on him than a helpless, bedridden shell of a man not strong enough to wipe his own ass.

"Ridge."

"Yes?" he asked, eyes full of hope. "What do you want? Me to call Owen? Get you to the hospital? Call your doctor?"

"No, I want you to call my lawyer."

He frowned at me. "You're sick. You need a doctor. Why would you…" He trailed off, the blood draining from his face.

"I need to adjust my will," I answered gently, because of how terrified he looked. "Owen… I need to know he'll be able to go to all those places I promised him I would take him. That he'll be able to explore life and enjoy it while it lasts."

Ridge's Adam's apple bobbed in his throat. "You can't be serious."

"I've never been more serious."

"No!" he shouted, backing away from me. "You're not going to give up, you stubborn ass! You're going to pick up the damn phone and call Owen. You're going to-to… you're going to call your doctor and make that appointment you canceled. Do you honestly think all that's going to matter to Owen after you're g-g-gone? You don't think he'd rather know you were here with him than dead, because you won't even fight for what you have together?"

"Ridge!"

But he was done listening. He stormed out of the house and slammed the door shut. I got out of bed to go after him, but the urge to hurl weighed heavy in my gut. With a curse, I headed for the bathroom instead, dreading the murky red that sealed my fate.

Is it so wrong to want to protect Owen from this?

35

OWEN

Anger surged inside me a couple days after Declan walked out on me, and I drove home after work to find his driver lounging in my driveway. Behind my anger at the way I had foolishly remained in the corner until ten minutes had passed, I couldn't help being relieved that he was here. I had worried over the last forty-eight hours, not knowing what was happening to him. I had tried calling him, but true to his word, he didn't answer.

Now that he was sitting in the car parked before my house, I was ready to give him the fight of my life. There was no way I was getting back in a relationship with him until he understood that I drew the line at him keeping things from me. I drew the line at him ordering me to stay in a corner when he was sick. I hadn't been able to sleep that night as I kept hearing the awful sounds of him throwing up in the bathroom.

He needed to trust me enough to let his guard down

around me. The realization that he didn't trust me enough was the hardest pill to swallow. I had given myself completely to him, opening up about my life while he kept his secrets guarded to his chest like a nun guarded her virginity.

I inched my car by his to park in front of the garage. I came out of the vehicle as the driver's door opened and Silas alighted the vehicle. I barely glanced past Silas as I checked the interior of the car, frowning when I saw no movement to indicate another life was in the vehicle.

"Silas, where is he?" I asked, alarm running through me when I noted he had come alone and without a rose. On the rare occasions he had dropped by when Declan was too busy to come, he always had roses. Now their absence bothered me. Scared me. Declan hadn't been in the best of conditions when he had left me in the corner. I shouldn't have let him talk me out of calling an ambulance.

"I'll take you to him," the somber driver answered.

The Silas I knew was always smiling. He was a pleasant driver who talked about his family when we were alone. He didn't usually have that worried look in his eyes. I was too frightened to move. Too afraid of the news he had carried.

"Wait." I placed a hand about his arm to halt him before he could move back to his car. He turned to face me, and he could barely meet my eyes. "Is he okay?" I enquired, breathing hard. "Did he send you?"

"He's okay," Silas answered, and when I let out a long sigh, he added. "For now."

I groaned. "Help me out here, Silas. Come on, you

must know how much I love him. You've driven us around plenty to be able to tell that. What's going on? What isn't he telling me? He is sick, isn't he? Is he…?" I trailed off, unable to say the word. I couldn't. It had to be anything but that.

"I don't know much," Silas replied. "I swear to you. I'll likely lose my job anyway because he forbade me to come to you, but I couldn't take it any longer. He is in so much pain, and he refuses to listen to reason. He refuses to seek medical attention." The man's eyes filled with tears. "I should have said something sooner. Maybe it wouldn't be too late, but now he's gotten worse. Now I can't stop thinking about his mother."

"You won't be fired," I remarked, squeezing the man's arm. "I'll make sure of it. Take me to him."

I left my car parked in the front of the garage and hopped into the car up front with Silas. I couldn't bear to sit in the back where I usually was with Declan, teasing and kissing.

"You were around when his mother died?" I asked Silas as he backed out of the driveway.

"I was," the driver answered. "I started working for his family when I was twenty-five. He was only five at the time when they placed him in my care. He was such a happy boy, very curious and always helping his mother in her rose garden. She would have been proud of what he's done with it. She would have been proud of the choice he's made in a partner. You've been good for him, Owen. I haven't seen him as genuinely happy as he's been since he met you."

"Did she suffer a lot?"

He shook his head. "I'm sorry, but it's not my story to tell. He should explain it to you. It was horrible for him though. His father nearly broke him."

We lapsed into silence as he continued the drive. Somber at all the thoughts rolling through my mind, I couldn't come up with any particular reason for Declan pushing me away. I needed him to trust me enough to confide in me.

Five minutes later, he turned onto the affluent Pleasant Street, the opposite direction from where Declan lived.

"Why are we on this street?" I asked.

"Two night's ago before he passed out, he asked me to take him here. Said he wanted his friend, Ridge, to know of his funeral arrangements and not have Charles plan the service."

"Jesus Christ!" My blood ran cold. *Oh god, Declan, what are you hiding from me?*

When we arrived at an elegant home nestled into a picturesque backdrop of trees in Mount Lookout, my hand shook as I pried the seatbelt loose. Before I was out of the car, the front door of the house opened, and Declan's friend, Ridge, walked out onto the porch to await my arrival. Silas remained in the car while I hurried along the steps of the wraparound porch.

"Thanks for coming," Ridge said, sounding grim. "Maybe you can talk some sense into him."

"Thanks for having Silas fetch me," I returned as he led me inside the house. I briefly registered it had a cozier feel than I would have thought for a man of Ridge's flamboyant taste, but I was too concerned about Declan to notice much of what was in his home.

"When he expected me to write you his last letter he was dictating, I decided to put my foot down," he said, leading me to a quarter turn staircase. I trudged after him, hanging on his every word. "He had a doctor's appointment yesterday, but he missed it. He's been stubborn, and I was all out of ideas. I'm hoping you can get him to be sensible about this since you obviously mean a lot to him."

I searched for malice in his words, but nodded when I found none. "He means a lot to me too. Without him, I wouldn't even know who I am."

And it was true. Declan had unlocked parts of me I would have thought nonexistent before him. He'd taught me how to be a little bit selfish and how to enjoy my life and my sexuality. He had taught me how to let go, and allowed him to take over, trusting him.

Now he had to learn to reciprocate.

At the top of the stairs, Ridge led me two doors down and popped the door open. The stale stench of illness hit my nostrils as soon as I entered the room, Ridge behind me. Declan lay propped up in bed by a mountain of pillows. His eyes opened, and I sensed a hint of relief before he shot a glare at Ridge.

"What the hell did you do, Ridge?" he demanded. "What is he doing here? Who brought him here?"

"I'm not going to assist you with your suicide wish!" Ridge hurled at him. "Get medical attention and let them cure you. It doesn't have to be what you think it is, but you're already giving up."

With that, Ridge spun on his heels and slammed the door shut. I listened to the reverberation before I stalked over to the bed where Declan struggled to sit up straighter, but I didn't miss the fresh sweat that broke out on his forehead nor his grimace.

"You stubborn, stubborn man," I said, halting at the side of the bed to stare down at him. "You need medical attention."

"You shouldn't be here," he growled at me.

"I'm exactly where I'm supposed to be," I shot back.

He scowled at me. "If you're not going to leave, then at least sit," he snapped. "I don't like you towering over me."

I sat at the edge of the bed and pressed the back of my hand to Declan's forehead despite the deepening of his scowl. Despite his forehead being clammy, he wasn't hot.

"I should have called the ambulance a couple of nights ago," I murmured, noticing how pale he was. "You're sick, Declan. You need medical attention."

"All I need is to be alone."

I reached for his hand and refused to let go when he tried to pull away. "Declan, I love you," I said softly to him. Shouting didn't work with him. It would only make him aggravated, so I tried another tactic. "Do you know how much it pains me seeing you home like this, knowing you could be getting the help you need? Why are you being so stubborn about this? Let me understand."

He closed his eyes and pinched his nose. "This is exactly why I didn't want you here."

"Why?"

"Because you give me false hope. I refuse to be a burden to anyone, Owen, especially you."

I frowned at him. "What? You think you being sick is a burden to me? It is not."

His eyes popped opened. "You spent the last fifteen years raising three kids on your, Owen. You took care of your responsibilities. The last thing I want you to do is treat me like another responsibility. I'd rather die."

"For god's sake, Dec, don't say stupid things like that."

He glared at me. "I'm not too sick to put you across my knee."

My chin jutted at him. "Actually, yes, you are. But I'll hold you to it, when you've recovered from whatever is making you feel like this. I'm taking you to the hospital, Declan. Don't fight me on this."

He opened his mouth to argue, but I cut him off. "Declan, this boy needs his Daddy to stick around a little longer than this. I just met you. I just met us. I am *not* ready to lose you, and if... if there's bad news that... that we need to face, then we'll face it together, because if we have limited time, I'd rather know... so I can spend every waking moment making you happy."

For a long time, he didn't say anything, and then I heard him sigh. He raised his eyes to the ceiling as if the answers were written there.

"I've let you down," he stated, and gave a bitter laugh which ended on a wince. "Everything was going so good. I enjoyed every moment of you being in my life. You are perfect, everything I could have asked for, but I've let you down. I'm not the confident, fearless, have-his-shit together Daddy you think I am. I'm a coward. Plain and simple. I'm too much of a coward to seek medical assistance and find out what is wrong with me."

"Daddy," I whispered, sensing he needed this more than ever. "That's who you are to me, Declan. I've no idea what other Daddy/boy relationships are like, but I don't expect you to be a superhero, solving all my problems while you pretend yours don't exist. Even if it's far and few between, you're human. You'll experience fear just like everybody else."

"But it's my job to take care of you," he said stubbornly.

"Then whose job is it to take care of *you*?" I demanded urgently. "You see, it goes both ways. Sometimes a boy has to take care of Daddy too. I think when you can allow me to see that vulnerable side of you and still expect me to see you as the same, that there will be no greater fulfillment to our relationship. Will you trust me to take care of you this time?"

36

DECLAN

I scowled up at the bright white ceiling of the hospital room, cursing beneath my breath at how I had ended up there. I had allowed Owen to talk me into admitting myself into the private hospital to find out what was causing my distress. Damn him and the speech he had given me. Now the fear was back, and I desperately wanted to find my clothes and check myself out of the hospital.

From the clicking of the doctor's tongue as he had examined me, it was obvious he had found the problem. However, instead of announcing that I had cancer, he had continued the routine check-up, urine analysis, abdominal x-ray, and endoscopy before stating he would be back within the hour to speak with me.

Owen had sat with me throughout all the tests. Despite his attempts at a cheerful mood, smiling and being positive, the worry lingered in his eyes. He was just as concerned that the news wouldn't be good, and with each test the doctor completed, I began to regret changing my mind. I had been resigned to await death in Ridge's home, hoping without prolonging the torture of medications it would come swifter.

Damn Owen for making me think of how much I would miss out on with him. He was right. The time we had together was way too short for it to end.

I measured the distance between the bed and the door, then glanced at the IV fluid I was hooked up to. Could I remove the fluid and leave the hospital before Owen returned? He had stepped out about twenty minutes ago to find something to eat, and I expected him back any minute now.

Unless the seriousness of the situation has hit him, and he isn't coming back. Maybe he has taken off, deciding after all that I'm not worth the trouble.

I peeled back the corner of the bed sheets, too restless to remain still anymore. I had one leg swung over the edge of the bed when the door opened, and Owen entered. I paused, unable to move at him catching me sneaking out of the hospital.

"Dec, what are you doing?" he cried, and hurried over to me, He grabbed my leg gently and eased me back onto the bed while I scowled at him.

Then I saw the small bouquet of flowers he had in his hand, and I was too distracted to try and make my getaway. I would try again after I found out about these flowers.

"I was…" I trailed off, trying to come up with an explanation of why I had been half-hanging off the bed.

"—trying to leave," Owen supplied for me on a

grunt. "Am I going to have to keep an eye on you twenty-four seven?" He didn't give me a chance to respond as he extended the flowers to me and smiled. "I found a flower shop just around the corner of the street. They didn't have roses, so I took these and hoped you'd like them."

I stared from the flowers to Owen. "I give the flowers," I stated, but the stubbornness in my voice had dimmed. Owen was breaking down all my walls and defining a new chapter in our relationship.

"Yes, you do," Owen agreed. "And I hope you never stop. I love receiving flowers from you, but now it's my time to reciprocate. You know what the word means don't you, Dec?"

I scowled at him. "As soon as they let me out of this hospital, you're on some serious punishment, Owen."

He grinned and leaned forward to kiss me. "See? That's why I need you to stick around. What's a boy without his Daddy to keep him in line?"

I flushed, not used to getting so much attention from a boy. Usually, I gave all the instructions. I did all the pampering. Owen had broken down my carefully constructed rules about how my relationship would pan out. And the most interesting thing was that he did it without me feeling like I had lost control. I still felt very much the same Daddy who had seen him for the first time that night and desired to make him mine.

He was mine, and it was time I explained everything to make him understand.

"Owen, sit." I patted the bed beside me. "In fact, think you can hop up into bed beside me? I want to feel you against me."

He toed off his shoes, and I backed up on the narrow bed to make room for him. Even in a private hospital, the bed was too small for both our bulks. I spooned Owen, tugging him close to me and kissed his neck. Having him so close to me made me feel calmer.

"My mother was a beautiful and happy woman," I said, breathing into his neck. His hand slipped over mine that was over his waist and although I struggled to get the words out, I wanted him to know the full story this time. "She laughed a lot, played a lot. My earliest memories are of us in her garden. But then she got sick , and although I didn't know what it was at the time, I understood it was bad. She lost all her beautiful hair, she lost weight, and she was eventually bedridden. Charles didn't hesitate to spend everything to get her better, but in the end, there was nothing they could do for her."

I paused to give myself some time to get past the lump in my throat. Owen stroked my arm comfortingly. "I'm so sorry. You were so young."

"But not so young I have forgotten," I answered, sighing into his neck. "Charles was a different man when my mother was well. My mother's illness took a toll on him. He became bitter and hateful. I'll never forget the day I discovered my mother dead. She was lying there in bed, and I had brought her a rose from the garden even though Charles forbade it. I thought she was just sleeping, but then I felt in my heart something was wrong, so I screamed for help. When Charles came running and saw her, he yelled at me that he had told me to stay out of her room."

Owen shifted, twisting around so we were facing each

other. I was practically lying half on top of him. He cupped a hand to my cheek. "That must have been horrible. You no doubt needed his comfort, and he pushed you away."

I brought his hand to my lips and kissed the center of his palm. "I told you this, Owen, because I want you to understand why I pushed you away. I didn't want you to be saddled with the responsibility of taking care of a dying partner. I would rather remember us as we are now than to see the toll such an illness would have on you. To watch your love turn to hatred. I know *you*, Owen. You would stay even if you weren't happy because you consider it your duty."

"You're right, Dec. I take my responsibilities to the people I care about very seriously, and I'm not going to apologize for that. It's never a burden caring for the people I love."

I frowned at him. "You're not listening, Owen. I watched my mother change completely before my eyes. Charles as well. I don't want that for you. For us. You must promise me that if the doctor announces that I have cancer, that you'll move on with your life. I could even recommend another Daddy who could make you happy."

Owen's nostrils flared. "So you won't mind the thought of having another Daddy giving me all the spankings I deserve?" he asked, cocking his head to one side. "You won't mind me begging to be fucked into the mattress? You won't mind another man bringing me roses that I'll freeze for sentimental reasons? You won't mind another man sleeping beside me in bed, and—"

"Enough!" I snapped at Owen, my heart aching with jealousy at the thought of Owen doing those things with someone else. "Okay then, I don't want you to be with anyone else. You're mine. Mine alone, Owen."

"Then stop fighting me on this," he said. "Please. I'm here to stand with you through whatever announcement the doctor makes. Whatever it is, we'll fight it together. You and me."

Fuck. I had to be the luckiest man in the world, I mused as I cupped Owen's face and kissed him slowly. My words were not sufficient to express my love for him. I wedged a leg between his and felt the hardness of his arousal against my hip. I would be dragging his jeans down his thighs if they weren't so complicated to get off and if I wasn't positive we would fall out of the narrow bed. The analgesic the doctor had me on was also wearing off, and the burning sensation in my stomach was returning.

A sharp rap sounded on the door followed by the doctor announcing himself. Owen vaulted out of the bed and gasped as he narrowly missed crashing to the floor.

"I'm going to feel that tomorrow," he groaned, rubbing at his knee.

Dr. Dover, a man in his fifties with salt and pepper hair, entered the room bringing a chart with him. He closed the door and approached my bed.

"How are you feeling, Mr. Moore?" he asked, shining his penlight into my eyes. "Any more dizzy spells?"

"No," I answered, keeping my answers curt. Owen pulled up a chair next to the bed and sat, searching for my hand. I squeezed his reassuringly.

He asked me a few more questions about my bathroom use and pain. I averted my eyes from Owen as I admitted the unpleasant sensations in my stomach were returning.

"Unfortunately, we won't be able to administer more painkillers," the doctor remarked. "We'll be prepping you for surgery shortly."

"Surgery?" Owen asked, his fingers tightening around mine. I clung back to his. "What for?"

The doctor glanced from Owen to me, and I sensed his hesitation in disclosing my condition. "You can speak freely before my partner," I encouraged him.

He nodded. "Very well then," he answered. "We have detected no sign of cancer which I know you were worried about. However, the diagnosis is clear. You have a peptic ulcer which has been left untreated for too long, hence the excessive bleeding from the ulcer site. That explains the blood in your vomit."

"Oh, thank god!" Owen gasped beside me, his eyes filling with tears as he grinned at me. "It's not cancer. If you hadn't been avoiding the doctors for so long this wouldn't even have reached the stage it's now at, Declan. Now do you really believe Daddy's always right?"

The doctor glanced from Owen to me in confusion. "Daddy? I don't understand."

Owen's face turned red, and I chuckled. "Trust me, Doc. You don't want to understand our very complicated relationship."

"It's not that complicated," Owen muttered before turning his attention to the doctor. "How long will the procedure take and what's the risk level, please?"

He asked all the right questions while I savored the news that my diagnosis wasn't cancer. The doctor was talking about the surgery and what to expect, but I wasn't even listening. My eyes were focused on Owen, seeing the intent look on his face as he took in every word the doctor said to him. He was so attentive, taking note of the aftercare I would need post-surgery.

"I'll ensure he gets the best of care when he comes home," Owen said, his tone determined.

I opened my mouth to burst his bubble, that I wouldn't need his care. I could hire medical assistance at the house for the six weeks it would take for me to recuperate after the surgery. But then Owen glanced at me, smile firmly in place, and I couldn't take this from him.

"A nurse will be by in an hour to get you prepped for the surgery, Mr. Moore," Dr. Dover announced, then made his way out of the room after I thanked him.

"I hope you're ready for the world's crankiest patient," I warned Owen when we were alone. "You don't get special treatment just because you're Daddy's favorite boy."

Owen scowled at me. "I better be Daddy's *only* boy."

I laughed, feeling light, feeling free despite the pain in my gut. "Come here, boy." I crooked my finger at him. "Think you can ride me before the nurse comes?"

He glanced at the closed door and chewed at his bottom lip. "But there's no latch. Someone can walk in any minute. Plus, I don't think you should get that excited before your surgery."

"But I could die under the umff—" I broke off as Owen punched my arm.

"Don't say shit like that, Dec."

"Don't make me send you into the corner, Owen," I growled at him.

"You know, I'm beginning to love being sent to the corner," he remarked.

My groin tightened. "Get up here, Owen, and at least suck my dick. Send me off to surgery with a happy satisfied smile on my face."

Owen laughed softly, his hand inching beneath the sheet down to cup my groin. I moaned as I thrust my hips up into the sweetest hold he had on my dick. He leaned over and kissed me, but when I reached a hand up to run over his chest, he captured it into his.

"Now, it's my time to take care of you," he mumbled on my lips. "Let me love you as a boy's meant to love his Daddy."

~

Now available book 2 and 3
Take Care of Me
Take Care of Us

ABOUT THE AUTHOR

Gianni Holmes is a high school Spanish teacher whose superhero strength is writing flawed characters who find love regardless of their imperfections. She is the Amazon bestselling author of the Corporate Pride series. She has been reading romance novels since the sixth grade when she got her hands on her first historical romance novel. She's been hooked ever since.

She likes to think of herself as an uncomplicated human being who may be just a little too simplistic for the complexities of life. In her mind, love conquers all. She enjoys roleplaying her characters as she believes their lives are far more exciting than hers. To this aim, she has created Characters Like Us, a Facebook group for authors who would like to roleplay their characters and for readers to interact with them.

Gianni loves to interact with her readers. If you would like, you can write to her a gianniholmes@gmail.com or join her Facebook group Gianni's Gems.

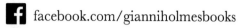

facebook.com/gianniholmesbooks

bookbub.com/authors/gianni-holmes

ALSO BY GIANNI HOLMES

Till There Was You series

Easy Does It Twice

Ollie on the Out

All Hearts on Deck

The Pick-Up (coming soon)

Corporate Pride Series

Falling for Mr. Corporate

My Dear Mr. Corporate

Corporate Bondage

Topped (a short story)

The Runway Project series

Unwrapping Ainsley

Where There's a Will

Fashionably, Frankie (coming soon)

A Marksman Tale

Marking What's Mine

Marking His Mask (Coming February 22, 2019)

Niccola

Bartering His Body: Prehistoric Man

Made in the USA
Columbia, SC
10 October 2020